THE QUEEN AND LORD M

On the morning of 20 June 1837, an eighteen-year-old girl is called from her bed to be told that she is Queen of England. The Victorian age has begun. The young queen's first few years are beset with court scandal and malicious gossip, the eternal conflict between Victoria and her mother, and her hatred for Sir John Conroy, her mother's close friend. Then there is the Prime Minister, Lord Melbourne – Lord M – worldly cynic and constant companion to the queen, and her guiding light – until the dashing Prince Albert appears and she falls hopelessly in love.

CRA

THE QUEEN AND LORD M

THE QUEEN AND LORD M

by

Jean Plaidy

Magna Large Print Books
Long Preston, North Yorkshire,
BD23 4ND, England.

British Library Cataloguing in Publication Data.

Plaidy, Jean
    The Queen and Lord M.

    A catalogue record of this book is
    available from the British Library

    ISBN   978-0-7505-3334-8

First published in Great Britain in 1973 by Robert Hale & Company

Copyright © Jean Plaidy, 1973

Cover illustration © Jill Battaglia by arrangement with
Arcangel Images

The Estate of Eleanor Hibbert has asserted its right to have Jean
Plaidy identified as the author of this work

Published in Large Print 2011 by arrangement with
Arrow, one of the publishers in the Random House Group Ltd.

Magna Large Print is an imprint of Library Magna Books Ltd.

Printed and bound in Great Britain by
T.J. (International) Ltd., Cornwall, PL28 8RW

Contents

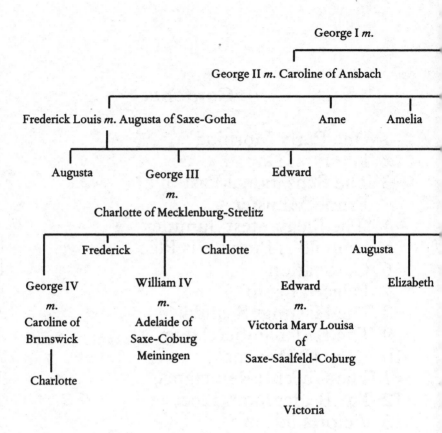

George I *m.*

George II *m.* Caroline of Ansbach

Frederick Louis *m.* Augusta of Saxe-Gotha   Anne   Amelia

Augusta   George III   Edward
m.
Charlotte of Mecklenburg-Strelitz

Frederick   Charlotte   Augusta

George IV   William IV   Edward   Elizabeth
m.   *m.*   *m.*
Caroline of   Adelaide of   Victoria Mary Louisa
Brunswick   Saxe-Coburg   of
Meiningen   Saxe-Saalfeld-Coburg

Charlotte

Victoria

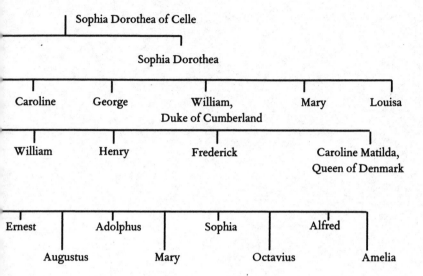

Chapter 1

ONE EARLY MORNING

That solemnity which etiquette, decorum and decency insisted should prevail could scarcely hide the excited expectation in the Palace of Kensington on that June morning in the year 1837.

The old King was dying. Ever since he had come to the throne seven years before it had been expected that either the tomb or the straitjacket would be his imminent fate, but he had survived those seven years as King of England largely due to the devotion of his Queen – the meek and virtuous Adelaide – who on account of her imperfect complexion had been known slightingly as 'Her Spotted Majesty' and whose gentle and unselfish nature had caused her to be regarded as insignificant which was far from the case.

The girl to whom the King's condition was of greater importance than to anyone else in the kingdom was very much aware of what was happening. She sat before a mirror while the Baroness Lehzen dressed her hair and there was a book on her lap from which she had been reading aloud, and trying to pretend that she was interested in it. She was no good at pretence of any kind, but perhaps on such an occasion a little duplicity could be forgiven. Oh dear, she thought, how shut in I am! I'm hardly allowed to think for myself.

It would be very different when she was Queen. She was of age now, having, a month before, on the 24th May, reached her eighteenth birthday; but it had made very little difference and she still thought of herself as a captive. But not for long. Perhaps, she thought, the best thing about being Queen will be that I am free.

'Lehzen,' she said, 'I wonder how he is.'

'He is dying,' said the Baroness.

'Poor dear Aunt Adelaide!'

'She has been a good wife to him.'

'And a good aunt to me, Lehzen. How I wish that I could have seen more of her. But of course...'

She sighed and Lehzen allowed the subject to lapse. The antagonism between the Baroness Lehzen and the Duchess of Kent was undoubted, but it was not to be mentioned. Victoria herself shared her dear Lehzen's resentment; and how unfortunate it was that she should feel thus about her own Mamma! Victoria wanted to be good; it was the object of her life; and surely it was a duty to love one's mother; but if that mother was a domineering flamboyant egoist, who really seemed to believe that she, not her daughter, was heiress to the throne, and if she was *very* friendly, far too friendly, with the most odious man in the world, what could even the most dutiful daughter be expected to do?

When I am Queen, thought Victoria, I shall have to show Mamma that I will not be coerced or persuaded by her and made to do anything I do not wish. The choice shall be mine.

'Poor Uncle William,' she mused. 'A kind gentleman but rather odd, don't you agree, Lehzen? His intentions are often ill interpreted. I suppose he is what one would call eccentric, and I do not think that is a good thing for a king to be ... or a queen.'

Lehzen said that His Majesty had never shown anything but kindness towards his niece.

'It was so good of him to send me that lovely piano for my birthday,' said the Princess. 'I think of him whenever I play on it. Oh dear, how sad that there should be these quarrels.'

Lehzen agreed that it was more than sad; it was tragic.

They were not exactly talking about the Duchess of Kent, which would have been disloyal, but they were skirting round the subject of her shortcomings; and not least of these was her attitude towards the Queen. She had been, quite rightly, so sure that nothing the King could do would oust her daughter Victoria from her position as heiress to the throne that she had been positively rude to him and had shown very obviously that she could not wait for him to die and leave the way clear for her daughter, by which she meant clear for herself; for the Duchess of Kent believed that when William died, although her daughter Victoria would be Queen in name, the real ruler would be the Duchess of Kent with *that man* as her chief adviser.

It shall not be, said Victoria firmly to herself.

She was silent, gazing down at the book while

Lehzen went on doing her hair. It was fitting on such an occasion that she should think of the past – of early memories in this Palace where she had been born and lived ever since, with visits of course to the sea and Uncle Leopold's home, Claremont; she thought of visiting Uncle King George at Windsor – a charming old gentleman, rouged, witty and very kind to his little niece Victoria, although being rather an amorous gentleman he preferred her half-sister Feodora who had been in her teens then, and very, very pretty; still he had taken Victoria into his carriage and been amused by her and she had been charmed by him; then she thought of the day when she had found the genealogical table concerning her family in her history book with her own name printed on it in large black letters and the sudden understanding of what that meant. When old Uncle George died, he would be followed by poor Uncle William and if William had no children then Victoria would mount the throne. She would never forget that moment when the significance of this was brought home to her. She had stared at the printed paper and Lehzen had come over to stand beside her, and placing a plump finger on the paper she had said: 'I could be the Queen.' Lehzen had replied that this was true. And she had said the first words which had come into her mind: 'I will be good.' And she must be good. For now William was dying and he had no children and when he died she, Victoria, just eighteen years old, would be Queen.

It was a sobering thought. She was not sure

whether she wanted it or not. Would she have been happier if she had not been so near the throne? Then she would not have been watched over day and night. Really, she thought resentfully, I can't move without one of them beside me! Would she have been allowed to go to Queen Adelaide's parties which Mamma had never permitted her to attend because always present were members of the FitzClarence family, Uncle William's sons and daughters by the actress Dorothy Jordan? The King doted on them and Queen Adelaide accepted them as though they were her own. Oh dear, thought Victoria, we are a very eccentric family I fear – particularly the Uncles. Everyone knew that Uncle George had lived scandalously; Uncle William of course was moderately respectable, at least he had been since he married Aunt Adelaide – if you could forget his living in sin with an actress for many years and raising a family of ten children with her. Comparatively respectable, temporised Victoria, and thought how shocked Mamma would be if she knew that Victoria was aware of such things.

Mamma would have to learn that as a Queen she must understand the significance of what went on around her. Mamma would have to learn a great deal. And one thing she must quickly understand was that her daughter had no intention of being treated as a child when she was a queen.

She would have many to advise her. One was Uncle Leopold, whom she regarded as her father – never having known her own. How, when she was a child, she had doted on Uncle Leopold! They used to walk together in the gardens of Claremont and he would tell her of his brief but ecstatic marriage with Charlotte, Uncle George's only daughter and heiress to the throne, of how she had loved him, how she had *relied* on him and how most tragically she had died having the child who would in turn have inherited the throne. And instead of being the husband of a Queen of England he would now be the uncle of one. Dear beautiful Uncle Leopold who was so delicate and who had told her that he had given up the crown of Greece to be near her, his little Victoria. But later he had accepted the crown of Belgium, which had meant that he was not so close to his little Victoria. Still, he wrote beautiful letters and he wanted her to know that he would always be beside her when she needed him. There had been such happy days at Claremont when after wallowing in an exchange of sentiment with Uncle Leopold she could go to dear old Louie who had been the devoted attendant of Princess Charlotte and had remained at Claremont afterwards as a kind of housekeeper. Louie talked endlessly of Charlotte, the naughtiness of Charlotte who was something of a hoyden, how she had struck ungraceful attitudes, had torn her clothes, had laughed very loudly, but who was adorable. More adorable than anyone else could ever be in Louie's opinion. Even Victoria, who had taken her place in Louie's affections, did not quite match up to Charlotte. It is very difficult to compete with the dead, Victoria consoled herself.

Everything must be different soon. When one

had been merely a princess and suddenly became a queen this must be so. She was thinking of Uncle Leopold's last letter to her, received only a few days ago. She knew phrases from it off by heart.

'*My beloved child* (she was always his beloved or his dearest child) *I shall today enter on the subject of what is to be done when the King ceases to live. The moment you get official communication of it you will entrust Lord Melbourne with the office of retaining the present Administration as your ministers...*'

Lord Melbourne! The Prime Minister! He was an extremely handsome man and he had had such an adventurous life. There was something very exciting about Lord Melbourne. He was essentially of that world from which all her life she had been shut away. His marriage had been a disaster; many people had said that his young wife, long since dead, had been mad; he had had a son who was not quite normal; he had been cited as co-respondent in two divorce cases. And yet he had come through all this victoriously. He was unscathed; in fact scandals had enhanced him. He was a magnificent man and the thought of sending for him and telling him that he was to continue as the chief of her ministers made her shiver with delight and apprehension.

With Lord Melbourne to advise her at home and Uncle Leopold with a benign, watchful eye and a ready pen from his Belgian kingdom she need have no fears. All she had to do was stand firm and not allow Mamma and That Man to dictate or attempt to persuade.

I shall decide on all matters, Victoria promised herself. I and my ministers.

My ministers! How wonderful that sounded. But as yet she must only say it to herself. She blushed at the thought of poor Uncle William on his death bed hearing her say that aloud.

'Dear Uncle William,' she said. 'How I wish that I might see him. But I suppose *that* is forbidden.'

And so she was back at Mamma.

Much better to think of Uncle Leopold who had ended his letter by saying that he would not come to her immediately, although at any time she desired his presence he would be there. If he came now people might think that he had come to enslave her; they might think that he had come to take a part in ruling the kingdom for his own advantage.

As if anyone could think that! she demanded of herself indignantly. But people could be difficult. There was Mamma's Comptroller of her Household, Sir John Conroy. 'That man', as she and Lehzen called him.

'*He* is capable of anything,' she said.

Lehzen said, 'Who is that?' And Victoria realised she had spoken aloud.

'I was thinking of Uncle Leopold's letter in which he says that if he came to me now his actions might be misconstrued and I am sure Sir John Conroy would be the first to misconstrue them.'

Lehzen's lips tightened. She would never forgive Sir John for trying to send her back to

Germany. She had fought hard to remain and Victoria – dear faithful princess – had threatened 'storms' and interference from the King, and so they had won an uneasy victory. But Lehzen did not share Victoria's blind adoration for Leopold. She often suspected his motives; she knew that he was very ambitious. She had deplored his departure for Belgium because that had made Sir John Conroy more powerful; but the truth was that Lehzen could not bear to share Victoria's affections with anyone. Fiercely possessive she lived for her charge.

'My dearest,' she said, 'when you are Queen and who knows you may be at this moment, you will have to tread very carefully and it may be difficult to know who is your friend.'

The rather prominent blue eyes were filled with tears. Victoria threw her arms about Lehzen's neck crying: 'There is one whom I shall *never* doubt. Dearest Lehzen, you and I will *never* be separated.'

Such demonstrations were the delight of Lehzen's life. They were not infrequent, for Victoria was affectionate by nature and too fundamentally honest to be able to hide her feelings even if she wished to.

'I pray that you will always feel as you do now,' said Lehzen fervently.

'But of course I shall. My crown will make no difference to my heart. We have been together for so long that it seems forever. Do you remember when I was so ill that my hair fell out in handfuls? Every time you dressed it you would assure me that it was getting thicker. And you made a funny little puff of it to make it *seem* thicker. Oh dear, *dearest* Lehzen!'

Lehzen was too moved for words. She composed her features but after a few moments said in her most authoritative governess's voice: 'I think it is time we went for our drive.'

'Yes,' said Victoria meekly; and as they went out she was thinking: It can't be long. Perhaps tomorrow. Perhaps even today. Queen of England ... at any moment.

The Duchess of Kent heard the clop-clop of horses' hoofs.

'The Princess and the Baroness are going for their morning drive,' she said to Lady Flora Hastings, one of the most devoted of her attendants. The Princess! mused the Duchess. How long before she was Queen? The thought filled her with an excitement she found difficult to control and the person to whom she could express her jubilation was naturally her dear Sir John Conroy, Comptroller of her Household and intimate friend. All through the difficult years of Victoria's childhood they had been together and now they should be approaching the culmination of their hopes. But were they?

'My dearest Duchess should contain her feelings,' said Sir John gently as she burst into his study. He liked the lack of ceremony and although it was noted throughout the household and caused a certain amount of scandal, that did not altogether displease him either. There was a mischievous streak in his nature which often appeared to force him into some action detrimental to his interests merely for the cynical pleasure it gave him.

'At such a time!' cried the Duchess. 'All our hopes and plans are about to be realised.'

'Your Grace must take into consideration the child herself.'

'Victoria! Do you know, my dear, I sometimes think that my daughter is lacking in gratitude.'

'A common failing,' smiled Sir John.

'It is not one I expect from my own daughter.'

'Alas, realisation often falls short of our expectations. My dear spy tells me that His Majesty is sinking fast.'

'It is fortunate that the Princess Sophia is so friendly towards us ... or perhaps I should say towards *you*.'

Sir John smirked. It was true that the Princess Sophia adored him and was ready to act as spy at Court. She had begged him to take charge of her accounts in addition to those of the Duchess, and this was well worthwhile, Sir John explained to his Duchess. The Princess Sophia could keep them informed of her brother William's actions and since the Duchess was on such bad terms with His Majesty that was not such a bad thing. Sir John always had excuses to offer her for his friendships with other women. He was of course very handsome, very clever and so many women seemed to find his somewhat sarcastic cynical manner fascinating. Even Lady Conyngham, George IV's mistress, had not been indifferent to him. So useful, Sir John had said then, to have a foot in the royal apartments; and so he said now, through the Princess Sophia. But the Duchess was well aware that his first loyalties were to her.

'He can't sink fast enough for me, the old buffoon,' snapped the Duchess.

Sir John raised an eyebrow. 'Perhaps we should not speak ill of the dead.'

'I only hope he is. It's certainly time he was.'

'Alas, that it did not happen a year or so earlier. Then we should have been on safer grounds. There have been too many storms lately.'

'I cannot understand her ingratitude.'

'She has been made aware of her importance.'

'I have always striven to make her realise what she owes to *us*.'

'Ah, there was a serpent in our Eden.'

'I'd hardly call that skinny caraway chewing spinster that!'

'Well our dear Princess herself has not been easy to lead. And now that she is past her eighteenth birthday...'

'By a month!'

'Alas that's of no moment. She has reached the milestone and passed it and if we are not very careful she will be flying away from us.'

'It must not be, John. After all we have done! Where have we failed?'

'Our failure is in the character of your daughter. My God, she can be obstinate; when she sets those little lips together and those blue eyes are stormy ... one fears the worst.'

'But a child! Surely...'

'I have written to Lord Liverpool asking him to advise her to instate a secretary.'

'Yourself?'

He nodded. 'She will not have it. She has

definitely made it clear there will be no post for me in her household.'

'And her mother?' The Duchess's eyes flashed. 'Is she to be banished?'

'She can hardly go as far as that. But we shall have to tread warily. Our little Princess has quite a considerable opinion of herself.'

'I wrote to her a few days ago, feeling that to set down my feelings in writing might have more effect than mere words. I told her that her popularity with the people is due to the way in which *I* have brought her up and that she should not have too high an opinion of her own cleverness.'

'I trust she realised the wisdom of those words, but I fear she did not in view of her actions. Ah, long ago we should have rid the household of the Baroness Lehzen. We should have been firm.'

'Lehzen has been a good watchdog. She would guard her with her life.'

'While making sure that she loses nothing by it.'

Sir John did not exactly reproach the Duchess but the reminder was in his words that had she followed his advice the Baroness would have been banished to Germany years ago.

The Duchess spread her hands. 'What can we do now?'

Sir John took them and smiled that cynical smile of his.

'We'll wait. When she realises what it means to be the Queen she may discover that she needs help ... and we shall be at hand to give it. You, her gracious mother, I her Secretary and Comptroller-to-be; and behind us good Baron Stockmar, who as your brother Leopold's ally, will surely be on our side. Do you think our German spinster can stand against such as we are?'

'There is ... Victoria,' said the Duchess.

'Ah, Victoria!' murmured Sir John.

The Princess Victoria had retired for the night and the Baroness Lehzen sat in her bedroom reading. Before getting into bed the Princess had opened her wardrobe door and gazed solemnly at the black bombazine dress which was hanging there in readiness.

Her eyes had filled with the tears which came so readily.

'Oh, Lehzen,' she said, 'it seems so *heartless* to have everything ready like this, as though we can't wait for it to happen. Poor Uncle William! I hope he doesn't realise it.'

'Kings are different from ordinary mortals,' soothed Lehzen.

'And queens too,' sighed Victoria. 'Lehzen, I fear I shall never sleep tonight.'

But like the child she would always seem to Lehzen, almost as soon as she had laid her head on her pillow she was fast asleep.

Lehzen had straightened the quilt and kissed the warm pink cheek. The Princess looked so young asleep, with those prominent blue eyes, which could be alternately softly sentimental and stormy, closed, and the little mouth with the rather prominent teeth and the receding chin, which mistakenly gave an impression of weakness, in repose.

My poor darling, thought Lehzen, what burdens of state will be laid upon those young shoulders. But I shall be there.

That was one thing on which Lehzen was quite determined. She would be there. She must be. To leave this beloved child would be like dying, for she had dedicated her life to Victoria. Everything that the child had become was due to her upbringing. The Duchess of Kent could take little credit.

It had been a wonderful day when she had come from Germany to serve in the household of the Duchess of Kent – a step upwards for the daughter of a Lutheran clergyman. She had been the governess of Feodora, the Duchess's elder daughter by her first marriage, but like everyone in that household she had succumbed to the charm of the pink-cheeked, plump little baby. And when that baby was five years old and Louise Lehzen had become her governess she was overjoyed. From that day Victoria was more important to her than anything else on earth. And the most endearing characteristic of this delightful child was her affection and her fidelity. Lehzen was to her the mother she had needed; and although the Duchess of Kent had watched over her daughter with the utmost care, never forgetting for one moment that there was a possibility that she would ascend the throne, she failed to give what Victoria needed most – love. Louise Lehzen was at hand to make up for the Duchess's deficiency in this respect.

Even the Duchess, who had, under Sir John's directions, attempted to banish her to Germany, was aware of her devotion to Victoria, and trusted her as she would no one else.

That was why she sat here in the Princess's bedroom now and would remain there until the Duchess came to bed; for it was a rule of the Palace that Victoria must never be alone; and when she retired for the night, Lehzen must sit in her room until the Duchess came to her bed, which was in the same room as Victoria's.

From the pocket of her gown she took a handful of caraway seeds and thoughtfully nibbled them. They were sent to her specially from her native Coburg and she rarely took any food without them. They were sprinkled on her bread and on her meat; some of her enemies at the Palace laughed at her and said this caraway seed habit was a loathsome one. She smelt of caraway seeds, they said, although the Baroness did not believe there was any odour attached to her favourite food. She knew she was not attractive; she was constantly unwell, a martyr to migraine; and she knew that many of the Duchess's women laughed at her behind her back. Never mind. What did it matter? She was dearly loved by the only person she cared about and whenever Victoria talked of her devotion for her dear Lehzen tears would fill her eyes. Lehzen smoothed her cap and stroked her rather hooked nose and let her thoughts dwell in the past and then fell to wondering what was happening in the sick room at Windsor.

In due course the Duchess appeared. This was the sign for Lehzen to depart. The Duchess, a colourful figure in her beribboned head-dress and gown a mass of lace and flounces was, Lehzen

26

supposed, a handsome woman. And the Duchess was well aware of it. No one could have had a higher opinion of herself than the mother of Victoria.

'She is asleep?' said the Duchess coldly.

'Yes, your Grace.'

'That is good. She is a child still. She cannot realise what this means.'

Lehzen did not contradict the Duchess; but she was aware that Victoria understood very well what this meant.

'It may be – tomorrow,' went on the Duchess. 'Think, Lehzen ... it may be at this very moment. It may be that we are in the presence of our Queen.'

The Duchess's expression was ecstatic. She should, thought Lehzen, show a little more decorum. Still it would have been hypocritical to have pretended remorse because her greatest enemy was dying.

'You may go now, Lehzen,' said the Duchess dropping her voice to a whisper, and Lehzen went out, wondering how much longer this custom of the years would continue. When the Princess became a queen surely she would insist on a little privacy? The child had never been alone in a room in the whole of her life; and Lehzen, who knew her so well, was aware that she found this irksome.

As she came through the Duchess's apartments the Baroness came face to face with Sir John Conroy and immediately regretted passing this way.

'Ah, the good Baroness,' he said. Lehzen always

had an idea – which she shared with Victoria – that he was sneering when he spoke to them. He was not alone. One of the Duchess's ladies was with him. This was Lady Flora, daughter of the Marquis of Hastings, a rather pallid woman in her early thirties whom the Baroness did not greatly care for, largely because she was friendly with Sir John and was a firm supporter of the Duchess.

'The watchdog is released from her duties,' went on Sir John. 'And I'll swear she'd rather not be.'

'I hope the dear Princess sleeps well tonight,' said Lady Flora.

'The Princess is sleeping peacefully,' said the Baroness.

'With such events about to break!' went on Sir John, raising his handsome eyes to the ceiling. A rogue if ever there was one, thought Lehzen. How could the Duchess be so deceived? But in view of their relationship...

Lehzen refused to go further even in her thoughts. Whether Sir John and the Duchess were lovers was open to conjecture, but many people were certain this was so, and if one were to judge from their behaviour it could be right. How she disliked him! He had tried to have her sent away from her beloved child.

'And when they do,' Sir John was saying, 'our little darling will have to break out from the nursery, will she not?'

Lehzen knew he meant that Victoria would no longer need a governess, but Victoria would never agree to her beloved Baroness's expulsion.

Was it possible that he had not yet learned how stubborn Victoria could be?

'Baroness,' said Lady Flora, 'there is something on your chin ... will you allow me?' She had taken a handkerchief and come closer, and to Lehzen's annoyance dabbed at her face.

'It's caraway seeds, I'll swear,' said Sir John laughing unpleasantly as though there was something obscene about them. He shook his finger playfully. 'We all know your passion, Baroness. Some women love men; some men love women; both women and men love power; but the Baroness remains faithful to her caraway seeds.'

She must get away before she lost her temper. How the Duchess could give her confidence to such a man was past understanding!

'If you will excuse me I will say goodnight.'

'Goodnight, Baroness Cara... Baroness Lehzen.'

She did not answer; she swept on. She hated them both. As for Lady Flora with her meek expression and gentle voice and delicate air, she was doubtless far from the virtuous spinster she pretended to be if she was so friendly with Sir John Conroy.

In his apartments in the Palace Baron Christian Friedrich von Stockmar found it difficult to sleep. Instead he took pen and paper and started to write to his patron and friend King Leopold of the Belgians. He hesitated. It could only be a few days at the most, he thought, before his real mission began. Perhaps therefore a letter would be a little premature. Exciting times were ahead. He was a man of dignified demeanour and he had spent years in the service of Leopold, sacrificing his own personal life to that of the King. Perhaps it meant a great deal to mould the destiny of nations rather than to share his life with his family. In any case he had chosen this way.

To Leopold he had been a faithful servant; but more than that – he was a king-maker. Ever since he had come to England at the time of Leopold's marriage to the Princess Charlotte he had had a hand in government. Leopold had quickly acknowledged his doctor's usefulness, for with his help, this clever, faintly hypocritical hypochondriac (so was Stockmar and this gave them an added interest in common) had become a power in Europe. A young son of the house of Saxe-Coburg, Leopold had somehow succeeded in marrying members of his family into most of the royal houses of Europe. But for a cruel fate he would have been ruling England now, for there was no doubt that the Princess Charlotte had doted on him and would have accepted his rule in everything. But Charlotte had died and Leopold would now rule through Victoria; for he and Stockmar had decided on a husband for her. Who but Prince Albert, Leopold's nephew, who should be guided by Stockmar, through Leopold of course. His niece and nephew on the throne of England! It would not be quite as satisfactory to be the uncle of the Queen and her Prince Consort as it would have been to be the husband of a queen. But it was no use repining. Charlotte was dead. And to govern England through Victoria and Albert must be the next best thing.

It was not only for political reasons that the

Baron enjoyed his role. He was fond of Victoria. Indeed who could help being fond of such a warm-hearted, innocent girl. He remembered her as the child who had visited Claremont years ago, rather solemn for her years, passionately devoted to Uncle Leopold and therefore ready to love anyone whom Leopold commanded her to.

'Dr Stockmar is a very dear friend of mine, my dearest child,' Leopold had explained. 'I want him to be yours too.'

'He shall be, Uncle.' The blue eyes brimmed over with love for Leopold and since Leopold commanded it, for Dr Stockmar too.

'He is the best doctor in the world and more than that, he is my clever friend.'

She believed it. She believed everything Leopold told her. One might have thought she was too pliable; but that was a mistake, as Stockmar had discovered on his return only a few weeks before. She had received him warmly. He had come from dearest Uncle Leopold and therefore was welcome. She remembered him years ago at Claremont and she was delighted to have him back.

He had told her that her uncle had asked him to come to Kensington because he thought his old friend might be of use to her.

'Dear Uncle Leopold,' she had said, 'is so careful of me.'

She had charm and when she was animated she was almost pretty; at other times she could be quite plain and rather homely; but she had such dignity in spite of her small stature that Stockmar could write to Leopold that he had every confidence in her.

Now she was on the brink of becoming Queen. A pity, thought Stockmar, that she was so young. Yet youth was appealing and he had noticed that the people liked her. What a change from the old King who was so undignified and who was called 'Pineapple Head' in some of the less respectable papers, and one only had to look at the King to be aware of the resemblance between his head and that fruit. And different, too, from the previous King, who had grown obese and upset his people by holding aloof from them.

'There is certainly not much competition from the Uncles,' wrote Stockmar, 'and she is so innocent and fresh, so easily moved to tears, that the people will love that.'

There was surely no monarch more appealing than a young female one – particularly after a succession of unattractive men.

It was well worth while, thought Stockmar, although the dampness of the climate did not agree with him and he suffered from rheumatic pains and a hundred mysterious ailments which he as a medical man – for it was as such that he had begun his career – could imagine were indications of dire diseases. And to think that he might be at home in Coburg with his family! Not that the climate there differed much from England and his physical sufferings would not diminish. He did not go so far as to admit that he did not want them to; and that if certain symptoms had disappeared others would have taken their place. One of the first interests he and Leopold had shared was discussing their ailments which

Leopold had so much enjoyed – and so had he. But they came a good second to politics.

Stockmar wanted nothing for himself. In that he was rare. He did not ask for great estates. What he wanted was power – power to do good. That gave him immense satisfaction. When he had seen how unhappy Leopold had been on the death of his wife after she had given birth to their still-born child, he had determined that Leopold should be compensated for his loss.

He it was who had advised Leopold not to accept the throne of Greece and had urged him to take that of Belgium. Leopold had had obvious evidence of the wisdom of Stockmar so it was natural that to him he should entrust one of the dearest of his projects – the marriage of Victoria.

So before coming to England he had made a study of Albert – a fine young fellow, as he had written to Leopold.

'Well grown for his age and agreeable. If things go well he may in time turn out a strong and handsome man of a kind, simple yet dignified manner.'

He was sure he had been wise in advising Leopold not to urge a marriage on Victoria until she had seen the Prince. So last year the Duke of Saxe-Coburg had visited Kensington with his two sons and Victoria had been delighted with them both – particularly Albert.

'The two young people are agreeable to each other,' Stockmar had written to Leopold, 'and that is good. But the Prince cannot receive in Coburg the education fitting to a Prince Consort of the greatest of monarchs.' So the Prince had gone to Brussels and Paris to study history and modern languages, and after that he had been sent to Bonn. Albert was there now, and being the astute young man Stockmar was sure he was, he would be another who was eagerly watching what was happening in England.

Of course Stockmar had been quick to grasp the friction in the Kensington apartments. The Duchess was Leopold's sister and one would have thought that the interests of both would have been identical; but it was obvious that what the Duchess wanted to do was guide her daughter in all things and thus become ruler of England ... Sir John Conroy to help her.

And the Duchess had not been strictly honest in her dealings with her daughter. There was that affair of the Regency which had taught Stockmar that it was impossible to serve the interests of the Duchess and those of her daughter at the same time; and Stockmar was not a man to divide his loyalties. He knew the Duchess. A vain woman and in many ways a foolish one; he did not care for her friendship with Sir John Conroy. He had come to England to serve Leopold's interests and now Victoria had engaged not only his interest but his affection.

Melbourne himself had told Stockmar that Victoria wished for a Regency even though she was of age; but Stockmar did not believe this and being on such friendly terms with the Princess it did not take him long to discover that she had made no such request, and that it had come from the Duchess in her daughter's name.

'Such action is dishonest,' cried Stockmar and

lost no time in telling Lord Melbourne the truth.

'My dear fellow,' said Melbourne, 'I am astounded. I was led to believe that the request came from the Princess herself.'

'And now that you know it does not?'

'It shall receive the attention it deserves,' said the urbane Melbourne and that was clear enough to Stockmar. There would certainly be no Regency. Victoria would rule with the help of Melbourne ... and Stockmar.

No, he thought. He would not write tonight. He would wait until their Princess was indeed a queen.

In the death chamber at Windsor Castle the King lay breathing with difficulty. The Queen sat beside him, her hand in his. On a table close to the bed was the flag which the Duke of Wellington sent to him every year to commemorate the victory at Waterloo. His eyes kept straying to it.

'Wasn't at the Waterloo banquet this year, Adelaide,' he murmured.

'No, William. But it took place on your orders.'

'Great victory,' murmured the King.

His eyes had become glazed, and Adelaide, bending closer, knew that his thoughts were wandering again. Dear William, who had been a good husband to her! She had failed him by not producing the heir for the sake of which they had been thrust into hasty marriage, and that was something she would always regret. She loved children and consequently had had to console herself with other people's. The palaces had always been full of William's grandchildren of the

FitzClarence family. What a devoted grandfather he had been to them even though they had been far from grateful. She was glad that at such a time as this they had forgotten their differences, and several of them were at Windsor now in case he should ask for them.

'Adelaide.'

She bent over the bed.

'You've been a good wife...'

'Don't talk, William. Lie still. Conserve your strength.'

The tears were on her cheeks. She loved him and he loved her; and that was strange in such a marriage. He had been faithful to her, which was perhaps because he was no longer young, and he would become furious with anyone who criticised her. Her gentle nature had won the regard which her lack of physical charms might have made impossible. It had been a happy marriage as such marriages go, and it was now nearly over.

'Glad I lived till she was of age,' murmured the King. 'Was determined to. I did it, Adelaide. The child will be Queen tomorrow.'

'William...'

'You're crying, Adelaide. Don't. You've been a good wife. Couldn't have been better. Wasn't going to let that woman rule the roost.' He gave a croaking cackle of laughter. 'She'll be mad with rage... Adelaide... She's been hoping I'd die before... Didn't I always say I'd wait till the child was eighteen?'

'You did, William.'

'And I kept my word. She'll be Queen and she'll know how to keep that woman where she

36

belongs. England will be great under her. Better than old men... Sailors will love a young queen. I know sailors. They'll fight the better for her than for a mad old man like my father, or for George and for me. Yes, they'll love a bonny girl...'

'William, don't try to talk...' It was useless to tell him this. He had always talked too much.

He closed his eyes; his lips moved but she could not hear what he said. She continued to sit by his bed. George Fitz-Clarence came into the room and stood in the shadows. George, his firstborn by Dorothy Jordan, the boy whom William so dearly loved, was now full of contrition for all the anxiety he had caused his father.

'How is he?' he whispered.

'Sinking I fear,' said Adelaide.

Somewhere a clock in the Castle chimed midnight. The Archbishop of Canterbury and Lord Conyngham, the Lord Chamberlain, were in the ante-room, waiting.

It couldn't be long now, they assured each other.

The King's physician, Sir Henry Halford, joined them.

'He is very near the end,' said Halford.

At one o'clock Sir Henry was at the King's bedside. William's breathing was stertorous; he was in a coma.

'There is nothing I can do,' said the doctor to the Queen, who continued to sit by the King's bedside.

The doctor joined the Archbishop and the Chamberlain. They talked in whispers of what this would mean at Kensington Palace.

Two o'clock struck.

'The end is very near,' said Sir Henry; and at twelve minutes past two William IV was dead.

As the carriage rattled along the highway from Windsor to Kensington, the Archbishop and the Lord Chamberlain talked in whispers although there was no need to do so, only to symbolise the solemnity of the occasion. A new reign was about to begin.

'A child,' whispered the Lord Chamberlain.

'Governed by her mother and that man Conroy!'

'Melbourne will know how to manage our affairs, I daresay.'

The dawn was beginning to show in the sky, and they could distinctly see the hedgerows now. They would be the first to greet her. Melbourne would say there was no need to wake her and tell her that she was Queen. That duty was for the Prime Minister. No, my lord, thought Lord Conyngham, she is after all the Queen although but a girl, and she will always remember those who first brought the news to her.

They had reached the Palace and as they rode through the gates the startled porter stared at them. He was about to demand their business when he recognised the robes of office of important men.

The bewildered maidservant stood before them.

'Please acquaint the Princess Victoria that we are here and wish to see her,' said Lord Conyngham.

'My lord, she is sleeping.'

'Tell her at once that the Archbishop of Canterbury and the Lord Chamberlain wish to speak to her.'

The maid, trembling and uncertain, made her way to the Duchess's apartments.

One of the Duchess's ladies rose sleepily from her bed.

'What is this?'

'There are gentlemen to see the Princess.'

'At this hour! It is only five o'clock. She is asleep.'

'It is the Lord Chamberlain and the Archbishop of Canterbury, Madam.'

'The Lord Chamberlain! Wait. I'll tell the Duchess.'

But the Duchess was already awake. She had been expecting something like this which could mean only one thing. She came out of the bedroom she shared with Victoria demanding: 'What is the meaning of this?'

'Your Grace, the Lord Chamberlain and the Archbishop of Canterbury are here demanding to see the Princess.'

To see the Princess! Indeed they would have to learn differently. If they wanted to impart important news to Victoria they must do it through her mother.

'Go and tell them that they will have to wait. The Princess is sleeping.'

The Duchess went back to her bedroom, her heart beating wildly. She slipped a robe over her nightgown. It has come, she thought, the moment I have waited for all these years. This is the most important day in my life. Everything depends on what happens today. We must start as we intend to go on. The King is dead! Jubilation shone in her eyes. Victoria must be made to obey her mother. Then for herself and John Conroy the years ahead would be glorious.

The lady was back.

'Your Grace, the Lord Chamberlain demands to see the *Queen*.'

The Duchess put a hand to her fluttering heart. At last those magic words had been spoken.

She went back to her bedroom, where Victoria lay sleeping. Bending over her daughter she kissed her.

'My darling,' murmured the Duchess.

Victoria opened her eyes. 'What is it, Mamma?'

'Your ministers are waiting to see you, my love.'

Her ministers! Victoria was wide awake immediately. Then it had indeed happened. Uncle William was dead and she was the Queen.

She looked at the tortoiseshell clock ticking away on the bedside table. It was not yet six o'clock.

'I will not keep them waiting,' she said. She took off her nightcap and let her long fair hair fall about her shoulders. The Duchess put a wrap about her daughter and she thrust her feet into slippers.

Someone else was at the door. It was the Baroness Lehzen carrying a candle and a bottle of smelling salts. Victoria threw a grateful glance at her governess. Trust Lehzen to be there. She would have been sleeping lightly, ready for the call. And there she was like a guardian angel waiting to protect her charge if need be. And smelling salts! Dear, foolish Lehzen! As though she needed those! What sort of a queen would she be if she were to need smelling salts on being told she was one.

'They are waiting in the sitting-room,' said the Duchess. 'We should go to them at once.'

'I will go alone, Mamma,' said Victoria firmly in a voice which struck the Duchess like a blow and warmed the heart of Lehzen.

'My darling!' began the Duchess.

Victoria said firmly: 'Yes, Mamma. *Alone.*'

They went down that awkward staircase, the three of them. Victoria had been forbidden even to walk down it alone and even at such a moment remembered this, for to be a queen meant to be free and freedom was one of the sweetest things her crown would bring her.

She glanced at the two women at the door of the sitting-room and her look was regal. Then alone she entered the room.

The two men were momentarily startled by the sight of the childlike figure, for with her bare feet thrust into heelless slippers she was very tiny indeed; and with her long fair hair hanging about her shoulders and her cotton dressing gown falling loosely about her she looked even less than her eighteen years.

But there was nothing childlike in the manner in which she received these men, and as soon as Lord Conyngham knelt and began 'Your Majesty' she held out her hand for him to kiss as though she had all her life been accustomed to the homage paid to a queen.

Conyngham immediately kissed the proffered

41

hand and went on to tell her that His Majesty King William IV had died at ten minutes past two that morning.

Then it was the Archbishop's turn. He too knelt and was given a small hand to kiss.

'Queen Adelaide desired that I should come and give Your Majesty details of the Kings last hours,' said the Archbishop. 'His sufferings were not great at the end and he died in a happy state of mind.'

'How relieved I am to hear that!' She was the affectionate niece then, her eyes full of tears remembering the kindness of dear Uncle William and Aunt Adelaide.

But there was no time for grief. Events would begin to move very fast and she must be prepared.

She thanked the Lord Chamberlain and the Archbishop for coming so promptly to acquaint her with the sad news from Windsor, and charging the Lord Chamberlain to return at once to the Castle to convey her condolences and sorrow to Queen Adelaide, she left the men.

Her mother was waiting for her at the door, Lehzen hovering, still clutching the smelling salts.

'Oh, Mamma,' said Victoria. 'Poor Uncle William!'

'My love!'

The Duchess took her daughter into her arms and laying her head on the maternal shoulder Victoria wept.

She needs comfort from her mother, thought the Duchess exultantly, but Victoria's next words dispelled that hope.

'I did not say goodbye to him. I did not visit him when he was so ill. He will think I did not *care*.'

That was a reproach, for who had prevented her visiting her uncle? Who had kept up a feud between Windsor and Kensington? Almost the last time the King had appeared in public he had delivered a reproach to the Duchess which had caused a great scandal.

The Duchess thought: I am losing her. Have I lost her already?

Her Majesty disengaged herself and saw Lehzen waiting.

'Dearest Lehzen,' she said, her tone becoming warm and affectionate, 'come with me. I must dress immediately.'

So she and Lehzen went back to the bedroom shared with the Duchess (for the last time, Victoria assured herself) and Lehzen took the black bombazine from the cupboard.

'Dear Uncle, I shall mourn him sadly, Lehzen.'

'Your heart does Your Majesty credit.'

'Your Majesty!' Victoria giggled. 'It's the first time you've said it, Lehzen.'

Lehzen turned away to hide her emotion and Victoria, to whom it never occurred to hide hers, seized her firmly and hugged her.

'Nothing ... simply *nothing* ... will make any difference to us, dear Lehzen.'

Lehzen sobbed. 'I'm so proud of you ... so proud.'

Victoria smiled and was immediately serious. 'I am so young, Lehzen, and perhaps in many ways

– though not in all things – inexperienced. But I shall do my utmost to fulfil my duty to my country. And even though I am young and shall make so many mistakes, nobody could have more goodwill and a desire to do what is right than I have.'

'Spoken like a queen ... my Queen,' said Lehzen.

And they clung together until Victoria said: 'Why, Lehzen, how foolish we are. I have business with *my* ministers. Come, I must dress. They will soon be here and I must be ready for them.'

'Yes, Your Majesty.'

'Majesty!' How nice to hear it. But I suppose, she thought, in time I shall become used to it.

Chapter 2

THE FIRST DAY

Even the excitement of having become Queen of England could not interfere with Victoria's appetite. She sat enjoying her breakfast while Lehzen hovered, adoring and marvelling, thinking how enchanting she looked with her fair hair and flushed cheeks which the rather dull black bombazine set off to perfection.

A letter had arrived for her Majesty. She read it as she ate.

'It is from Lord Melbourne, my Prime Minister. He is going to call on me a little before nine.'

She smiled. A very exciting man, Lord Melbourne. *My* Prime Minister, she thought.

There was a knock on the door.

'Is Your Majesty to have no peace?' cried Lehzen in a martyred tone of voice which made Victoria want to giggle. But she remembered her dignity in time.

'Pray see who is there, Lehzen dear.'

'It is the Baron Stockmar,' said Lehzen. 'Her Majesty is at breakfast, Baron. Perhaps you would care to wait.'

'No, no,' cried Victoria. 'Come in, dear Baron. You can talk to me while I eat.'

Stockmar entered and she rose, regal all at once, and held out her hand for him to kiss.

He kissed it, and as she commented afterwards to Lehzen, 'His affection for me shone in his dear faithful eyes.' Lehzen said she always thought the best of everyone, but so many people were kind and good. There were exceptions of course, and one of her first tasks would be to set about dismissing That Man.

'Dear Baron, have you eaten? Can I give you breakfast?'

The Baron replied that he had breakfasted and like Lehzen was astonished to see her making such a good meal. Like Lehzen he had thought the smelling salts might have been more to her taste. He sat down smiling with admiration. She was so young. She did not realise the difficulties which lay ahead. But she was amenable and with him to guide her she would come through.

'This is a great day in our lives,' said Stockmar. 'I hope it will be one which no one will ever 'regret,' she said solemnly, and he thought the transition from frivolous girl to serious monarch was very endearing.

'I will prophesy you will make a very great queen.'

'Dear Baron! I know I shall have many kind helpers. Lord Melbourne will shortly be calling upon me.'

'He has sent word of this?'

'Yes, a charming note to say that he hopes it will be convenient for him to call just before nine.'

'And will it be?'

'Dear Baron, he is *my* Prime Minister.'

'I believe His Majesty the King of the Belgians has confidence in him.'

'Dear Uncle! As soon as I have finished breakfast I shall write to him and tell him it has happened, though I daresay he will not need me to tell him.'

'He will be most eager to hear from *you*.'

'It is wonderful to know that he is there.'

'Your Majesty will have to be very discreet ... now.'

'Oh yes, Uncle is continually impressing that upon me.'

'You will need a secretary. You will have to choose him with the utmost care.'

She laughed, girlish again. 'I can tell you one thing, Baron, that secretary will *not* be Sir John Conroy. In fact I intend to rid myself of that man at the earliest possible moment.'

'Have you mentioned this to your mother?'

'No. I consider it to be *my* affair.'

Yes, the regality was undoubtedly there. Little

46

Victoria might not be as easy to handle as some people had imagined. All the more reason why he should make known his desires as early as possible.

'This matter of a secretary. Has Your Majesty anyone in mind for the post?'

'I have not given the matter any thought yet.'

'I have been your friend as much as that of your uncle. Your Majesty could trust me. Do you not think so?'

She was direct. She had never liked innuendo. 'Are you suggesting yourself for the post, Baron?'

'That was in my mind,' said the Baron.

She was on the point of telling him that of course he must be her secretary. He was her dear friend and beloved Uncle Leopold doted on him and trusted him. Who better than Stockmar? But wait. She was no longer the impetuous Princess Victoria. She was the Queen of England. The decisions she made now were important.

'I will consider it,' she said.

Expecting immediate acquiescence, the Baron was dismayed. He had intended to get her promise before it became a matter for the Government; and now she, who had been his admiring pupil, and had loved and respected him because her Uncle Leopold had wished her to, was telling him that she would consider it.

She had finished her breakfast. She knew he would understand but she had some letters to write and the Prime Minister was calling shortly. Stockmar could only bow and retire. The Queen had spoken.

20th June 1839 Half past eight a.m.

'*Dearest most beloved Uncle,*' wrote the Queen, '*Two words only to tell you that my poor Uncle, the King, expired this morning at twelve minutes past two. The melancholy news was brought to me by Lord Conyngham and the Archbishop of Canterbury at six. I expect Lord Melbourne almost immediately and I shall hold a Council at eleven. Ever my beloved Uncle your devoted and attached niece,*

Victoria R.'

What a comfort, she thought as she sealed the letter, to know that dear Uncle Leopold was there to guide her.

And now a word to her half sister, dear Feodora, who in her German castle would be so happy to have a note from her on this day. How Victoria had loved her sister when they were together in Kensington and how heartbroken she had been when darling Feddy had married and gone away! They had only their letters to comfort each other for their absence – so she must write and tell her that she was now the Queen.

She was sealing the letters when Lord Melbourne arrived.

'I will receive him as I intend to receive all my ministers ... *alone,*' she said.

As soon as he came into the room she was aware of a lifting of her spirits. He was tall and very good-looking and because of the solemnity of the occasion he was in Court dress. She noticed the hair beginning to whiten at the

48

temples, the thick dark eyebrows, the sensitive lips. He bowed and as she gave him her hand to kiss and he murmured 'Your Majesty', she saw that his eyes filled with tears and she was won immediately by those tears. She thought: He is beautiful and more than beautiful, he is *good.*

'Your Majesty is kind to receive me at such an early hour.' His eyes were expressing admiration, and she felt herself blushing. How she wished she could conquer that ridiculous childish habit – so absurd in a *queen.*

'I wish to tell you, Lord Melbourne, that it is my intention to retain you and the rest of the present Ministry at the head of affairs.'

He bowed his head, and how gracefully he did it. She was comparing him with Sir John Conroy. It was the contrast which struck her so forcibly. There could not be two men less alike.

'And I am sure,' she said warmly, 'that it could not be in better hands.'

'Your Majesty is gracious,' he said, with the most beautiful smile which conveyed that while he was every bit as respectful as any subject could be to his Queen, he was secretly aware of her youth and inexperience and was ready to place himself entirely at her service. How fortunate I am, she thought, to have such a man at the head of affairs. *My* Prime Minister!

'I have prepared the Declaration which Your Majesty will read to the Council. Would you like me to read it now so that you may give it your approval?'

'That would please me very much, Lord Melbourne.'

So he read the Declaration in his beautiful voice and she was sure that it was a fine Declaration and could not have been improved in any way. She told him so and it was apparent that they were delighted with each other.

'Your Majesty would not wish to detain me longer so if I may have your permission to retire, I will call on you again this morning at eleven o'clock just before the Council meeting when Your Majesty may wish to speak to me on various matters.'

She thought that was exactly what should be done and bowing, he took his leave. She noted the tears were in his eyes again as he left her.

When the Prime Minister had left she sat down and wrote a letter to Queen Adelaide. She wanted the Dowager Queen to know that she was not unmindful of past kindnesses. As she wrote she remembered the balls which Adelaide had arranged for her and which Mamma had not always allowed her to attend, and when they *had* been present there had often been unfortunate incidents for which Victoria had to admit the Duchess had been responsible. It was Adelaide who had presented her with the Big Doll, one of the most treasured members of her doll family, and had never forgotten to ask after her as though she felt, as Victoria did, that the doll was a living person. Those were matters which Victoria would never forget, so she wrote with gentle kindness towards her bereaved aunt as her loving niece, not as her Queen. But as she wrote her thoughts strayed continually to the man who had recently visited her and who would shortly be calling again. '*My* Prime Minister,' she murmured.

True to his word he came a quarter of an hour before the Council meeting was due to start in case there were any points on which she might wish to consult him. So thoughtful, Victoria assured herself.

'Your Majesty!' His bow was perfect, and yes, there were tears in his eyes once more as he regarded her.

'It is so good of you, Lord Melbourne, to come again so soon.'

'Your Majesty must know that it shall always be my pleasure as well as my duty to wait on your wishes.'

'That is a great comfort. I am, I fear, rather young.'

'Youth is the greatest of gifts. I pray you, Ma'am, don't deplore it. You remember what Shakespeare said: "Youth I do adore thee. Age I do abhor thee."'

She did not remember; indeed had never heard the quotation; and she said so in spite of a temptation to pretend she had. She added that she thought this was one of the occasions when Shakespeare erred, for age often carried with it experience, and that seemed to her the greatest of gifts – if one made proper use of it, of course.

'Your Majesty has wisdom as well as youth – an invincible combination,' said the Prime Minister.

What a delightful conversation! He made her feel clever rather than young and innocent; and that, of course, was exactly how she wanted to

51

feel before facing her first Council meeting.

She said: 'Baron Stockmar called on me while I was at breakfast this morning.'

Lord Melbourne's beautifully arched eyebrows shot up. 'So soon?'

'He has always been a very good friend to me.'

'And to your Uncle, the King of the Belgians.'

'Precisely. He has offered his services as my Secretary. I have said that I will consider appointing him.'

'Which was wisely diplomatic of Your Majesty, for I know you have decided that such an appointment would not be well received in the country nor by Your Majesty's Government in view of the fact that although Baron Stockmar is a good friend to Your Majesty, he is a foreigner and known to be the devoted servant of a monarch of another country. Ah, King Leopold is your own uncle, but Your Majesty will realise that the people would imagine that with such a secretary, a foreign power would most certainly be having some effect on Your Majesty's opinions.'

'But this had not occurred to me.'

Lord Melbourne's smile was indulgent. 'But it does now. I see Your Majesty has quickly grasped the significance such an appointment would have.'

'Well, I do see now...'

'Then I am sure you will agree that this matter of a Secretary may be temporarily shelved. I myself am at your service and could do all – and I daresay more – than a Secretary could do at this stage, so if Your Majesty will trust me...'

Trust Lord Melbourne! With her life and crown

if need be. She said with great feeling: 'Oh, absolutely, Lord Melbourne.'

He looked so moved that she felt she would betray her emotion so she said quickly: 'Shall we run through the Declaration once more? I want to make certain that I do not disappoint them.'

So they went through the Declaration until her two uncles, the Dukes of Cumberland and Sussex, arrived. It was a few minutes before eleven o'clock when they, with Lord Melbourne, conducted her to the red salon where the Council meeting was to be held.

All eyes were on her – this tiny eighteen-year-old girl who had only today become their Queen. Before the door had opened all those assembled in the red salon had been feeling a certain tension. She was too young, they feared. Moreover she had been brought up in the seclusion of Kensington Palace; she had rarely come to Court though it had been the wish of the late King that she should do so. She would be overwhelmed, bewildered; it was most unfortunate that William had not lived a year or so longer until the girl could have come to a greater maturity, or perhaps had been married and had a husband's counsel to help her in a difficult task. But alas, she was barely eighteen. They could expect difficulties.

Now she stood before them in her black bombazine dress, and although she was but eighteen – and certainly looked no older – she had all the appearance of a queen.

She took her seat and the ceremony began. First the Privy Councillors were sworn in and there were a great many of them and they all must come and swear fealty to her. She found this very moving, particularly when her own uncles came to pay their homage. Uncle Ernest, Duke of Cumberland, had automatically become King of Hanover on the death of King William, for the salic law persisted in Hanover and the throne could therefore only pass to male heirs, which precluded Victoria from taking sovereignty there. Now that the King of Hanover must accept the fact that he could not be King of England because the daughter of his elder brother had become the Queen, he no longer seemed the menacing old ogre he once had; he was merely an excessively ugly old man and Victoria greeted him warmly.

All the time these proceedings were taking place, she was apprehensive but gradually becoming reassured, and finally proud.

She glowed with pleasure. It was of the utmost importance to her that she did not disappoint Lord Melbourne.

She knew that those lords who had assembled in the red salon were astonished by her demeanour. They had waited in trepidation for a young girl and had found a queen. She was conscious of a power she had not thought possible. Could she have behaved with the same poise if she had not been primed by Lord Melbourne? Dear kind man! Already she owed him a great deal. How lucky that she had *him* for her Prime Minister. She would tell him so when she next saw him.

She left the red salon, her uncles and Lord

Melbourne following her, and there in the ante-room was her mother, her face flushed, her eyes brilliant, her jewels glittering and feathers shaking. The warm glow, which thinking of Lord Melbourne had engendered, faded. Victoria felt cool and aloof, but the Duchess was too excited to notice her daughter's manner.

'My love!' she cried, seeking to embrace Victoria, 'I am so proud of you.'

Victoria dutifully allowed herself to be crushed against that superb bosom for a few seconds but she was thinking: Mamma will have to remember that I am the Queen.

The Duchess was quivering with questions and advice. She wanted to carry off her daughter, advise her, warn her, in general lay before her the plans which she and Sir John had devised for the future. Victoria's attitude of the past months might have prepared her for the difficulties she was facing, but the Duchess refused to accept this. Victoria was her child and she would always be so.

'Thank you, Mamma,' said Victoria coolly.

'My darling, there is so much to talk about.' The Duchess shot a glance at the Uncles and Lord Melbourne. Sir John had said: 'Victoria must be warned against Melbourne. He is not on our side.'

And there he was, thought the Duchess, taking charge, having paid two calls on Victoria already this morning although she had not been Queen more than half a day. Oh yes, Victoria must certainly be warned against Lord Melbourne.

'Mamma,' said Victoria, 'am I really and truly Queen?'

'But, my love, you have seen that you are.'

'Then, Mamma, I hope you will grant the first request I make to you as Queen.'

The Duchess's smile was indulgent. A request? Some honour she was going to bestow on her dear Mamma in appreciation of all that had been done for her? 'Dearest Mamma, I beg of you to accept...' Now what would she be most likely to offer?

'My love, I shall of course be delighted and now I suppose I should say honoured, for you are our little Queen, are you not? I shall be delighted to grant any request.'

'Then, Mamma, let me be by myself for an hour.'

The Queen passed on, leaving an astonished Duchess staring after her. Lord Melbourne was bowing to her with a slightly ironic smile on his handsome face.

The Duchess was accustomed to scenes, having been responsible for many, but even she knew that this was not the moment to make one. The ingratitude! she was thinking. How could she ... a daughter of mine!

But Victoria was the Queen now and capable of anything.

In Victoria's room Lehzen was waiting for her.

'I was a success, Lehzen,' she cried. 'All those men were expecting me to blush and stammer and show my fear of this great responsibility, but I did no such thing. I showed them quite clearly that having for so long been accustomed to the *idea* of being Queen, I know exactly how to act.'

'As I always said you would.'

'And I have just spoken to Mamma.'

Lehzen was alert. It would never do for the Duchess to gain ascendancy over Victoria for that would mean that Lehzen was relegated to the background.

'Do you realise, Lehzen, that all my life I have never been in a room alone?'

'It was the Duchess's orders that you should not be.'

'I know, and we had to accept it. *Now*, Lehzen, I do not *have* to accept anything. I might decide to, if Lord Melbourne desired it, but that is a very different matter. So I told Mamma that I had a request to make which was that I be allowed to be alone for an hour.'

'And the Duchess agreed–?'

'My dear Lehzen, how could she do otherwise? I am the Queen.'

Lehzen could take a hint. It would never do for her to become a nuisance.

'I understand your feelings,' she said. 'It is so natural that you should wish to be alone. You will have so much to think about. So I will leave you to yourself.'

If she were hoping for a protest she did not get it. This was indeed the Queen.

Lehzen shut the door quietly and Victoria looked blissfully about the room.

'Alone!' she said aloud. 'For the first time in my life.'

It would not be for long, she knew, as her Ministers would soon begin to arrive and she must give them audience; but from now on if she ever wished for an hour's solitude it could be hers.

I never knew what a prisoner I was until now that I am free, she told herself. Free, that is, as ever a monarch can be.

She would never be free to consider her own wishes if these conflicted with the needs of the State. There would be no question of that *ever*, and she would tell Lord Melbourne so at their very next meeting, which would be later this day of course. How fortunate to come to the throne to find such a good, kind, amusing, witty, handsome man waiting to advise. Indeed, one ran out of adjectives when describing Lord Melbourne. She had no qualms, no fears when she considered that *he* was there beside her, to guide her and keep her informed on all matters of state.

And now during this brief respite – this hour of being alone – she must consider her new position and always remember that she was the Queen. Everyone must realise this – and by everyone she meant Mamma, for Mamma was the only member of the household who would question her right to command. It was unfortunate because it was one's duty to love one's parents and Victoria wanted always to do her duty, so she must remind herself of her mother's behaviour during the last years when she had deliberately kept Victoria from Court and had prevented her learning so much which would have been useful to her; and it was not as Mamma implied, that she did not wish her to meet the illegitimate FitzClarences but because she feared that her Uncle William and her Aunt Adelaide might have had too much influence over her. And so Victoria had come to the throne knowing little of Court life and had it not been for the presence of dear, good, kind Lord Melbourne, she would have been lost indeed. Nor was this the only grievance against her mother. She hated to think of what the Duchess's relationship was with Sir John Conroy, for that man was allowed a familiarity which suggested that he could scarcely be merely her Comptroller of the Household. Lehzen became very significantly silent when the matter was referred to and she must not forget that her mother – she was sure on the advice of That Man – had tried to banish Lehzen to Germany as they had dear old Baroness Spath.

She was, of course, reminding herself of all this so that she could justify herself in what she was about to do. 'And to think,' she said aloud, 'that I, the Queen, have reached the age of eighteen and never had a bedroom to myself.'

She summoned one of her servants and noted with pleasure the awe in the woman's eyes. She no longer served the Princess but the Queen.

'My bed is to be removed from the Duchess's room,' she said, 'and this must be done without delay. It should be put in the room next to that of the Baroness Lehzen.'

The Duchess was in angry tears. In vain Lady Flora Hastings tried to comfort her.

'When I think of all I've done! The ingratitude! From the time her father died I have sacrificed myself...'

Lady Flora made soothing sounds as she thrust

the smelling salts under the Duchess's quivering nose.

'Perhaps at first she is feeling her power, Your Grace,' suggested Flora. 'She is so young.'

'It is for this reason that she needs me. And to flout me in this way! First she wants to be alone. Then without consulting me she has her bed removed from my room. Why did I watch over her as I did? Because I cared so much for her safety! Why, Flora, there was a time when we feared for her life. That rogue Cumberland was capable of anything. And because I gave my life to her, now I am despised and flouted.'

'She cannot despise Your Grace.'

'There is no knowing what she will do. If Lord Melbourne tells her to be cruel to her mother, she will. She was always ready to be led by men. It was the same with my brother Leopold. She doted on him – still does. He only has to say something is so and she believes him.'

'His Majesty always had her good in mind.'

'I'm not so sure, Flora. Leopold always wanted to rule. He's my brother, yes, but he sent Stockmar over and I must confess that I am not all that sure of Stockmar. There is only one man whom I can trust.'

Flora nodded. She shared the Duchess's admiration for Sir John Conroy.

'If Her Majesty were not so much under the influence of the Baroness...'

'Ah!' snapped the Duchess. 'There you have it. The Baroness gives herself *airs*, and these have become more intolerable during the last weeks.'

'The Baroness, Your Grace, is a woman of low

birth and this is often apparent. It seems incongruous that the Queen's confidante – who advises her against her real friends – should be the daughter of a pastor!'

'We bestowed the title of Baroness on her when she had proved herself a good nurse as it was unseemly that an untitled person should wait on a Princess – as Victoria was then.'

'She has the title but not the dignity of a Baroness,' commented Lady Flora.

'Sir John always wanted to be rid of her, but Victoria went into a storm at the merest mention of her departure and although she was malleable in some ways she was adamant in this.'

'The pastor's daughter always had a great influence with Her Majesty.'

'*Has*, Flora, has!'

'But Your Grace will not allow her influence with the Queen to supersede your own?'

'I had thought that impossible, Flora, but to move her bed ... without consulting me!'

'If Her Majesty wishes to be alone she will not want the company of the Baroness.'

'That's true. But I feel there is a special animus towards *me*.'

'Forgive me, Your Grace, but surely not towards her own mother!'

'Victoria can be so stubborn and she is in the hands of these people. I had to protect her from that old buffoon William and insipid Adelaide. Heaven knows what ideas they would have put into her head ... and now this!'

The Duchess was so distressed that Lady Flora suggested calling in Sir John, to which the

Duchess readily agreed.

Without question Victoria's bed had been removed.

I am truly the Queen! she thought triumphantly.

Lord Melbourne was asking if she would do him the honour of granting another audience.

'With the utmost pleasure,' she cried.

And there he was, her good Prime Minister, tears in his eyes, as he congratulated her on her performance at the Council meeting.

'One would have thought Your Majesty had been attending Council Meetings every day of your life.'

'If I did well it was entirely due to my Prime Minister's thoughtful instructions.'

'Everyone is commenting on your magnificent performance. You were every inch a queen.'

'I fear there are very few inches. How I wish I were taller!'

'Your small stature is very appealing, Ma'am. It but adds to your dignity. Now have I your permission to mention a little business?'

'Pray do, Lord Melbourne.'

'I must be brief as others of Your Majesty's servants are waiting to present themselves. I hope you will give me permission to call on you later. This evening at half past eight o'clock would be agreeable to me if that suited Your Majesty.'

'It would suit me very well, Lord Melbourne.'

'Then we can talk comfortably, if Your Majesty wishes.' She glowed with pleasure. What could be more enjoyable than a comfortable talk with her dear Prime Minister?

'Your Majesty will wish to name your physician. Perhaps Sir James Clark? If you find him to your taste.'

'I do indeed.'

'And your Master of Horse – Albemarle perhaps?'

She was ready to think that anything Lord Melbourne suggested must be for the best.

'Lord John Russell is waiting for an audience. So is the Archbishop of Canterbury. I fear Your Majesty is being overwhelmed by these duties.'

'By no means, Lord Melbourne. Indeed, if I were not so sorrowful on account of Uncle's death, I could feel stimulated ... elated almost.'

Lord Melbourne's eyes glazed with the inevitable tears and she thought: Oh, you dear good man!

'Your Majesty was born to be a queen,' he said with emotion.

'Did you know, Lord Melbourne, that before I was born a gypsy told my father that his child would be a girl – he hoped for a boy of course – but, said the gypsy, a girl and a queen.'

Lord Melbourne did know of course. Lord Melbourne knew everything.

He added: 'And I will tell Your Majesty something else. She also said: "A *great* Queen!" and now it is my turn to make a prophecy. It is this: Hers will be fulfilled in its entirety.'

How happy he made her feel and how sad that this interview must be short! And though worthy, how dull were Lord John, Albemarle and the Archbishop in comparison with dear Lord Melbourne!

The long day was drawing to its end. So many duties had been performed; she had seen all her important ministers and all alone (as I shall *always* see my ministers in future, she assured herself). She fancied that she had (prompted by Lord Melbourne, of course) made a favourable impression; she had written several letters and noted the day's events in her Journal.

'And now,' she announced to the Baroness Lehzen. 'I will take my dinner *alone* upstairs.'

No one questioned her order. How glorious to be a queen!

After dinner Baron Stockmar called and congratulated her on the day's activities. She had done well and everyone was applauding her.

'Lord Melbourne has already told me,' she assured the Baron; and she could not help thinking how much more graciously and with what *telling* compliments and without ridiculous flattery. Of course, one could not expect poor Stockmar to compare with Lord Melbourne. *Poor* Stockmar? It was the first time she had ever thought of him thus. It must be because she was comparing him with the incomparable Lord Melbourne.

'It is a great credit to yourself and to us all,' said the Baron. She wished they would not keep reminding her of all they had done for her.

The Baron went on: 'You will have had time to think of that matter we discussed earlier today?'

'Which matter?'

'We agreed that you would need a secretary.'

'My dear Baron, I have had no time to think of anything but my duties this day.'

'Of course. Of course.'

And then because she could never prevaricate she said: 'But it may well be that the people, knowing your connection with my Uncle Leopold and he being the King of a foreign power, might not feel that you would be a wise choice'

Poor Baron! He looked so crestfallen but Lord Melbourne was certainly right. She went on kindly: 'It is so different now that I am the Queen. I have to be very careful and you, dear Baron, will be the first to realise this.'

The Baron took a somewhat bewildered leave. He feared that the King of the Belgians would not be pleased. So did Victoria. But it is different now, she told herself and of course Lord Melbourne is right.

She was delighted when that dear good lord himself appeared at twenty minutes to nine and after kissing her hand with such courteous gallantry settled down for a cosy talk. And it really was cosy. He was like an uncle or even a father far more than a Prime Minister. He complimented her again on her performance and begged her to let him know if at any time he could be of service to her in any capacity whatsoever. They would naturally have State business to discuss and as her Prime Minister he would wait on her every day. She had no secretary and he believed that for a while she should delay appointing one to that post for why should she need a secretary when her Prime Minister was at hand to explain all State business, to read all documents to her and to give her his counsel on any matter over which she felt she needed it. Certainly she did not need a secretary as yet.

'In any matters of difficulty consult Lord Melbourne,' he said with a gay laugh. He laughed a great deal, being not at all solemn. That was one of the things she liked so much; and he had a most amusing way of expressing himself. But best of all he made her feel that when he was beside her she had nothing to fear whatsoever.

Yes, that was a very *comfortable* interview.

She went straight to her room when he left at ten o'clock and wrote in her Journal:

'Each time I see him I feel more confidence in him. I find him very kind in his manner.'

Her thoughts were full of him. What, without him, would have seemed a formidable task, with him was an exciting adventure.

Lehzen came in and said anxiously that it had been such a long tiring day and she must be exhausted.

'I feel exhilarated, Lehzen,' replied Victoria. 'But I agree that it has been the strangest day of my life. I thank God that I have the best of Prime Ministers to guide me. Lehzen, you must have some post in my household.'

'I don't think that would be right,' said Lehzen slowly.

'Lehzen! You're not thinking of leaving me!'

'Never while I can be of the slightest use to you.'

'Use! Don't talk of use! You are my friend and always will be. Do not imagine that the Queen will forget the Princess's dearest friend.'

'Your generosity and good nature touches me as always. Let me remain with you as your friend, to help you when you need help, to comfort you when you need comfort. That's all I ask.'

Victoria threw her arms round Lehzen's neck. 'You are right,' she said. 'You shall always remain with me as my *friend*.'

Victoria suddenly remembered her mother.

'I should go down to Mamma and say goodnight, I suppose, for after all she is my mother.'

Lehzen agreed, secretly delighting in the humiliation of the Duchess.

So the Queen descended to the Duchess's apartments and bade goodnight to her mother. There was some display of affection because that was necessary, Victoria decided, but it was a very formal goodnight.

Then Victoria ascended the stairs to her own room. Gleefully she looked at the bed – the only bed in the room.

'Fancy,' she murmured. 'I had to be eighteen and a queen before I was allowed to have a room to myself.'

Then to bed, her thoughts full of that strange day and they were dominated, of course, by her handsome though ageing Prime Minister who was undoubtedly the most charming and attractive man she had ever met.

Chapter 3

THE SENSATIONAL PAST OF A PRIME MINISTER

On his way to Melbourne House from Kensington, Lord Melbourne considered the events of the day and felt exhausted by his own emotions. He was extremely sensitive and if his feelings were somewhat superficial while he suffered them they were real enough. The tears came easily to his eyes – as Victoria had noticed and had warmed towards him because of this – but they did not spring from very deep wells. At the same time he had been deeply touched today by the prospect of this young girl who had never really emerged from the schoolroom, yet who had become overnight the Queen of England.

An enchanting creature he thought her, so natural, so honest. Caroline had been much younger when he had first met her. What a contrast! Caroline seemed to materialise on the carriage seat beside him to mock him as she had so often during the years when they were together. A mischievous sprite – he had always thought her, not entirely human – with her enormous hazel eyes and her hair the colour of ripe corn. How she had shocked everyone by cutting it off and wearing it like a boy's! Caroline was unique. There would never be anyone else like her. Thank

God, said the cynical Melbourne. No one could afford two Carolines in one lifetime, few could survive one; but he being himself – suave, civilised, intellectually superior to so many of his colleagues – had done so. Not without some cost. He shuddered faintly to recall the days of passion, of hopes, of quarrels and reconciliations, and the wild mad fascination of Caroline Lamb.

A new reign was about to begin and he had lived through three of them already: not a very admirable trio, he thought with a smile. Victoria's grandfather, poor mad George III; her gouty extravagant uncle George IV – who though he might have been a Prince Charming in his youth had become a pitiable, querulous be-rouged mountain of decaying flesh by the time he was King – and William IV, certainly the most unkingly of them all, a man whom his people tolerated with a certain indulgence but who was suspected often of suffering from his father's malady and certainly behaved in a manner to suggest this was true.

So was it not moving after a succession of unprepossessing half or wholly crazy old men, to find on the throne an eager young girl, anxious to do what was right and showing a willingness – one might say eagerness – to be guided?

He thought of her dispassionately not as a queen but as a girl. She was by no means beautiful, though at moments she could look almost pretty; her blue eyes were too prominent, her chin too small and receding; her nose was a trifle arrogant and when she laughed she showed her gums in a way which was not very attractive. But there was a determination there. Was it an obstinacy? There was an eagerness and above all an innocence. The Queen knew little of the world; she was too ready to trust; she was sentimental; life seen through her eyes would be a simple matter of right and wrong. What delightful material for a man satiated with experience, having lived life to the point beyond which there had seemed little of novelty to attract him, to mould into a queen! Here was a new interest in life. He was convinced that he knew exactly how to handle Victoria and he had not been so excited since the day he had married Caroline.

As soon as he had come face to face with the Queen he had been aware of the possibilities of a new relationship. He was a man who was very fond of the society of women; all his life he had had many friends among the opposite sex, which had on two occasions – three counting his marriage – brought him to the edge of disaster. It was due to his own inimitable insouciance that he had come through these scandals unscathed; and it was due to that same characteristic that the little Queen had met him and decided without preamble that he was the man she would choose for her favour and her confidence.

It was gratifying to know that the old charm was not lost and at the age of fifty-eight he could have this effect on a young girl.

There had been three great influences in his life – politics, literature and women; and perhaps women came first. It was not that he was a particularly sensual man; he indulged in female friendships and nothing could be proved against him in two divorce cases in which he had figured. When his wife had shocked London society with Lord Byron he had remained at home studying the classics; no man in Parliament had so many Greek and Latin quotations at his fingertips. His conversation was both racy and erudite; he peppered it with oaths and salted it with quotations; hostesses clamoured for his company knowing that any party at which Lord Melbourne was a guest would certainly be stimulating.

He could not have felt the same interest in the new monarch if her sex had been different. A young boy would not have been half as appealing, nor so susceptible to the charms of Lord Melbourne, he was sure. Therefore he was glad that the new monarch was a girl, but was he being premature to find a few short meetings in one day so significant? He did not really think so. They had in truth been overwhelmed by each other. But for the differences of age and the fact that she was a queen and he a Prime Minister one might have called it love at first sight. The phrase brought a smile to his lips.

How fanciful and yet not exactly untrue. He was looking forward with the greatest exhilaration to further meetings. It was just the fillip he needed to resume his appetite for living.

He had not been altogether surprised by his success although he had not expected it to be so unreserved. She really was a delightful young creature. It was that candour, that innocence, which made her so; all young, intelligent girls were attractive for their very youth if nothing else; but Victoria had a great deal besides youth –

71

including a crown.

He supposed his life had been dominated by women. First there had been his mother. An unusual woman, brilliant and attractive, though scarcely moral, she had guided him through his childhood, surrounding him with cultivated people, made him into the man of fastidious taste that he had become. He could not say the same for Peniston Lamb, the first Viscount Melbourne who as his mother's husband was reputed to be his father, but his mother (according to some reports) had obligingly supplied him with a sire far more distinguished than her own husband. It had been a long-standing matter of gossip that his real father was the Earl of Egremont. Well, he considered, it might well be so, for who the devil could tell who was anyone's father? And the first Viscount Melbourne had never had the same feeling for his second son as he had for the other members of the family; but his mother had made up for any lack of affection her husband may have felt towards the boy whom he no doubt considered to be a changeling.

Yes, he owed a great deal to his mother. What an amazing woman and one to be proud of. Her salons were a centre for the wits of the day and she had entertained lavishly in both Melbourne Hall, near Derby, and her London residence, Melbourne House. The Prince of Wales had been a frequent guest and it was said the friendship between him and Lady Melbourne was of a very intimate nature.

Lady Melbourne doted on William, who was far more intelligent than Peniston her firstborn.

Gracefully he had passed through Eton and Cambridge and had spent a year or so at Glasgow University where work was taken more seriously than at Oxford and Cambridge. He emerged as cultured a product as Lady Melbourne could wish, ready to take his place in the world of high society.

He remembered the talk they had had together in her boudoir at Melbourne House where he supposed she had entertained a lover or so. The Prince of Wales perhaps? The Earl of Egremont? How proud of her he had been! She was such a fascinating woman with sharp wit and knowledge of affairs.

'William,' she had said, 'you are a son of whom to be proud, but a second son, alas.'

He murmured that she was deuced hard on poor Peniston who had done nothing but get himself born first.

'A second son, William,' she had said. 'It's not what I would have wished for you. I'd like to see you inherit the title and that which goes with it.'

'Well, that will be Pen's, of course.'

She had looked up at the picture of herself and Peniston at the age of one year. Poor Pen in chubby nudity was embracing her and she was looking serene and presumably at Sir Joshua Reynolds who was responsible for the painting.

'A pity,' she had said briefly. 'Because it means, William, that you will have to have a career. I have been thinking a great deal about it.'

He had waited without undue concern. He was lazy by nature he supposed; and at that time would cheerfully have adopted almost any career

73

she chose for him.

'I had considered Holy Orders.'

'Good God!' he had said, startled out of his calm.

'You always did use too many oaths, William.'

'Sorry, Mamma, but Holy Orders! Do you really think I'd be suitable for such a calling?'

'No. Neither does Lord Egremont.'

He had not asked why the Earl should be consulted, because the inference was obvious.

'He is all for the Bar,' she had added.

The Bar! It was not displeasing. The idea of studying law interested him. It seemed a profession ideally suited to his character. He had said so and she had been pleased.

'You will be brilliant. You could become Lord Chancellor with your ability and *my* influence.'

He had agreed.

'You should not, of course, consider marrying as yet.'

He had looked at her sharply and knew that she was thinking of Caroline, for he had met Caroline by then and been fascinated by her. Caroline had been only thirteen when he had first seen her – a strange elf-like creature, wild eyed and fey. She had looked like a slim young boy with her short hair and those enormous brilliant eyes.

'William Lamb,' she had said to him, 'I have heard of you. Your mother talks a great deal of her brilliant son. He is good as well as being brilliant.' She had laughed; he would never forget her laughter which had so often ended in hysterical tears. 'Good people fascinate me,' she had gone on. 'Because you see I am far from good.'

She had been thirteen and he twenty. She had mocked him for his virtuous way of life even then. *Good* William Lamb, she called him and the adjective was disparaging.

'I fell in love with you before I met you,' she told him once. 'You were so good ... and I was bad ... so that made an attraction of opposites.'

Looking back he wondered how he had allowed himself to become her victim, for that was what he had been. He should have been wiser but if he had been, what an experience he would have missed.

She had been strange from her childhood. Her grandmother, Lady Spencer, had feared that her eccentricities amounted to madness and had consulted a doctor about her. That was when she was a child. So he should have been warned.

His feelings for her were known. Caroline talked constantly and freely about her emotions and her experiences. She made no secret of the fact that she was in love with and intended to marry *good* William Lamb.

The Bessboroughs, Caroline's parents, were not very pleased. Who were the Lambs? demanded Lady Bessborough and her husband, the third Earl, echoed her words. Their origin was wrapped in obscurity but there was money there; and Lady Melbourne had a place in high society. She was the only daughter of Sir Ralph Milbanke and came from Yorkshire. But who were the *Lambs?* They had somehow acquired a fortune, but one could not see very far back into their ancestry and Caroline was the daughter of Frederick Ponsonby, third Earl of Bessborough, and his wife had been

Lady Henrietta Spencer, daughter of an Earl. No, the Bessboroughs were not exactly delighted with the possibility of a match with a *second* son.

Caroline was not one to take heed of parents; she was in love; she was reckless. It was William who had been the cautious one.

'I would marry you tomorrow, Caroline, if I could afford it,' he had told her. 'But as a second son...'

She had laughed at him, mocked him in that wildly passionate and disturbing way, so that in his wiser moments he had reasoned that it was just as well that he was not in a position to marry; but again and again he had gone back to her.

In the year 1805 his future had been decided for him, for his eldest brother, Peniston, had died. Lady Melbourne, though devoted to her other children – Frederick, George and Emily – and eager to see them all well placed in the world – more than that, determined that they should be – could not be completely bowed down with sorrow because the removal of poor Pen, who was so much like his father, made the way clear for her favourite second son, William. He would now inherit title, wealth and what was more important, the power to do without a lucrative career, which would make life so much more interesting for him. William could do what she had always hoped he would, and what she was well aware he wanted himself, for no doubt with his personality and fluency he had an aptitude for the life – he could go into politics.

So she drowned her sorrow in poor Pen's death by making plans for William.

As for William, now that he was no longer a second son he would inherit Lord Melbourne's title and most of his wealth; he would doubtless make a brilliant career in Parliament. He would also marry, he told his mother, and his chosen bride was Lady Caroline Ponsonby, the daughter of the Earl of Bessborough.

Lady Melbourne was not displeased. In fact, apart from the fact that Lady Caroline was a little wild, he could not have made a better choice, politically speaking. William had always been a Whig; he had admired Charles James Fox to idolatry; and of course Caroline's aunt was the Duchess of Devonshire, who had been one of the most ardent Whig supporters of all time. William would be well received with open arms in Whig circles, for there could be no doubt of his cleverness, and once Lady Bessborough and the Earl realised what a brilliant son-in-law they had there would be no obstacles to his advancement.

'Prime Minister, no less,' declared Lady Melbourne, and later years proved her to be a true prophetess.

But that had been years ahead. Life with Caroline came in between and the battle uphill had to be won. He was not a great fighter; he was a better observer; he liked to stand outside the conflict and look on, finding the right moment to seize an advantage. He was too fastidious for the battle. Indeed, it was his aloof insouciance which had brought him through trials which would have finished a more sanguinary man.

Lord Melbourne had been less helpful than his wife. Such a stupid man! commented Lady Mel-

77

bourne. He could not see what a credit their son William would be to them. Her husband's rise in society had been due to her. She had pulled him up with her. And on the occasion of William's marriage and his entry into politics with the whole force of the Whigs behind him one might say, the first Viscount Melbourne declared that William should have only £2,000 a year on which to set up house with the daughter of the Earl of Bessborough.

'How was that possible?' demanded the irate Lady Melbourne; and she had some high words with her husband in which the Earl of Egremont's name was mentioned.

But the result was that Lord Melbourne would not budge from that £2,000 and all that Lady Melbourne could do was offer the young couple a floor in Melbourne House as their home. She began to feel almost immediately that this was not such a bad idea as she could keep an eye on them; and as she was one of the most popular hostesses in society and entertained people of such fame as Fox, Sheridan and of course the Prince of Wales, what could be better for William's advancement than to live in such an environment?

She proved to be right. William began to advance. Even Lady Bessborough changed her opinion about her son-in-law and was delighted with his performance in the House of Commons (he had won the seat of Leominster); and with the death of Fox, it was realised that fresh blood was needed to stimulate the party and eyes were turned on William Lamb, who with his energetic mother and connections with the Devonshires, plus his own erudition and obvious talent, was indeed a man to watch. Society was soon watching him for another reason.

Oh, Caroline, he thought, as the carriage jogged onwards, what a dance you led me! And what an indication of his feeling for her that he should still remember her so vividly although it was nine years since she had died.

He was thinking of her now because of that other young girl; yet their only similarity was their age. Caroline had been nearly twenty when they married; Victoria was eighteen. He laughed aloud and murmured an oath. Victoria, somewhat prim, an innocent knowing little of the world and determined to be good, and Caroline, outrageous in word and deed, knowing so much of the frailties of human nature, except her own ungovernable temperament, and determined to be bad.

Yet he had thought he would mould Caroline into the perfect woman just as now he was thinking of moulding Victoria into the perfect queen. Did he see himself as a Pygmalion?

'I hope, William,' he said (he had a habit of addressing himself), 'that you will make a bigger success of creating a queen than you did a wife.'

Certainly he would. The material was so different. Victoria would be so sweetly docile, whereas Caroline was a wild, irresponsible creature at the mercy of her illogical instincts. Victoria would be predictable; it would only be a matter of understanding how that clever little mind worked; and how could one ever be sure what went on in

Caroline's disordered one. 'There you were doomed from the start, William. Oh, no, it was not you who were doomed. It was Caroline.' And he thought of her living as she did with their poor tragic Augustus, their only child who had survived to live out his life in his own childish world, poor defeated Caroline waiting for the end in Melbourne Hall, while he, William Lamb, went on to become Lord Melbourne and Prime Minister of his country.

Caroline was unfaithful. How could it ever have been otherwise? Lady Melbourne, keeping a watchful eye on her daughter-in-law from the floor above in Melbourne House, was censorious.

'Dear Mamma-in-law,' Caroline had cried, 'can you really blame me for liking the society of gentlemen? Surely *you* understand how alluring that can be.'

And Lady Melbourne, who was well aware that her own name had been linked with men like the Earl of Egremont and the Prince of Wales, tried to instil into Caroline something of the nice distinctions of adultery. She had been married to a fool, a man who would have been nothing without her. Caroline was married to William Lamb, a future Cabinet Minister. And who knew what rank awaited him? Romantic attachments enhanced some while they destroyed others. Caroline must learn.

As if Caroline would ever learn!

And he himself; how had he felt? It was hard to say. She had exasperated him, but he had begun to know himself and the superficiality of his emotions. He began to realise that he could never mould Caroline into the perfect wife; and that she was unfaithful to him had ceased to disturb him greatly. He had accepted her infidelity, for afterwards she would be contrite, devoted, swearing that she loved him only. 'Always first with me will be William Lamb,' she had told him. And in spite of his cynicism, he was still attracted by her. That very strangeness which was to destroy her and would undoubtedly have destroyed a weaker man had been clear to him. He had seen the dangers; and his mother was constantly calling his attention to them. But in his calm detached way he was fascinated. So he always forgave and was ready to start again.

Then Lord Byron, the wicked fascinating poet, had limped into society and set Caroline firmly on the road to madness.

What a romantic figure Byron had been! Three years younger than Caroline, he was not only a famous poet (*Childe Harold* was being discussed everywhere) but he had possessed great personal beauty. His grey eyes had been set off by enormously long dark lashes and his dark brown hair was a riot of curls over a high forehead; his teeth had been white and perfect; but it had been his expression which could be aloof, cold, vital and passionate all in the space of a few moments that people had talked of. Women had been immediately attracted by him – a challenge which Caroline had found irresistible. She wrote in her diary of him: 'He is mad, bad and dangerous to know' and therefore her great desire had been to know him.

Being as eager for notoriety as herself, Byron

had not been averse. The wife of William Lamb would have seemed to be a worthy conquest, for it would be one which would excite the interest of society. It did. She and Byron were together everywhere; they quarrelled violently and publicly; they were reconciled and quarrelled again; and society watched with avid interest the growing indifference of Byron, the increasing passion of Lady Caroline and the seeming aloof indifference of William Lamb.

He had not been as detached as he had appeared to be, for it was at this time that he had begun seriously to consider a separation. His mother believed this should be arranged.

'You have proved yourself in Parliament,' she had declared. 'You have your Whig standing. No one would blame you if you broke free of her. In fact society expects it, and this latest Byron affair perhaps makes it a necessity.'

Yet he had continued to smile and make no comment on Caroline's behaviour. He shut himself away with his books and found great satisfaction in the Greek and Latin classics. At first they had been a drug to make him forget the difficulties of his marriage; later they became a necessity. While William improved his mind Lady Caroline had begun to lose her place in her lover's affections. Lord Byron was bored; those dramatic and passionate scenes which had amused him in the beginning began to pall. He had had enough of Lady Caroline Lamb, and he told her so.

'My poor Caroline,' mused Melbourne, 'why did you always take the road to self destruction?'

But then had she been a normal rational being she would have never exposed herself to such a scandal as she had. She had been completely frank; she had never stopped to consider. 'I love Byron,' she had told him, herself and the world, and she would not pretend otherwise.

She had tried to explain to her husband. 'I love Byron, yes, and I love you, William Lamb. But it is enough to know you are there and always will be there. I don't feel this mad craving for your company. I *must* see Byron or I shall go mad.'

And he had looked at her quizzically and thought: But Caroline my dear, you are already mad and can you be sure that I shall always be there?

He had shrugged his shoulders and gone back to Aeschylus which was more rewarding than the ramblings of a mad woman.

Perhaps his indifference had goaded her. Perhaps he had been wrong to shrug his shoulders. Perhaps she needed him to take her firmly in hand as other men would have done; either to have discarded her or to have fought to bring her back to him. But he did neither; his indifference had been clear; it was that which had saved him.

That was the most difficult of all times, when the whole of society, the whole of London was talking about Caroline Lamb's crazy passion for Lord Byron who was trying to elude her. Neither of them had made concessions to conventional behaviour. They had cared nothing for the fact that their affair was made public. They insulted each other in company; they quarrelled in the open so that all might know how their relationship progressed. She pleaded; he scorned. She offered him all her jewels; she would wait outside his house for him to come home and then plead with him; she bribed his servants to let her into his house. There was no end to the follies of Caroline. She could not see that Byron was tired of her and that the more she pursued him the more she bored him.

Then there was that scene which was recalled even now when, finding herself at a party at which the poet was a guest, Caroline had accosted him, had accused him of neglect and quarrelled noisily with him to the outward consternation and inward delight of the other guests. He had expressed his contempt, his dislike and his great desire never to see her again, at which she had picked up a knife and tried to stab herself, and when this was wrested from her, crying passionately that she had no desire to live, she had snatched a glass, broken it and tried to cut her wrists

William's fortunes had seemed low then; he had lost his seat owing to his support of the Catholic Emancipation Bill and had remained out of the House of Commons for four years. He was not sure how he would have come through that trying time but for his love of literature. He became familiar with Tacitus and Horace, Aristotle and Cicero. His obsession with the past enabled him to be a detached observer of the present. It became clear during that period of Caroline's maddest escapades that he was an unusual man. There was his mother to advise and comfort him. She applauded his attitude but continued to urge a separation from Caroline. There would be a time when he would come back to the House of Commons, she told him, and Caroline would be an unsuitable wife for a Prime Minister. She had not thought it incongruous to consider that he would attain this goal, and had the utmost confidence that one day he would be the leader of the Whigs.

'Dear Mamma,' he murmured. 'Right as usual.'

And after that disastrous scene of Caroline's attempted suicide he had taken her to Ireland and sought to calm her. Surprisingly, she had seemed tolerably happy there. He had always wanted a son and he had one, although two other children had died in infancy. When was it he had first been forced to admit that Augustus was not normal? The boy was only six years old at the time of Caroline's attempted public suicide. 'He's a little backward,' they had said. 'Some children are.' But of course later he knew that Augustus would go through life with the mind of a child.

What tragedy, people said, for William Lamb! A mad wife, his only child mentally deficient and his political career in ruins. But his charming indifference had made him as outstanding as their dynamic energy did most men.

Caroline had continued to fret for Byron and Lady Melbourne had decided it would be useful if the fascinating poet were married, so with characteristic verve she produced a wife for him – her own niece Annabella Milbanke – and rather to everyone's astonishment Byron agreed to the match.

Caroline had been overtaken by melancholy

when the marriage took place; she shut herself away in her rooms and did not emerge for days; it transpired later how she had occupied herself and in the meantime Lady Melbourne made William see that he must agree to a separation from his wife if he were to continue with his career. So he had agreed; and the deeds of separation had been drawn up. How Caroline had wept and thrown herself at his feet and clung to him and demanded to know what she would do without him! She was fascinated by Lord Byron, she declared; she was ready to die when he deserted her, and would have done so if she had not been prevented. But if William Lamb deserted her she would surely die. She was wild; she was mad; but he knew that she meant what she said. The loss of Byron had filled her with passionate rage; the loss of William Lamb would fill her with melancholy; and the latter was the more dangerous of the two.

He had tried to reason with her, but who had ever reasoned with Caroline? She was his creature; he had sought to mould her; he had failed; but he could not forget her as he had seen her at thirteen and later when they had married – slim, boyish, with the short golden hair and the enormous wild eyes; she exasperated but she enchanted. She was a tragedy to herself and to him; but he supposed he could never be unmoved by her.

So he had capitulated and when the lawyers had come with the papers for him to sign they had found them together, she laughing, insisting on feeding him with thin slices of bread and butter.

'The papers are ready for your signature,' he had been told, and she had watched him, puckish, impudent and pleading all at once.

'Take them away,' he had said. 'We have no need of them now.'

Then she had danced and flung her arms about his neck and had been passionate and gay – and mad of course, always mad.

But when it transpired that during those nights she had shut herself away she had been writing a novel, this was too much even for him to forgive. For the book told the story of herself, her husband and Lord Byron, highly exaggerated and romanticised. How could she have done this? It seemed as though she had deliberately sought ways and means of humiliating him and destroying them both. He had only learned of the book's existence when it was on the point of being published and he went to her at once. 'It can't be true,' he had cried. 'You could not be so foolish.'

She had given him that puckish look as she retorted: 'Haven't you yet learned that there is no end to my foolishness?'

'I have stood by you through great difficulties,' he had told her then. 'But if it is true that this novel is published I will never see you again.'

And he left her sobbing, wildly begging him not to desert her, but the book was published; all their friends, all his political enemies read it. It had indeed been more than any man could endure. Yet once more he had given way.

He recalled vividly the day when his mother had died; he could feel even at that moment the numbed desolation which had sent him to his

87

books, his only consolation and refuge against the blows with which life was buffeting him. She had left him the stately old mansion of Brocket Hall near Hatfield and there he took Caroline with poor Augustus their son. Lord Melbourne, his mother's husband, joined them; and in the quiet of the country he had tried to bring some serenity into his life. He had devoted himself to Augustus, trying with great patience to awaken the boy's intelligence. When his son had uttered an intelligent sentence it had been a good day. His devotion to his son and his passion for the classics he supposed now had been his salvation. If only Caroline could have subdued her wild nature, if only she would have allowed him to be at peace, he could have made a tolerable life for them all. But being Caroline how could she? She grew wilder; she wrote more books; and his friends declared that she was making her husband the laughing stock of the country.

Then, in the year 1824, she chanced to be out riding when a funeral cortège came into sight. When she asked whose it was and was told 'Lord Byron's' she had burst into hysterical tears, and collapsing with passionate grief had been brought home in a state of raving madness. After that she had been ill for months and when she had recovered a little of her physical health she no longer wished to visit London. She would be a recluse, she had said, and stayed in her own apartments at the Hall, not emerging for days. She had not come down to the dining-room; remains of meals which she would not allow the servants to remove had littered her bedroom; she tore the curtains at her windows and let them hang in rents; she kept bottles of brandy – in her room – under the bed, in cupboards, on the mantelpiece, anywhere which would hold them; she would weep all day and then her hysterical laughter would be heard all over the house; and all the time she had been writing her books and diaries and the theme which ran through them all was her relationship with Lord Byron and William Lamb.

He marvelled at the manner in which he had been able to come through and find his way back into politics. He had seen that his mother was right when she had insisted that if he were going to lead a successful public life there must be a legal separation from Caroline. Caroline, shut in her room, taking liberal doses of laudanum to make her sleep and brandy to make her gay, had listened dully when he told her that it was now inevitable, and had not seemed to understand. When she discovered what had happened she had declared but without vehemence: 'My heart is broken.'

Even then he had not deserted her. He was often at Brocket Hall. There had been his son Augustus to be cared for and he had gone on hoping that one day he would find the key to unlock what he believed to be that latent intelligence. At least the boy was gentle, unlike his mother; although the taint she had passed on had affected his brain.

So, there had been politics which began to absorb him. Canning, the new Prime Minister, had given him his first government post. Chief Secretary for Ireland was a long way from being Prime Minister but at least he was in the Government and that was an indication that the barren years were over. He was not free from Caroline then but the bonds were slackening; down at Brocket Hall she was drinking heavily and taking laudanum to forget her sorrows; and he was not surprised when he was summoned back because she was dying. She was forty-two. 'Oh God!' he had cried, 'what a waste of a life.'

He was glad that he was in time to see her alive and that her last hours were lucid.

'Oh, William Lamb,' she had cried while the tears slipped down her cheeks and her sunken hazel eyes were mournful, 'what have I done to you?'

She must not fret, he had told her. The past was forgotten and forgiven. He loved her. He always would love her. No woman would mean to him what she had always been.

And she had smiled, happier perhaps than she had ever been in her frenzied attachments.

She was buried in Hatfield Church; he could only feel sorrow although he now was free. No longer would there be this force to undermine him, to humiliate him, to shatter his hopes.

Lord Melbourne had died soon after, and he succeeded to the title. He came home from Ireland and was often at Brocket Hall with Augustus. It had been a peaceful household now that Caroline was dead; the boy had looked forward to his visits, and had been better when he came; and always he had hopes of awakening his intelligence. Sometimes he had dreamed of having a son who could discuss the classics with him – an absurd dream. If Augustus could have read the simplest children's book and understood it he would have been grateful enough.

And then scandal again when an Irish peer, Lord Brandon, brought a case against him. It was true he *had* been rather friendly with Lady Brandon. He had always liked the society of women, and after Caroline's death had acquired a growing circle of women friends. A member of the Government to be involved in such an affair ('improper intimacy with Lady Brandon' was the charge) would almost inevitably be death to his career. In consternation he had employed the best possible lawyer and the case had been dismissed by the Lord Chief Justice who had stated that no one could give a word of proof against Lord Melbourne.

He took a handkerchief from his pocket and wiped his brow at the memory of that affair. But it was nothing of course compared with that which came later. He had been friendly with the Nortons for some time, when in 1830 Lord Grey took office and had offered him the post of Secretary for Home Affairs. The Honourable George Norton was a Tory but he had a beautiful young wife, Caroline (ill-fated name), who was a Whig. Caroline Norton was the granddaughter of the playwright Sheridan and magnificently equipped both mentally and physically. Tall, dark, with enormous luminous eyes, and a voluptuous figure, she had become a well-known personality, and Lord Melbourne had found her very attractive. He had visited the Nortons frequently and was known as a friend of them both.

George Norton was not very successful and he became so hard pressed for money that his wife had asked Melbourne if he could do something for him. Consequently Melbourne had found him an appointment as a magistrate with a salary of £1,000 a year, and the friendship between the Home Secretary and the Nortons had grown. Nor had it slackened when in 1834, in spite of his lurid past, Melbourne became Prime Minister.

What solace he had found at Storey's Gate, the Nortons' somewhat humble – by Melbourne's standards – London home. There he and Caroline had spent hours in spirited discussion; they did not always agree, but what pleasure to be able to discuss art and literature with an intelligent woman; George lacked his wife's brilliance. Caroline was a poetess; she was also a noted beauty. Of course he had known that her marriage with George was not successful; George Norton was by no means worthy of Caroline. Perhaps he had thought that had she not been a married woman they might have made a match of it. She would have made an excellent wife for a Prime Minister. What a pleasure it had been after a wearying session at the House to call in and be received unceremoniously in her untidy drawing-room where she might be writing or painting. But what a terrible blow when Norton announced that he was going to sue for a divorce and named the Prime Minister as the co-respondent.

Here was a scandal as bad as anything that had happened with Lady Caroline. At least she had been his wife. The case had been a *cause célèbre*. He remembered now his acute distaste for the affair, his anxiety for Caroline Norton of whom he was genuinely fond, and his speculation as to what this would mean to his career.

Resignation seemed inevitable. He remembered the occasion when he had called on the King. He and peppery William had never much liked each other but the King was a firm supporter of justice and he declared that in his opinion this case they were bringing smacked of conspiracy of some sort. If Melbourne said his relations with the Hon. Mrs Norton were platonic, then the King believed him.

He never wanted to go through that again. The humiliation of listening to the accounts of his and Mrs Norton's conduct was intense and would have been worse if they had not been so ridiculous as to prejudice the case in his favour. Drunken servants, servants who had been dismissed for stealing, servants with a grievance, they all came along to testify against the Prime Minister and the woman who had employed them. And the case was won as it must have been with any justice; for he was innocent and would never allow Mrs Norton's innocence to be questioned. Indeed the case had fallen down on the evidence or lack of it; and the King and Wellington both congratulated him and declared it had been brought through jealousy.

He had had great fortune; for the scandals which had threatened his career and would have finished most men's had left his unscathed; and when the case was over Melbourne was still

Prime Minister.

But tragedy had not finished with him. This time it was his son who died quietly one evening when they were together. His mad wife was dead; his mentally deficient son was dead; he was fifty-eight years old, and eighteen-year-old Victoria had ascended the throne. So young, so eager to learn, wanting to be good. What a challenge for an ageing man who had failed so bitterly in his marriage. But why must he think of that bitter failure on such a day as this?

The carriage had come to a halt at Melbourne House.

'Caroline is dead,' he said to himself. 'And now ... Victoria.'

Chapter 4

'THE PLEASANTEST SUMMER'

After a good night's sleep when Victoria awoke to the second day of her reign, her first thoughts were: 'I shall see Lord Melbourne today.' She laughed delightedly to herself. Of course she would see Lord Melbourne today; she would see him *every* day. He was her chief minister.

'My Prime Minister,' she said aloud. 'How exciting!'

Lehzen hovered while she ate her breakfast, fussing in the most delightful way. She had not seen the Duchess yet. Nor shall I, she thought. In

94

future I shall say whom I shall see and when.

'And not in the least nervous,' Lehzen was saying. 'It is quite wonderful.' Lehzen nibbling at bread and butter sprinkled with caraway seeds regarded her young mistress with admiration.

'I think I enjoy it, Lehzen,' she said calmly, getting on with her breakfast and reflecting that Lehzen dared not tell her now not to gobble. For gobble I shall if I want to, Victoria told herself. 'I love the dear people and it will be no more of an ordeal for me to face them than it was my ministers.'

'They will love you,' said Lehzen. 'The people love a young queen.'

'That is exactly what Lord Melbourne said,' replied the Queen; and Lehzen realised that was a compliment. But she was a little uneasy. We don't want too much Lord Melbourne, she thought.

After breakfast the Prime Minister called. The Queen was to be proclaimed from a window of St James's Palace and he wanted to prepare her. He knew of course that she was not nervous.

'Not in the least,' she told him, which made his eyes glaze over with the tears she had come to expect. *Dear* Lord Melbourne!

'The right attitude is to smile at the people and make them believe you're enjoying it all even if you're not.'

She loved the way he talked; he was so frank, so natural.

'Oh, but *I am* enjoying it. And would it be *right* to pretend if I were not? I have always *hated* pretence in any form.'

'A queen cannot afford to hate what the people

95

love,' he told her, 'even if it entails a little pretence now and then.'

And she thought: How clever he is! I must remember his sayings and write them in my Journal.

'I remember the Coronation of your Uncle George IV,' he told her. 'Ah, there was an occasion!'

'There was trouble with the Queen, I believe.'

'Your Majesty was then a babe in arms.'

'And unable therefore to be present,' she said with a giggle. How easy it was to laugh with her Prime Minister!

'Which was perhaps a blessing.'

'Wouldn't it have been well for me to have some experience of coronations since I shall have one of my own?'

'There never was such a coronation as that one, and it would not be possible for Your Majesty's to resemble it in the least.'

She laughed. She had heard how her Aunt Caroline of Brunswick had tried to storm the Abbey and had been kept out on Uncle King George's orders. What exciting relations she had had, and rather wicked too! Lord Melbourne would, of course, know a great deal about them. And exciting things had happened to him. She had heard rumours. That wife of his, those two divorce scandals. The world was waiting to be explored and how comforting to remember that she had her Prime Minister beside her – such a dear, good, *experienced* man.

But this was not the time to talk of past scandals. Perhaps they would later. Oh no, that would doubtless be very improper. A queen and her Prime Minister must discuss State matters; but the scandals of King George and Queen Caroline had been a State matter, so State matters could be scandalous too.

'But,' went on Lord Melbourne, 'this is not a matter of a coronation but a proclamation. Your Majesty will ride to St James's and there be proclaimed Queen of England. So that on this occasion all you have to do is smile and look pleasant, which you will accomplish with the greatest ease. You need have no qualms.'

'None at all.'

His expression was sentimental.

'I know Your Majesty will delight all your subjects as you do this one.'

So she set out for St James's; and the dear people lined the streets to see her carriage pass and they showed, in no uncertain way, their delight in the young Queen with her wide blue eyes and ready smile.

'What a little thing she is!' she heard them say.

'Different from her uncles.'

It was as Lord Melbourne had said. The nation was delighted with a young attractive girl after the gross old men who had occupied the throne for so many years.

And from an open window of St James's Palace she stood while the Proclamation was read and the trumpets sounded and the guns fired their salutes.

'God bless the Queen!' Those words echoed all round her.

'Oh, God,' she prayed, 'help me to do what is

right. Help me to be *good*.'

A letter had arrived from Uncle Leopold.

'My beloved child,
Your new dignities will not change or increase my
old affection for you. May Heaven assist you and
may I have the happiness of being able to be of use to
you...'

Dear Uncle Leopold! She had not thought of him very much since her accession. He was far away and she had dear Lord Melbourne close at hand; and she must not forget, as Lord Melbourne had pointed out, that Uncle Leopold was the head of a foreign power. At the same time she must not forget either the affection she had had for this beloved Uncle during her childhood when he had been a father to her. That reminded her that Lord Melbourne had known her own father. She must ask him to talk to her of him at some time. Oh dear, her thoughts were straying from Uncle Leopold's letter.

He went on to congratulate her on how she had conducted herself.

Then:

'I have been most happy to hear that the swearing-in
of the Council passed so well. The Declaration in the
newspapers I find simple and appropriate. The trans-
lation in the papers says: 'J'ai été éevée en
Angleterre.'' I should advise you to say as often as
possible that you are born *in England...'*

She saw the point of this but Lord Melbourne had approved the Declaration and had not mentioned it.

Uncle Leopold went on to remind her that she could never say too much in praise of her own country and its people.

'Two nations in Europe are really almost ridiculous in their own exaggerated praises of themselves; the English and the French...'

Was he a little critical of her country and her people?

How strange that she should begin to criticise to herself – she would never do it openly – that dear good Uncle who had been the god of her childhood.

But then of course she was growing up; she had become the Queen; and she had Lord Melbourne to advise her. An Englishman like her Prime Minister would naturally understand the English and their affairs better than a foreigner.

She wrote in return:

'My beloved Uncle,
Though I have an immense *deal of business to do I shall write a few lines to thank you for your kind and useful letter of the 23rd which I have just received...'*

She paused to think of those happy days at Claremont in which she had so delighted and of dear Louie who had always been so pleased to see her and had given her the place in her affections which had once been occupied by Princess Charlotte – or almost given it. No one could quite replace Charlotte with Louie, of course. Dear Louie! I must find time to go and see her. I must not let her think that now I am Queen it will make any difference to our relationship.

Again her thoughts were straying from Uncle Leopold.

'Before I go further let me pause to tell you how fortunate I am to have at the head of the Government a man like Lord Melbourne. I have seen him now every day, with the exception of Friday, and the more I see him, the more confidence I have in him. He is not only a clever statesman and an honest man, but a good and kindhearted man, whose aim is to do his duty for his country and not for a party. He is the greatest use to me both politically and privately.'

She sat back in her chair. She did hope Uncle Leopold would realise the merits of Lord Melbourne and that it was the advice of her Prime Minister she must take rather than that of the head of a foreign power even if he was an uncle.

In growing closer to Lord Melbourne it was inevitable that she should move farther away from Uncle Leopold.

The Duchess was in despair, and she naturally sought comfort from Sir John Conroy.

'I would not have believed it possible,' she moaned. 'What have I done to deserve this?'

Sir John looked at her ruefully. The ruin of his hopes was more to be deplored than hers. She

100

was at least the widow of the Duke of Kent and the mother of the Queen. What had he?

Victoria had shown clearly enough that she had no love for him; and now the Regency which he and the Duchess had hoped for would never be, for Victoria had been proclaimed Queen and was determined to have no interference.

'She changed overnight,' wailed the Duchess.

But that was not true. She had always been aware of her dignity; nor had she ever prevaricated; she had accepted their rule unwillingly and as soon as it was over she had escaped.

'I shall never forget going into my bedroom and finding her bed gone,' cried the Duchess. "Where is my daughter's bed?" I demanded. "Removed Your Grace", I was informed, "on the *Queen's* orders." How could she!'

'Simply, dear Duchess, by giving the order. She only has to give orders now.'

He regarded the Duchess sadly. Their plans had come to nothing and he was not a man to stand still. He had to make new ones.

'I will send Flora to you,' he said.

She did not answer and he left. When Lady Flora Hastings appeared the Duchess reiterated her resentment and found some comfort in enumerating the benefits she had bestowed on her daughter and the indications of that daughter's ingratitude.

'Lehzen is to blame,' declared Lady Flora. 'She has far too much influence with the Queen. But what can one expect from a low born pastor's daughter?'

There was some comfort in reviling the

Baroness and the Duchess felt a little better.

Meanwhile Sir John was reviewing his own position. There was not much left to him. He and the Duchess had had a joint plan which had been formulated in Victoria's childhood. There was to be a Regency of which the Duchess was to be the titular head; and he, through her, would rule the country, although she and the rest of the world would believe that he was merely advising her.

It was not a sudden shock – this repudiation by Victoria. He had seen it coming for a very long time and so had his dear Duchess, so she need not pretend – at least to him – to be so surprised by it.

Victoria had made it clear that she was not going to be guided – by them at least. She was obstinate and so incapable of deceit that she made no secret of her dislike for him. She had told him firmly some time ago that she could not accept him as her secretary and that meant he would have no place in her household. Well, if he were to have no place in her household he had better make other plans and quickly.

I have given years of my life in the Duchess's service, he told himself with a smirk. I have therefore looked after the Queen's affairs. I deserve a reward which will make my retirement worth while.

There was no point in under-estimating himself and as soon as possible he should make his wishes known.

He would have liked to make them to the Queen but she would most certainly refuse to see him, or at best delay doing so. Melbourne? Melbourne was wily; he did not think he wanted to approach the Prime Minister direct. Baron Stockmar was the man. The Baron was the born intermediary and he would know how to couch Sir John's request in diplomatic terms.

He went at once to see Stockmar. Sir John sniggered inwardly. We are allies in misfortune in a way, he thought. The Baron had also aspired to the secretaryship and been declined – more politely in his case but nevertheless he was refused the post, so it came to the same thing in the end.

'Baron,' he said, 'I have reached the conclusion that the time for my retirement has come.' He smiled deprecatingly. 'I have reason to believe that there are some in the royal household who will not greatly regret my departure – in other words they may well be glad to see me go, and inclined to reward me for doing so. Therefore I will not beat about the bush. I am ready to go in exchange for the following considerations: a peerage, naturally; a pension of three thousand pounds a year; a seat on the Privy Council and the Grand Cross of the Bath.'

'You must be joking,' said Stockmar.

'I never joke on a serious subject.'

'My dear Sir John, do you really think these requests will be granted?'

'I have every confidence, Baron.'

'There is no harm in being confident,' replied the Baron.

'Certainly no harm ... only good. So you will place my terms before Lord Melbourne?'

His terms! thought the Baron. It was as though this were some disreputable bargain. Was it? There had been a certain amount of scandal concerning Sir John and the Duchess. Could it possibly be that this man was suggesting it would be necessary for the Queen to meet these demands because of her mother's relationship with him?

It was certainly a matter to lay before the Prime Minister.

'You may be assured,' said the Baron, 'that I shall lose no time in giving your suggestions to Lord Melbourne.'

'Good God!' cried the Prime Minister. 'Have you ever heard of such demands? The insolence! Why a Cabinet Minister would not expect so much.'

The Baron lifted his shoulders. 'Conroy was in a very special position in the Duchess's household.'

'Good God,' said the Prime Minister again. 'It's a form of blackmail.'

'One might call it that.'

'The fellow's a rogue.'

'I fear you may be right.'

'The Queen will not have him near her.' He smiled tenderly. 'She is very shrewd, which is quite miraculous in one so young.'

'She has always disliked him.'

'And rightly so. The blackguard. A seat on the Privy Council! I never heard anything like it.'

'You will know how to deal with the matter, Prime Minister.' Melbourne hesitated. 'In view of the rather delicate situation it will need some devilish clever handling.'

'I thought you would see it that way.'

'I'll consider it. Leave the matter with me.'

In spite of her youth she was the Queen and Melbourne could not conceal from Victoria the fact that Conroy had made his demands.

Victoria flushed with indignation when she heard. 'I always hated him. He told me once that I resembled Queen Charlotte and the Duke of Gloucester.'

Lord Melbourne burst out laughing. Victoria looked astonished but when Lord Melbourne laughed she always wanted to, so she laughed with him.

'Odious creature!' said Lord Melbourne. 'And an obvious liar. How could you possibly look like Queen Charlotte and the Duke of Gloucester?'

'You knew them both. What were they like?'

'As unlike Your Majesty as it is possible to be.'

More laughter. How happy he made her feel even at this time.

'What should be done about this man?' she asked.

'Nothing in a hurry,' replied her Prime Minister.

'I was hoping you would say dismiss him from Court.'

'That is what I should like to say, but the desire does not always coincide with the necessity.'

'I wish I need never see him again.'

'We might arrange that.'

'Then you will have arranged something very much to my liking.'

'We shall have to *consider* his demands in view of ... er ... his position in your mother's household.'

She blushed rather charmingly as she said: 'I know I can talk to you frankly, Lord Melbourne.'

'I trust Your Majesty is able to do that because it is very necessary to our relationship that we should be entirely frank with each other at all times.'

'A certain amount of scandal has been whispered about Mamma.'

'Ah! Scandal,' murmured Lord Melbourne, and she thought of his own very colourful life in which so many scandals had existed. Yet, she thought, he is the most perfect gentleman. But she was sorry she had mentioned the word if it brought back unhappy memories to dear Lord Melbourne.

'There are some people,' she said loyally, 'whom scandal cannot touch. But that is, of course, if they are *innocent*.'

Grasping the implication Lord Melbourne gave her a grateful look. How well we understand each other! she thought blissfully.

'But to return to this odious man,' said Lord Melbourne. 'He has been in the household of the Duchess of Kent for many years. I suppose a certain reward should be given him. Besides, it would be worthwhile to rid ourselves of him, would it not?'

'I should be delighted to be rid of him.'

'All Your Majesty need do is refuse to see him in any circumstances. But *I* would like to exile him to the country.'

She nodded.

'In the meantime,' said Lord Melbourne, 'we will shelve the matter by considering it. It is always better to let these things simmer and avoid rash actions.'

She was sure he was right. He always was right in any case.

When Lord Melbourne left, a messenger came to tell her that her mother the Duchess of Kent wished to see her.

She knew what this meant. Mamma was going to ask her to agree to Sir John's terms. Having no desire to be embroiled in one of her mother's scenes, remembered with such distaste from the days when she was, as she now began to consider herself, 'Mamma's prisoner', she sent back a message to say that she was too busy to grant the interview.

Then she sat down to think about Sir John and what a menace he had been in her childhood. If Mamma had not allowed that odious man to dominate her household, how different everything might have been and how glad she was that she now had Lord Melbourne to deal with this most disagreeable affair.

The Duchess's fury was turning to despair. To receive a note from her daughter saying she was too busy to see her own mother was the last straw, she declared to Sir John.

'She is dominated by Melbourne,' he told her. 'You can depend upon it. He is the one who is responsible for this highhanded behaviour.'

'Who does he think he is ... the King?'

Conroy grinned. 'Well, he might well be aspiring to that position.'

'You are not suggesting that she would marry the man!'

'Oh, no, even I wouldn't go as far as that. There's forty years difference in their ages and the Queen can't marry a commoner.'

'I should think not. The sooner she is married to one of her Coburg cousins the better.'

'Your brother Leopold will see to that, and I gather he still has some influence though he may well be ousted by Melbourne.'

'It shall be Ernest or Albert. She shall have the choice. And the sooner the better, I believe.'

'She is surrounded by our enemies, that is the trouble.'

'And she is so easy to lead.'

'We did not find it easy to lead her,' Sir John reminded her.

'By some people,' amended the Duchess. 'Melbourne ... Lehzen...'

'Ah, Lehzen,' sighed Sir John a little reproachfully. 'What a pity you cannot get someone more sympathetic to us into her household.'

'I will beg her to take in Flora.'

'That's a good notion.'

'And I shall ask her to see you sometimes. Her not doing so, in such a pointed way, makes it a little embarrassing for me.'

Sir John nodded. He knew that people were already whispering that the Queen's aversion to Sir John was due to her mother's relationship with him.

'I will write to her since she is too busy to see

108

her own mother.'

'Write calmly,' said Sir John.

'You may trust me.'

She sat down at her desk and feathers quivering with emotion she wrote to her daughter. She hoped that she was not letting Melbourne know how much she disliked her mother's Comptroller of the Household. In fact was she confiding too much in Lord Melbourne? Did she not think it might be wiser to see a little less of her Prime Minister?

'Take care,' she wrote, 'that Lord Melbourne is not *King*.'

When Victoria received the letter she blushed hotly.

How dared they! She included Sir John in her condemnation because she knew he would have had a hand in this. He made outrageous demands which were like blackmail, and then they dared speak so of Lord Melbourne!

Definitely she would never see Sir John Conroy again if she could help it; as for her mother, she would have to learn that her daughter was no longer her prisoner but the Queen of England!

Lord Melbourne said that it was not very suitable for the Queen to continue to live in Kensington Palace.

'Kensington Palace is all very well for the heiress presumptive to the throne; but when that heiress becomes the Queen that is a very different matter.'

Victoria was wistful. 'It is no easy matter to leave one's home.'

'But it is an easier matter to leave one of your

homes when you have many. And you can always come back for a spell to Kensington. Why your grandfather George III and his wife Queen Charlotte...' She made a little grimace. '...who incidentally bore no resemblance whatsoever to Your Majesty...' Victoria joined Lord Melbourne in his laughter. 'Your grandfather George III and Queen Charlotte loved Kew and they were very glad to leave Windsor to escape to it. They would walk about the place like a country squire and his lady and the King so interested himself in the farmers thereabouts that he often gave a hand with the butter-making.'

How their conversation strayed from the main point at issue and how fascinating that was! They had begun by talking of this move and ended up with King George at his butter-making.

'So,' went on Lord Melbourne, having succeeded in lifting the slight sadness which the prospect of moving had made her feel, 'Your Majesty will remember that you can always come back to Kensington when you wish.'

So she could but Lord Melbourne would understand that it was not *quite* the same.

'If you surround yourself with familiar objects – and why should you not? – it will make little difference to you whether you are in Kensington or Buckingham Palace.'

'You will come and see me every day?'

'That will be my duty and my pleasure.'

And so she had been wise and given her attention to the packing, for as she pointed out to Lehzen, there were so many personal possessions which one wished to look after oneself.

She and Lehzen spent a happy hour packing her dolls because although she rarely looked at them now it was inconceivable that they should be left behind. Lehzen was nothing loath. She had made quite a number of the dolls which represented characters from history – Queen Elizabeth was conspicuous among them.

'I never liked her,' said Victoria. 'She was really very cruel. I believe she was a great queen and perhaps I should try to be like her in some ways, but *I* shall try to be *good*. I want to make my people happy, Lehzen, and comfortable.'

Lehzen said that was a very worthy desire and she believed that Victoria in years to come would be known as 'Victoria the Good'.

What a pleasant thought! And there was her little dog Dash looking at her rather disconsolately as though he knew something was afoot.

'We are going to leave Kensington, Dashy,' she told him; and he put his head on one side and regarded her in that bright and intelligent way which she loved.

'The only good thing Conroy ever did,' she announced, 'was to give Mamma Dashy.'

'And he, being a wise dog, immediately decided to be yours.'

And Dash hearing his name mentioned gave his little series of joyous barks.

'Oh, Dashy,' she said, 'I do hope you are going to like Buckingham Palace.'

'We all shall, I've no doubt,' comforted Lehzen.

'All the same it is rather a solemn moment when one leaves one's birthplace. Just think,

111

Lehzen, for eighteen years this has been my home. Think of all that has happened here. Do you remember how we used to sit up here and play with the dolls?'

Lehzen remembered very well. 'I believe Amy Robsart was your favourite.'

'Well yes, because she was so sad and tragic.' Victoria picked up Queen Elizabeth and gave her a little shake, as she used to in the old days. 'Do you believe that Amy was murdered?'

'That is something we shall never know.'

'I remember dear Feodora's wedding. She is very happy now with her darling children. What fun it would be, Lehzen, if they could come and visit us. I'm sure they would love it.'

'You have only to ask them.'

'I shall, Lehzen, I shall. Oh dear, I *am* going to miss dear Kensington.'

'Buckingham Palace, as Lord Melbourne said, is far more suitable.'

So of course if Lord Melbourne said it, it must be so, and there should be no more regrets.

It was, naturally, more grand than Kensington. Her Uncle George IV had applied his considerable artistic talents to making it so, but when Uncle William and Aunt Adelaide had moved in and Adelaide had chosen some of the decor it had been voted decidedly vulgar.

With satisfaction Victoria examined her room; it was lofty, stately, and she would be alone, for she had made sure that the Duchess should have a quite separate set of apartments as far removed from her own as possible.

Standing at her window looking out across the gardens, she admitted that this was indeed a royal palace, although she still regretted Kensington for it was so hard to forget one's birthplace and the scene of one's childhood, girlhood and accession.

And when in bed that first night and the quiet of the Palace closed in on her she thought of the cosiness of Kensington and all the terrors of darkness descended on her. She had craved to be alone, but now the loneliness frightened her. She thought of the little Princes in the Tower – one of them the King of England. Stealthy footsteps in the night; a pillow pressed over the face. There had been scares in her childhood when a rumour had been in circulation that her uncle Cumberland had wanted the throne and was determined to get her out of the way. Uncle Cumberland was a man with an evil reputation. It was believed that he had committed one murder at least, and his wife had been married twice before and there was a certain mystery surrounding both her husbands' deaths. That was why Mamma had said she was never to be alone; and even when she had gone down the little twisting staircase she had had to be accompanied.

Now she was the Queen. 'Uneasy lies the head that wears a crown,' said Shakespeare, and he was a very wise man.

It was so very quiet in the room that one might be in the heart of the country, and although many people were sleeping in the Palace, tonight they seemed far away.

Oh, yes, Lehzen was in the next room but a wall

separated them and Buckingham Palace was so different from dear cosy Kensington.

Dash was sleeping in his basket. If anyone came in he would start to bark furiously. Dear, *dear* Dashy!

Tomorrow, she thought, I will have a door made in the wall so that Lehzen's room can communicate directly with mine. If it was desired, that door could be left open.

On that comforting thought she went to sleep.

When Lord Melbourne asked her how she liked Buckingham Palace she told him that she liked it; it was, as he said, so much more suitable for a royal residence; and Dashy *loved* the gardens.

The Duchess was far from pleased with her apartments. They were too cramped, she declared. But what really angered her was that Victoria had ordered that they should be separate and some distance from her own.

It was an insult! declared the Duchess.

Sir John, who was anxious about his future, suggested that it would be unwise to make too much fuss. They had to act with tact for Victoria had shown very clearly that she had forgotten all they had done for her during her childhood and she was completely under the spell of her Prime Minister.

Sir John was sure though that his demands would be met. After all it was a delicate situation and the new Queen would be made to understand that the less talk there was about the man who was reputed to be her mother's lover the better. The worldly wise Prime Minister would realise that;

and as that same gentleman was noted for a somewhat easy-going attitude towards difficult problems Sir John felt that he was right to be optimistic.

Meanwhile Victoria was finding life agreeable, and was very eager to forget Sir John Conroy.

She had taken the Duchess of Sutherland into her household and was greatly attracted to her. Harriet Leveson Gower, Duchess of Sutherland, was at the time in her early thirties, admired for her beauty, respected for her intellect, and being a Whig she had seemed an ideal choice for Mistress of the Robes. Such a good *feeling* person, Victoria confided to the Baroness; and indeed dear Harriet was constantly telling her about the evils in the country that she was sometimes quite depressed about it. Harriet believed that it was everyone's duty to improve the lot of the poor and needy and Victoria was horrified to hear of the terrible things that were happening in her realm.

She was so upset that she spoke of this to Lord Melbourne, but he was as comforting as ever.

'Little children are being dragged from their beds at three in the morning to go to the mines and on all fours drag the carts of coal through underground passages in the coal mines!'

'Whoever told you such stories?'

'Harriet did. She knows a great deal about such things. She is very concerned with them.'

'I think it better not to concern oneself with such matters.'

'Oh, but do you, Lord Melbourne? Surely my subjects' welfare is my concern?'

'It is, indeed it is. But this subject does not like to see his Queen distressed.'

'*Dear* Lord Melbourne, but is it not my duty...?'

'Your duty is to smile for the people, to let them see how happy you are to be their Queen.'

'Oh, I am, but the thought of those poor children ... *little* children, no older than dear Lord John Russell's babies ... dragging carriages through the mines ... it is terrible.'

'They enjoy it. It is a game to them.'

'Can it really be?'

'You can depend upon it.'

And of course one had to depend upon Lord Melbourne.

'Harriet is also worried about the way lunatics are treated in our asylums, and the people working in mills and factories. Her great friend, the Earl of Shaftesbury, is determined to do something about it. He cares so much for the poor.'

'Shaftesbury. He is not so fond of his own family. What a pity he doesn't concern himself with making life easier for them!'

'But dear Lord Melbourne, I feel that I should know about these things.'

'They are things which are best left alone. Change often makes things a thousand times worse.'

Then Lord Melbourne started to tell her a funny story about Grandfather George III who visiting a cottage found a woman baking dumplings and could not understand how an apple got into a dumpling.

She rocked with laughter. Lord Melbourne could be so amusing.

She was also very fond of Lord John Russell – 'Little Johnny' as he was called. Lord Melbourne told her in a very humorous manner how Johnny was so small that when he stood up to speak in Parliament he could scarcely be seen above the boxes on the table. He was the Leader of the House of Commons and Victoria, although not as delighted with him as she was with her Prime Minister (that would have been impossible), found him delightful. She liked Lady John and one of the reasons she saw a great deal of the Russell family was because of the children. Little Johnny had married quite late in life, Lord Melbourne had told her, for now she and her Prime Minister discussed not only State matters but as Lord Melbourne put it, 'everything under the sun', which meant quite racy stories about some of his fellow members of Parliament. Not that there was anything racy about Little Johnny, who had married a widow at the age of forty-three. She already had four children by her first husband and now she and Lord John had a little girl of their own. 'Five young children! How very happy you must be,' cried Victoria to Lady John; and realised that one of the things she wanted most was to have children. Whenever Lady John was due to call, Victoria asked: 'Please bring the babies.' And what fun she had with them, racing up and down the corridors of the Palace.

'Really,' said Lehzen indulgently, 'is this the Queen of England?'

And laughingly Victoria pointed out that one of the pleasures of being Queen of England was that in matters that did not interfere with State policy, a queen could do exactly as she wished.

The first little difference with Lord Melbourne came over the matter of the review of her troops in Hyde Park.

'I will do so on horseback,' she told her Prime Minister.

'I think it would be better to do the review in a carriage,' said Lord Melbourne.

'My dear Lord Melbourne, I shall certainly *not* ride to review my troops in a carriage!'

'I should tremble for your safety if you rode on horseback. It's some time since you rode. It would be most unsafe.'

'Then it is certainly time I showed you that I know how to manage a horse.'

For once her mother and Melbourne were in agreement. 'It would be most improper,' said the Duchess.

'It would be most undignified for the Queen to ride in a carriage,' retorted Victoria.

'I'm afraid I cannot advise you to ride on horseback,' replied Lord Melbourne firmly.

'This is not a matter of State,' she answered.

'Begging Your Majesty's pardon I consider it to be,' said the Prime Minister.

She had held her head high and the colour was hot on her cheeks. 'I refuse to ride in a carriage,' she declared. 'And if there is to be no horse for me there will be no review.'

Lord Melbourne thought it best to cancel the review; the news leaked out; the papers took up the story and there were rhymes about the stubborn little Queen's disagreement with her Prime Minister; but they liked her for it. She might be tiny but she had a high spirit.

'As for Lord Melbourne,' Victoria commented to Lehzen, 'he was concerned for *my* safety which proves once more what a good, kind, *feeling* man he is.'

Now that she had been proclaimed Queen and had seen her Ministers there was no reason why she should stay in London. Lord Melbourne suggested that the Court should move to Windsor, which would give Her Majesty an opportunity of enjoying the country and taking rides in the forest. A sly allusion to the review contretemps which had amused them both

How she loved Windsor! What a fine old place and here again she must thank Uncle George IV.

'In the days of your grandfather, the third George,' Lord Melbourne told her, 'it was the most uncomfortable place on earth. They used to say there was enough draught in the corridors to sail a battleship; and in the winter only your grandfather was hardy enough to go to the Chapel. It was like being in the Arctic circle.'

She so much enjoyed hearing stories of the family and what a wonderful raconteur Lord Melbourne was.

Every day he was closeted with her while they discussed State business, which was enlivened by these pleasant little anecdotes.

'You should know these details about your family,' said Lord Melbourne. 'It's history.'

She enjoyed the mornings because then she had him all to herself; it was so cosy, so friendly, so stimulating and interesting; and what more

119

proper than that the Queen should discuss business with her Prime Minister? Nobody could explain the tiresome details of politics as lucidly as Lord M. It seemed so much more friendly to think of him by this abbreviated form of his name. He made everything so easy to understand and would never let her worry about anything.

'It's a mistake to worry,' he said. 'Worry never cured anything. Let events take their course.'

That was his motto; he was lazy, easy-going and nothing seemed so vital that one must have the smallest anxiety about it, and so many things were amusing that one could laugh at them. So much of the morning was spent in laughing. But of course she was learning all the time. She learned to love the Whigs and hate the Tories; but alas, said Lord Melbourne, the Whigs were not as strong in the House of Commons as they would like to be, but now that people were beginning to realise how friendly the Queen felt towards the Whigs, the next election would doubtless change that.

His sayings were so original. He never carried a watch, she discovered. 'But, dear Lord M, how do you know the time?' she asked.

'I always ask a servant and he tells me what he likes.'

She roared with laughter. Perhaps it was the droll way Lord Melbourne made these observations which seemed so funny or perhaps she laughed so much because she was happy. She was constantly telling herself how fortunate she was to have come to the throne when Lord Melbourne was Prime Minister, for it might so easily have

120

been grim old Lord Grey (how dreary!) or the old Duke of Wellington (how terrifying!). But it was neither of these. It was the kindest, best, most wonderful *feeling* man in the world.

Every afternoon they went riding in the forest, she and Lord M leading the cavalcade. The Prime Minister looked magnificent, in Victoria's opinion, on a very fine black mare which he had had sent down from London. Behind came other members of her Government who happened to be staying at Windsor, with some of her household and guests. She herself usually rode the spirited Barbara who was a little frisky, and she was glad of this because she was eager to show Lord Melbourne that he need have no qualms about her riding. The Baroness Lehzen was sometimes of the party, following the riders in a little pony cart.

Those afternoon rides were the best part of the day... No, that was the morning, or perhaps in the evening when she would sit with Lord Melbourne beside her and they would chat and laugh in the happiest manner.

After the ride they would return to the Castle and there was a little time to be filled in before dinner. Sometimes she played games – not with Lord Melbourne this time, but with some of the younger members of the Court. One could hardly expect the Prime Minister to indulge in a game of battledore or shuttlecock. If the John Russells were there she would play with their children for a while or any other young people who were in the Palace; and after that dinner.

Sometimes important guests would be at the

Castle and she must devote a certain amount of time to them; but if a distinguished visitor must sit on her right hand it was always Lord Melbourne who sat on her left. That had come to be regarded as his special place.

The Duchess was at Windsor, of course, and while Victoria always showed affection towards her in public, there it stopped. They rarely saw each other in private.

The disappointed Duchess would sit nodding drowsily until the whist started. It was said that only the game kept her awake.

They were wonderful days; Victoria had never been so happy in the whole of her life.

What a triumphant day it was when she reviewed the troops at Windsor on horseback! There was a little tussle with Lord Melbourne about this. He said that her favourite Barbara was too frisky; she declared that she loved to ride Barbara best of all.

'Leopold would be much safer,' commented Lord Melbourne.

'Then I shall ride Barbara to show you that I am not such a poor horsewoman as you appear to imagine.'

Lord Melbourne replied that he knew she was a superb horsewoman; their riding together had convinced him of that; but he was a fussy old man and he simply would not have a moment's peace until the review was over if the Queen rode Barbara.

Since he put it in such a way what could she do but ride Leopold? Secretly she had to admit that once again Lord Melbourne was right for the review had lasted over two hours and she knew that frisky Barbara would have objected most strongly to that while Leopold had come through, his docility unimpaired.

Afterwards, taking a ride on Barbara with Lord Melbourne beside her, she had demanded: 'And now, Lord M, have you such a poor opinion of my performance on horseback?'

'My opinion is, as it always was, that Your Majesty performs all her duties to perfection. And when she listens to an old man who in his devotion cannot suppress his fears, unfounded as they are I am sure, then she adds understanding to her other talents and that is a rare quality.'

Trust Lord M to say *exactly* what one most liked to hear.

As though to make everything perfect in this very happy time, Uncle Leopold decided it was time he paid a visit, so he and Aunt Louise arrived in England.

Victoria was excited; she told Lord Melbourne of another occasion when she and Mamma had gone to Ramsgate to meet her uncle and aunt and how the people had cheered.

'Uncle Leopold is *so* popular in England. I think everyone was very attached to him because of the terrible tragedy of my cousin Charlotte's death.'

'That was a long time ago,' said Lord Melbourne, and she was not sure whether he was referring to Princess Charlotte's death or Uncle Leopold's popularity, and before she could ask he went on: 'You cannot expect the people to go on mourning for an event which gave them their present most beloved Queen.'

'Charlotte would have been a good Queen I am sure with Uncle Leopold to help her.'

'I believe he is very eager to help Your Majesty ... as others are.'

'Oh, I am *so* lucky.'

This conversation had taken place in the blue closet, the spot she had chosen for her meetings with the Prime Minister, and therefore her favourite room. It had been even more cosy since Dash had attended the meetings.

'Do you mind Dashy being here, Lord M?' she had asked.

'I am secretly delighted to see him. We share our greatest enthusiasm – devotion to Your Majesty.'

'He *is* devoted. No one would think he started by being Mamma's dog. And that horrid Sir John gave him to her. What is happening about his affairs?'

'The gift of Dash was indeed a satisfactory act on his part but I doubt whether Your Majesty's Government would think it worthy of a baronetcy, the income he demands, plus the Grand Order of the Bath.'

Victoria began to giggle. Trust Lord M to introduce a humorous note into the conversation!

Dash came up to sniff Lord Melbourne's boots and when the Prime Minister patted him he licked his hands.

'All dogs like me,' said Lord Melbourne.

'They are noted for their sagacity,' replied the Queen.

And there they were laughing again. Oh, the

meetings in the blue closet were such fun!

When Leopold and Louise arrived, she noticed that her uncle looked much older. So did poor Aunt Louise, and she seemed much less gay than she had been during that other visit. Of course Uncle Leopold *was* a little solemn. She hadn't been aware of this before but now that she had grown accustomed to Lord Melbourne's most amusing and original conversation she noticed these things.

They had many private conversations during which Uncle Leopold harked back somewhat to the days when she had called him her second father and how much they had always meant to each other. They wept a little but even Leopold's tears weren't quite the same as Lord M's. Lord Melbourne's appeared in his eyes and made him look so kind; whereas one felt Uncle Leopold's meant he was sorry for himself.

Uncle Leopold was tortured by his various ailments but he did not look as ill as he implied. Lord Melbourne told her a story about Uncle Leopold and Aunt Louise which was that when Aunt Louise had said something amusing Uncle Leopold was reputed to have retorted sharply: 'No jokes please, Madam.' He didn't like jokes but what harm was there in laughing? She and Lord Melbourne continually laughed but she did not think the country suffered because of that. But these faint criticisms were never allowed to be examined very closely. Victoria was essentially loyal and she would never forget her devotion to Uncle Leopold.

During her talks with him he expressed his

admiration for Lord Melbourne which immediately removed that little tarnish which had touched his image. He was delighted, he said, that she had such an excellent adviser.

'I have no doubt that he will do everything in his power to be useful to you,' he said. 'He was in a very awkward position with the late King who didn't like him at all.'

'Uncle William was so unwise in many ways, I fear.'

'But it is very happy for Lord Melbourne now that he has your confidence and support.'

'He shall always have it,' she answered fervently.

At which Leopold retorted: 'My dearest child, only while he deserves it, I hope.'

'Of course,' she replied, and felt faintly disloyal until she reminded herself that Lord Melbourne would *always* deserve it.

Uncle Leopold was disappointed that she had not taken Stockmar more into her confidence.

'Now there is a man you *can* trust.'

'I am certain of that, Uncle.'

'I think it is possible that the letters between us may be intercepted. I must try to arrange something through Stockmar.'

He went on to say that he hoped the friendship between England and Belgium would always be strong.

'I cannot imagine it otherwise,' said the Queen.

'Trouble is blowing up in Europe and the support of England may be necessary to us.'

'I am sure Lord Melbourne will be most anxious to give it.'

'I am sure he will if it is the wish of the Queen.'

Oh dear, she thought, it is true that dear as Uncle Leopold is to me he *is* the King of a foreign power; and being a princess unconcerned with politics is very different from being the Queen. She would have to talk with Lord Melbourne and ask him to explain the European situation before she could make any promises.

Still, Uncle Leopold seemed certain of her support so she left it at that. She really wanted to think of the entertainments she would offer them while they were visitors at her Court.

Lord Palmerston joined them at Windsor. She liked Palmerston, the Foreign Secretary, and of course Uncle Leopold had a great deal to say to him. Lord Palmerston was a wizard, Lord Melbourne told her; he had raised the prestige of England greatly since he had joined the Foreign Office seven years before. He was a fluent linguist and that, as Lord Melbourne said, enabled him to understand what the foreigners were getting at. Lord Melbourne told her that he was nicknamed 'Cupid' and that spoke for itself. He was a very gay bachelor. She replied that she really did enjoy the company of gay people.

The evenings could on occasions be a little disappointing; that was because there were usually so many people present. She would have liked more dances for she loved to dance and could do so all through the night until four in the morning without tiring of it. Unfortunately there were so few people who were considered worthy to dance with her, which was a pity. The Duchess was a continual reproach too, sitting there yawning and almost falling asleep until she felt forced to call out: 'Dear Mamma, do go to your whist if you wish. I am sure you are longing to play.'

That would take care of the Duchess and then the Queen could indulge in some other game. Sometimes they played draughts and even chess. She challenged Aunt Louise to a game of the latter which really was amusing since they were both queens and she knew that the company were making allusions to this as the game progressed. It was particularly significant when Lord Melbourne and Palmerston hovered over her and advised her how to checkmate Aunt Louise, and Uncle Leopold advised his wife. She was so amused and laughed so much that she lost the game, which made dear Lord Melbourne look quite disconsolate.

In due course Leopold left and when he had gone she realised how much she loved him. She really did miss him.

'*My dearest most beloved Uncle,*' she wrote,

One line to express to you imperfectly *my thanks for all your very great kindness to me and my* great great *grief at your departure.* How *I shall miss you, my dearest dear uncle,* every every where. *I feel* very very *sad and cannot speak of you both without crying...*'

She was pleased that she did feel so strongly and she hoped the accentuating of important words would convince her uncle.

But it only made her all the more thankful that she had dear Lord M to turn to. And reflecting on all that had happened. since her accession she wrote in her Journal... 'This is the pleasantest summer I *ever* passed in my life and I shall never forget the first summer of my reign.'

Chapter 5

LEOPOLD IS PUT IN HIS PLACE

One could not stay forever at Windsor and in October it was necessary to return to London. On Lord Mayor's Day she must attend the dinner at the Guildhall, which was to be a glorious occasion given in her honour.

It was pleasant riding through the streets and seeing how she pleased the people.

'The little duck,' she heard one woman say, which wasn't really very respectful, as she remarked afterwards to Lord Melbourne.

'Oh, I don't know,' was his answer, 'I have always had a great respect for ducks.'

Which made her rock with laughter, and reflect that Uncle Leopold would never have said such a thing.

After the dinner when she returned to the Palace there was a letter awaiting her from her mother. She recognised the handwriting of Sir John, who was still in her mother's household waiting for his impossible demands to be met.

The Duchess was shocked and deeply wounded. She had, she wrote, been insulted at the Guildhall

129

and it was humiliating for the mother of the Queen to be placed after minor relations. Was she to expect similar treatment at the Coronation? She knew that for a subject to expect audience of the Queen might seem an impertinence but she had yet to learn that the request of a mother to a daughter could be described in those terms, and she wished to see Victoria without delay.

When Baroness Lehzen read the letter, which Victoria passed to her, she was pleased. The Court had divided into two domestic factions – that of the Queen and her ladies, at the head of whom was Baroness Lehzen, and the Duchess with Sir John and hers. Lehzen particularly disliked Lady Flora Hastings who was constantly making sly allusions to her enemy's origins. It was gratifying, therefore, that the Duchess had to beg for an interview with the Queen when she, the companion or whatever name was attached to her, for she had no official title, was allowed to come to the Queen at all times in the most unceremonious fashion.

'I suppose I shall have to see her,' sighed Victoria.

'You are the Queen,' said Lehzen significantly.

'I know, but she's right. She *is* my mother and nothing can alter that.'

Which was a pity, thought Lehzen, but knew that Victoria would not wish to hear her say so. The Queen was very much aware of her duties in life and honouring her mother was one of them.

So the Duchess came to her apartments and Victoria was held in a suffocating embrace.

'My dearest angel!'

'Dear Mamma.'

'You are a stranger almost. Let me look at you. I only see you in public nowadays.'

'Mamma, you have no idea how busy I am kept.'

'I know I am the perfect ignoramus.'

'Oh, not that, Mamma, no. But before my accession *I* had no idea what hundreds of duties there would be. What I should do without the help of Lord Melbourne, I can't imagine.'

'*He* has become very important in the last few months.'

'Dear Mamma, a Prime Minister is always important.'

'There could rarely have been such an important Prime Minister as this one.'

'He takes his duties very seriously.'

'Much more seriously since we have had a new Sovereign.'

'Because the good man realises that with an inexperienced girl on the throne his duties are naturally greater.'

'Yes, my dearest love, you *are* inexperienced. That is why I must speak to you. Your attitude to me is not liked by the people, you know. *I* am very popular. People noticed at the Guildhall how I was slighted and they didn't like it. They didn't like it at all. You will not impress them by neglecting your mother who did everything for you... yes, *everything...*'

They were back on a familiar theme and Victoria said regally, 'I have no time to quarrel, Mamma.'

'Quarrel! Who is quarrelling, I should like to know?'

'You are, Mamma. And I have simply no time to indulge in scenes like this. I will speak to Lord Melbourne.'

'Of course you will. You do little else.'

'I will ask my Prime Minister to make sure that you are given your rightful place at the Coronation.'

'And there is one thing else. Do you think it wise to ignore Sir John as you do?'

'I have no wish to do anything else but ignore him.'

'People talk because of your attitude. They gossip and ask each other why you will not receive Sir John and are so unkind to me.'

'If your conscience is clear, Mamma, you have no need to be concerned about gossip.'

'We all have need to be concerned about gossip if it touches us.'

'Well, Mamma, I will not receive Sir John. That I have always made clear.'

'Are you going to help him? Do you forget what he has done for me and for you, too.'

'I am unsure what he has done for either of us that has been to his credit or our benefit.'

'You have become hard. Is that Lord Melbourne's teaching?'

'I wish you would not continually bring Lord Melbourne's name into the conversation. And I advise you to be very careful because Parliament will soon be discussing the Civil List which could bring some benefit to you, Mamma.'

'It is nothing more than I deserve,' said the Duchess somewhat mollified as she always was at the prospect of money, and Victoria was able to bring the interview to a close on a more peaceful note.

When the Duchess left, the Baroness, who had been waiting in the next room, came out.

'Oh dear,' said Victoria. 'What a scene! It reminded me of the old days at Kensington.'

Leopold had noticed nothing different in Victoria's attitude towards him during his visit to England and her letter written after his departure confirmed her continued adoration for and devotion to him.

He was determined that England should be Belgium's ally and at this moment Belgium needed allies. On his return he passed through France and saw the French Prime Minister and Foreign Secretary, Count Molé, and in his usual somewhat arrogant way warned him as to the action France would be wise to take towards Spain, Portugal and Greece.

He hoped, he wrote to Victoria, that the English Government would fall into line with the French and he wished her to tell her ministers so. She would understand that the Monarchy was a little uneasy in France. That it had been restored was a matter for rejoicing in all royal houses through-out Europe, and it must be the concern of all royalists to keep it steady. With regard to the Peninsula she would agree that there could be action there which England might take more easily than France and she might agree that it was wise to ask her ministers to decide that it was a necessary action.

When Victoria read this letter she was bewildered. Uncle Leopold, it seemed, was trying to lead English foreign policy. Of course he was only advising her for her own good, but Uncle Leopold did seem to forget that she was not merely a niece to be taught a lesson or two about the world; she was a Queen with her own Government.

The obvious action was to show the letter to Lord Melbourne and this she did at the earliest possible moment.

Lord Melbourne was a little grave and told her that he would discuss Leopold's letter with Lord Palmerston.

Her Majesty will understand readily enough I know, he pointed out, that it is not policy to discuss a possible foreign policy with the head of another country however close in kinship that head might be with the Sovereign. There were close family ties between many European countries and if they discussed foreign affairs with one another they might as well be conducted in the open and there would be no such thing as diplomacy. He trusted Her Majesty understood and approved.

She did, even though this concerned her dearest Uncle.

'Perhaps Your Majesty would care to write to the King of the Belgians and tell him that you are placing these political enquiries in the hands of your Prime Minister and the Foreign Secretary?'

'That is exactly the right thing to do,' she said with relief.

And this she did, but Leopold did not mean to relinquish his influence with his niece. He continued to write to her pointing out the need for

134

English support in Belgian projects; and at Lord Melbourne's suggestion she wrote back and told him that it was impossible for her to give her word that England would act in such and such a way, for she could not be sure what her Government might find it necessary to do in an emergency before that emergency arose.

Leopold was uneasy. He wrote to her:

'My dearest child.
You were somewhat irritable when you wrote to me...'

He was very disappointed in her, she knew, because he did not discuss political issues further. Instead he wrote about her cousin Albert She remembered Albert, of course, the young cousin whom she had so much admired when he visited England the previous year; Uncle Leopold had made it quite clear then that he hoped one day they would marry, although if she preferred Albert's brother there would be no objection.

Last year when life had been very dull, she had been quite happy with the idea; but it was rather different now. She had not given marriage a thought since she had mounted the throne, though now she supposed she would have to consider taking a husband for to provide an heir was a Queen's vital duty to the State. She would love to have babies. She thought of the little Russells, who were so often at the Palace, and the little Conynghams who called her the 'Tween', the darlings! But a husband? No, she did not think she wanted a husband. He might interfere. She was quite happy to have Lord M to advise her.

All the same it was much better that Uncle Leopold, rather than write of politics, should tell her what Albert was doing in Bonn where he was undertaking special studies to 'prepare himself' as Uncle Leopold called it. To prepare him for what? Marriage? Well, if she did not want marriage she would not have it ... yet.

She did hope Uncle Leopold would understand that he must not meddle too much in English affairs. That was Lord Palmerston's province – and of course dear Lord Melbourne's.

Lord Melbourne came to tell her that the new Civil List had been passed through Parliament.

'We have got them to agree to £375,000 a year, £60,000 of which will be for Your Majesty's privy purse.'

'What a lot of money!'

'In addition to that of course you have the revenues from the Duchies of Cornwall and Lancaster.'

'So much money!' cried the Queen, her blue eyes wide.

'You are the first Sovereign who has thought it so much.'

'Surely anyone would think it a great deal?'

'Oh, you are very careful with money. You will never be in debt as your uncles continually were, and even your grandfather George III, parsimonious as he was, couldn't make ends meet!'

'I always budgeted,' said the Queen. 'That dreadful man Conroy laughed at me for it.'

'He couldn't understand wise spending. He has

been a poor choice for Household Comptroller as your mother's affairs have shown.'

'He was supposed to have settled my father's debts but he never did. Now that I have so much money that is what I shall do. All my father's creditors shall be paid in full.'

Lord Melbourne's eyes filled with tears.

'A noble suggestion,' he said, 'and one that does not surprise me one little bit.'

'It is very unfair to one's creditors not to pay one's debts. I am surprised that my father did it.'

'It is a tradition of princes to live beyond their means.'

'A sad tradition for the poor tradesmen.'

'Oh, they expect it.'

'They must also expect to be paid sometimes.'

'But not by Royalty.'

'Then I shall surprise them. Was my father very extravagant?'

'No more so than his brothers. He resembled King George IV more than King William. He was charming and affable and very popular.'

'I'm glad of that. But I'm sorry he was extravagant. I should like to think he was a good man.'

Lord Melbourne smiled benignly at her and wondered if she had heard rumours of her father's liaison with Madame Saint Laurent. It had, it was true, been as respectable in its way as William's with Dorothy Jordan; and like William on his State marriage he had abandoned the woman who had been as a wife to him for ... was it twenty years or so? These Royal Dukes would have been faithful husbands if the State had allowed them to be. But it had all happened a long time ago and although Victoria must have asked her mother, and those who would have known him, what her father was like, it was almost certain that no one would have mentioned Madame Saint Laurent.

'Your mother might take charge of those debts. She has been granted an extra £8,000 which means she will now have an annual income of £30,000.'

'That should please her. But I can see I must be the one to pay my father's debts because if I left it to her Comptroller (I can scarcely bring myself to say his name!) he would never do it. I must think of those poor creditors.'

'I can tell you that the sole reason why she was granted this money was out of respect for you. So she has you to thank for it.'

Lord Melbourne fixed his tenderly tearful gaze upon her and she was happy.

Life could not be all happiness and Victoria was very sad because news had come to her that old Louie was very ill and not expected to live.

'Of course she is very old,' said Lord Melbourne.

'But it is very sad all the same.'

'We all have to go sometime,' replied Lord Melbourne.

He was right, of course, but she was very unhappy. She kept thinking of those visits to Claremont when Louie had greeted her with her own special kind of curtsy and then had carried her off to her own room and had chatted about Princess Charlotte.

The Court was leaving for Windsor, but before she went she must go and see dear Louie.

What a shock to find her so changed! She was quite distressed because she could not rise from her bed and make that very special curtsy.

'Dearest Louie,' cried Victoria, kissing her.

'Your Majesty!' murmured Louie, overcome by the honour.

'Foolish Louie! Did you expect me to love you less because I am the Queen?'

'It's wrong that I should be lying here and Your Majesty standing.'

'Then I'll sit and you lie still. That is an order. I give orders now.'

Louie laughed. 'You always did.'

'Oh yes. I could be very demanding, I am sure. Oh, they were happy days and how I used to look forward to them! I remember so well your having breakfast in your room in your neat morning gown and then in the evening dressed in your best. You always stood up so straight and the curtsy you gave me was so dignified ... it was like no one else's. I think you thought me a little like Charlotte.'

Louie nodded.

'And sometimes I declare you mistook me for her.'

'Yet you are so different. Charlotte could be very naughty and you were on the whole such a good little girl.'

'Mamma would not agree. She was constantly accusing me of having storms.'

'Ah, that temper of yours. Is it still as fiery?'

'I fear it is, Louie. I am very hot-tempered. I get

really angry sometimes. Although not so much lately. Perhaps it is because I am Queen or it may be because Lord Melbourne makes everything so easy for me.'

'You have good advisers. You will be a great queen. I wish I could live to see it.'

'Oh, Louie,' said Victoria and the tears began to fall down her cheeks.

'But Your Little Majesty mustn't cry for me,' said Louie shocked.

Victoria leant over her and kissed her. She couldn't stop crying because she knew that it was for the last time.

She was at Windsor when the news came of Louie's death. She wept bitterly and sat down at once to write to Uncle Leopold about it because of Louie's having been so close to Princess Charlotte, she was sure he would want to know.

'I don't think I have ever been so much overcome or distressed by anything as by the death of my earliest friend... I always loved Louie and shall cherish her memory...'

Lord Melbourne, finding her red-eyed and disconsolate, immediately expressed his concern.

'She was really my earliest friend,' explained Victoria. 'I feel that the first link has been broken with my childhood.'

'As we get older,' said the philosophical Lord Melbourne, 'such broken links are so numerous that one scarcely notices them.'

'How terrible!'

'Nothing is so bad when one becomes accustomed to it,' replied Lord Melbourne. 'You have lost an old friend but you have new ones. That is the compensation of life.'

So she looked at dear Lord Melbourne and was comforted, reminding herself that poor Louie *was* old, her time had come and she went peacefully.

'She was prepared I am sure, although she thought she would get better,' she explained. 'What I mean is she was so good all her life that she was ready at any time to die.'

'She was always very neat and her soul would be in as orderly a condition as her kitchen.'

Lord Melbourne was rather wickedly flippant, but one would not expect him to make *ordinary* remarks; and he never shocked her, although he did some people, because she knew what a good kind man he was. In any case his light-hearted comments made her feel less unhappy and she told him so. She was therefore comforted.

'To bring comfort to Your Majesty is the main purpose of my life,' he answered.

So of course she had to smile and try to put aside her grief. 'There is the matter of a Coronation,' went on Lord Melbourne.

'Have you fixed a date for it?'

'Most certainly it must be June – the month of your accession.'

'I hope I shall not disappoint anyone.'

'I have no fear whatsoever of such an occurrence. Now,' he went on briskly, 'if Your Majesty will be kind enough to give me a list of the ladies whom you would like to carry your train, that will

141

be a beginning. You will, I know, consider the position of the young ladies and select them with that in mind.'

'I shall try not to offend anyone.'

'That will, I fear, be an impossibility because every young lady at Court will wish for the honour of carrying Your Majesty's train, and will be offended if she is not chosen.'

'Oh dear, how sad that one cannot please everyone.'

'As one can't, let us think of those who will be pleased and forget the others.'

'It seems a little *unfeeling*.'

'Good sound sense often does to those whom it affects adversely,' said Lord Melbourne.

'I hope I shall look well in my Coronation robes. How I wish I were even a few inches taller. Everyone seems to grow but me.'

'I think you have grown in the last months.'

'Do you really think so or are you being kind?'

'If I were not kind I should deserve to be kicked out of the Castle; and when I say you have grown I am not necessarily referring to inches. Of what importance are they? You have grown in wisdom, dignity, understanding, sympathy. These are the qualities of sovereignty, not inches.'

'Dear Lord Melbourne. You are *such* a comfort. But I do wish I were good looking – like Harriet Leveson Gower for instance.'

'She is an old woman compared with you. She would make a very poor Queen.'

'Now why do you say that, Lord M?'

'Because she would never take the advice of her Prime Minister.'

She threw back her head and laughed. Then she was sorry because she should really be crying for Louie. Trust Lord Melbourne to amuse her so much that she forgot her sorrow.

Victoria's first thought when she awoke in her bedroom in Buckingham Palace on the 19th of May was: This is my birthday. My first birthday as Queen of England!

What a sobering thought. She had been Queen for eleven months and she was nineteen years old.

This was going to be a very special birthday, different from the last when she had been under the control of her mother. Now she would say what the celebrations would be and she had already chosen a ball.

We shall dance all night, she thought, and I shall not go to bed until four in the morning ... five if I wish.

She remembered the ball Uncle William and Aunt Adelaide had given for her and how Mamma had been so angry that she had made the Kensington Palace party leave when it had only been in progress an hour. How angry Uncle William had been, but Mamma had very rudely ignored the fact that he was King, just as she now forgot that Victoria was Queen.

Well, there would be no interference this time. It would be her first State ball as Queen of England, and it was going to be the grandest and most magnificent occasion. Everyone was going to enjoy it thoroughly – most of all the Queen.

First of all there would be the receiving of

presents. Mamma had always been a great giver of presents. In the old days at Kensington they used to be set out on tables and at Christmas she, Feodora and Mamma had had their own tables. How fond Mamma was of giving bracelets and brooches containing a lock of her own hair!

There was a knock on the communicating door which she had had cut in the wall between her bedroom and that of Lehzen.

The Baroness entered.

'Many happy returns of the day.'

'Oh, thank you, Lehzen.'

They embraced.

'Nineteen. Really I am growing up, but at no time more than this past year. Lord Melbourne says there is a great change in me.'

Not wanting her to start on a eulogy of Lord Melbourne – the easiest thing in the world for her to do it seemed – the Baroness reminded her of the busy day ahead of her and asked if Her Majesty would care to get up now and if she wished to breakfast alone.

It was rather a solemn day. There were so many people to see and so many congratulations to receive. The guns fired a salute in the Park and she went on to the balcony to wave to the crowds. The people were charmed with her. 'Like a little doll,' they said. 'No more than a girl.'

This was clearly a very important occasion, but one of Mamma's presents gave her a few uneasy moments. It was a copy of King Lear.

Oh dear, thought Victoria, I never really liked King Lear. It's rather an *unpleasant* play. Besides it is about ungrateful daughters. I do hope Mamma is not trying to *spoil* this day.

It was impossible to spoil the State ball. The ballroom was beautiful and the ladies in their laces and ribbons, satins and velvets, feathers and diamonds, were charming.

They were all waiting for her and she went through the saloon to the ballroom feeling a little nervous (but she remembered that Lord Melbourne had said that all people with high and *right* feelings were sometimes nervous) and there the dazzling scene met her eyes; everyone watched her as she made her entrance; the men bowed and the ladies curtsied as she took her place on the sofa.

The band played Strauss music and she thought she had never heard anything so beautiful as a Strauss band.

Alas that she could not join in the waltz. That was too intimate and as there was no young Royalty present no one was worthy to put an arm about her waist as was done in this rather daring dance. So she could only join in the quadrilles and the gavottes and such dances, which she did with gusto.

She would never *never* tire of dancing, she told her partners. And she hoped every one of her guests was enjoying this *lovely* ball as much as she was.

There was one disappointment. She had expected Lord Melbourne to come and pay his respects. How pleasant it would have been to sit beside him on the sofa while the waltz was in progress which would have been almost as good

145

as dancing. But Lord Melbourne was not at the ball, which was very odd indeed.

While she was dancing she forgot Lord Melbourne. Lord Alfred Paget really was most amusing and very handsome. She had been slightly aware of him when out riding but had been too absorbed in Lord Melbourne's brilliant conversation to take much notice of him. Now she could appreciate his good looks and his devotion; he really was rather charming.

He was twenty-one, he told her, two years older than she was; and he had a retriever called Mrs Bumps. Victoria laughed at the name.

'What an odd name! I daresay she is very dignified and adores you.'

Lord Alfred thought this might be true of Mrs Bumps; he admitted that he had a portrait of Her Majesty which he carried with him always and that Mrs Bumps, whom he was determined should be as staunch an admirer of Her Majesty as he was himself, also wore a portrait of the Queen about her neck.

'What a wonderful idea!' cried Victoria. 'I think that is excellent. A dog to wear my portrait!'

'Why not?' demanded Lord Alfred. 'Mrs Bumps is one of your subjects also.'

She was enchanted. *What* a wonderful ball! But now they were playing the waltz and she must sit on her sofa and watch them, when she would so much have loved to be dancing the waltz – perhaps with Lord Alfred.

Then her thoughts turned to Lord Melbourne. It really was strange that he should be absent.

It was supper time and she led the way into the

banqueting room where the royal liveried foot-men were waiting to serve. Everyone seemed to want to have a word with the Queen and she was eager to speak to as many as possible for she was not in the least tired.

'Oh, no,' she cried to solicitous enquiries, 'I could go on dancing all night.'

And she did, for it was four o'clock before the ball was over.

When she was very young, before her accession, one of her greatest treats had been to stay up late and she still felt excited to do so. It had been a heavenly ball, and it shall be the first of many, she promised herself.

She was too excited to sleep so she decided to write in her Journal:

'A charming ball. I have spent the happiest birthday that I have had for many years. I have been dancing till past four o'clock. Only one regret I had and that was that my excellent good kind friend Lord Melbourne was not there.'

The next day while she was at breakfast a note arrived from Lord Melbourne. It contained profuse apologies and stated that he had been unable to attend the ball because he was both unwell and disturbed.

Lord Melbourne unwell! Lord Melbourne disturbed! She was in a panic.

'I *knew* he did not take enough care of himself,' she told the Baroness. 'I have told him often that he must not go out in the cold wind.'

'The wind is scarcely lethal at this time of the

year,' commented Lehzen.

'But it is precisely at this time of the year that we have to be *most* careful. Oh, I do hope he is not ill. I must send a messenger. I must know.'

'Even if he is ill the Queen of England can't very well act as his nurse, you know.'

Victoria turned troubled eyes on Lehzen. Good Heavens! thought Lehzen, how far do her feelings go for this man? Is she in love with him?

Absurd! Preposterous! Little innocent Victoria and a man of fifty-eight ... fifty-nine more likely. Nearly sixty, cited in two divorce cases, involved in a *cause célèbre* with his wife. Melbourne and the Queen of England!

Lehzen was beginning to feel worried.

During the morning Lord Melbourne called at the Palace. Victoria could not wait to greet him. Her expression was very serious but she was immediately relieved to find that he looked much the same as usual.

'My dear Lord M, you are unwell.'

Lord Melbourne touched his brow with a beautiful graceful motion.

'A little disturbed,' he said.

'Only disturbed ... not ill?'

'I was very, very anxious last evening because I fear a crisis in the House of Commons.'

'Oh, is that all? I was afraid you were sick.'

'Sick with anxiety perhaps,' he said.

'Is it so bad?'

'You remember that we have perpetual trouble with Ireland. It's a complicated situation, always on the simmer, ready to boil over into trouble. The tithe system and the poverty of the people, the state of their municipal government, all these are such as to make an uneasy country. They're an excitable people. One feels that if their land were turned into Utopia they'd find fault with something. There is a continual conflict between the Catholic and Protestant population. They can't settle down together as they do in England. They have to be at each other's throats all the time. We can be sure of one thing only. Whatever legislation was brought in there would be trouble about it. The resolution regarding the Church is now under discussion as to whether or not it should be rescinded. You know we have a very small majority in the House, and a thing like this could bring down the Government.'

'No!'

'It's true. If the vote went against us and we were defeated we should fall and Sir Robert Peel, the Leader of the Opposition, would come along and ask Your Majesty's permission to form a new Government.'

'I should never give my permission.'

'But that is something you would be obliged to do.'

'I ... the Queen!' Her eyes were brilliant, her cheeks flushed. 'I never would.'

'Your Majesty's temper is a little choleric,' he said with a tender smile.

'Do you expect me to agree to this when I know what it would mean? *You* would cease to be my Prime Minister.'

He nodded, making one of his grimaces which usually amused her but did not do so on this occasion.

'That,' she said firmly, 'is something I should never allow.'

Lord Melbourne's eyes filled with tears and at the sight of them she wanted to repeat her determination even more emphatically.

'Alas that you cannot enforce your sweet will,' he said, so poetically, she thought, that she could have burst into tears. 'Ours is a Constitutional Monarchy and that means that we all – even our Sovereign – must obey the rules of the Constitution. The Government is elected by the people and since our Reform Bill all sorts and conditions have been allowed to vote. Therefore Your Majesty's Government cannot always be of your choosing.'

'But to change Governments. How foolish! Why?'

'Because ours is not a strong Government. Our majority is small and popular feeling is against us. Sir Robert Peel is waiting to jump into my shoes.'

'I will never allow that!'

He shook his head at her.

'Your Majesty will have no choice. If I go out, he will come in.'

'And all because of this silly Irish question!'

'Many consider it of importance.'

'I would rather lose Ireland than let you go.'

He was touched, but he pretended to treat the matter lightly.

'It will most certainly give you more trouble than I ever shall, but you will not be asked to make the choice. I have wanted to speak to you on this matter for some time and now seems an appropriate moment. I fear the day will come – and it may be that that day is not so far distant – when I may not be your Prime Minister.'

'Oh, no!' She stamped her foot. Anger was the only emotion she dared show. 'I will *not* have that.'

'Well, it is not yet happened. I have been talking to Lord John this morning and he feels optimistic. He thinks we'll scrape through with a small majority.'

'And you agree with him?'

'He may be right on this occasion, but I think Your Majesty must bear in mind the weakness of our party. If we get through on Ireland nemesis may overtake us over Canada.'

'Who cares for Ireland and Canada?'

'Your Majesty's Government cares deeply for them.'

She turned away from him. A few discreet tears in the eyes were delightful but now she felt that she would be unable to prevent herself from bursting into noisy sobs.

Lord Melbourne with his exquisite tact seemed to realise this for he said he would take his leave and would of course keep her informed. At some other time he would explain the Canadian situation to her. It might well be that Lord John was right to be optimistic, and they would get through on this occasion, but he had felt for some time that he wanted her to be prepared.

When he had left she went to her bedroom and shut herself in.

If Lord Melbourne were not her Prime Minister how could he call on her every day? She

151

knew that the Opposition which would then be the Government would object. Sir Robert Peel would come in his place! She had met him briefly. *A horrid* man, she thought, as much like her dear Prime Minister as... as Sir John Conroy. She *hated* Sir Robert Peel and would never accept him.

Don't be ridiculous, she answered herself, if they make him Prime Minister you will *have* to accept him.

Her grief was choking her.

A few days later she received a note from Lord John Russell. It was brief but it sent her into an ecstasy of delight.

The Whigs had come through safely on a majority of nineteen. 'It was far more than I expected,' wrote Sir John.

So they were safe.

She ran to Dash and knocked over his basket.

'Come on, you lazy old Dashy. It's time for a run in the gardens.'

Dash barked joyfully.

'They've won, Dashy. A majority of nineteen! That'll show Sir Robert Peel.'

Out in the grounds she raced across the lawns with Dash in pursuit.

'Not much like the Queen of England,' commented Lehzen when she came in.

'It's a wonderful day,' said Victoria. 'The Government had a majority of nineteen. *They* thought they were going to beat *us*. But a majority of nineteen is quite a considerable figure.'

She was laughing. All was well once more.

Trouble came from another direction.

Lord Melbourne, during the course of some of their interesting and amusing conversations, had told the Queen that the Dutch, the French and the Belgians were being somewhat tiresome over Luxembourg. The Dutch and the Belgians desired possession of this Province and the French who had signed a Treaty with Belgium were supporting that country's claims against those of Holland.

'I am sure Uncle Leopold will take the right action,' Victoria had said.

But now came a disturbing letter from her royal Uncle. He wanted the support of England for Belgium in this matter, and he was appealing, not through her ambassador to her Foreign Minister, but to her as his niece.

'You have given me so many proofs of affection ... that it would be very wrong in me to think that in so short a time and without any cause, those feelings which are so precious *to me could have changed. This makes me appeal to these sentiments.'*

She frowned. Of course she loved her Uncle and would never forget that he had been a second father to her, but this was not a matter for tenderness or sentiment. She was experienced enough to know that matters which concern the welfare of the country were not to be settled because of her private family feelings. He went on:

'The independent existence of the Provinces which

153

form this Kingdom has always been an object of importance to England... The last time I saw the late King at Windsor, in 1836, he said to me: "If ever France or any other Power invades your country it will be a question of immediate war for England; we cannot suffer that..." All I want from your kind Majesty is, that you will occasionally express to your Ministers, and particularly to good Lord Melbourne, that as far as is compatible with the interests of your own dominions you do not wish that your Government should take the lead in such measures as might in a short time bring on the destruction of this country as well as that of your Uncle and his family...'

She was very disturbed. He was asking her to *advise* her Government on a matter of which she was well aware that she knew very little. One of her great qualities, Lord Melbourne had told her, was her awareness of her inexperience and her ability to listen and take advice. She wanted very much to please Uncle Leopold and it would have been easy to write and say: 'Yes, I will speak to Lord Melbourne and I will tell him that I wish him to do as you say,' but that would be unwise.

When Lord Melbourne called that day he knew at once that she was disturbed.

'I think I cannot do better,' she said, 'than to show you a letter I have received from my Uncle, the King of the Belgians.'

Lord Melbourne took the letter and when he read it, his expression became a little grave.

'How wise of you,' he said, 'to show me this letter before answering it. Indeed, it is what I have come to expect of Your Majesty. You quite rightly assume that this is a matter for Lord Palmerston and your Government and I will take the matter up immediately with your Foreign Secretary.'

She sighed with relief, but she was apprehensive.

'You see,' she explained, 'he was so good to me when I was young, and you know how insecure I always felt at Kensington.'

'It was most unfortunate,' replied Lord Melbourne tenderly. 'How much better it would have been had *that* Uncle the late King William and his Queen Adelaide been able to show you something of Court ways before you ascended the throne.'

'I was always very much aware of it.'

'This insecurity made you turn to your Uncle Leopold, of course, and it was, at the time, a very satisfactory relationship, but nothing remains static. *Tempora mutantur, nos et mutamur in illis.* The times are changed and we with them.' Lord Melbourne always thoughtfully translated his Greek and Latin to her to save her the embarrassment of asking if she did not happen to know. 'Now of course the King of the Belgians is still a dear relation and Your Majesty's loyalty and fidelity are strong, but we have to see him as two in one – the charming relation and the head of a foreign power.'

'How right you are ... as always.'

'So,' went on Lord Melbourne, 'Cupid and I will put our heads together over this.'

The reference to the Foreign Secretary's nickname was an indication that the matter was no

155

longer very serious and lightness returned to the conversation.

As she had spoken of her childhood Lord Melbourne talked of his days at Eton and described how on one occasion he had eaten too many sweet cakes and come out in spots because of this indulgence.

'I fear you were very greedy,' said the Queen severely.

'Those spots cured me of greed in that direction.'

Then he told her how he had his hair cut and picturing him in his Eton uniform she thought he must have looked very handsome indeed. Thus she was able to shelve the unpleasant matter of Uncle Leopold.

Lord Melbourne again referred to the Belgian affair but characteristically threw it in lightly. She had been asking him how her Court compared with those of her predecessors and Lord Melbourne had launched into one of his amusing accounts of the past. He told her how her Uncle William had once gone to the Royal Academy and threatened to throw the President into the street because he said the picture of a certain sea-going gentleman was good, and William did not admire the gentleman.

'But what had the picture to do with the man's character?' asked Victoria.

'Precisely nothing,' replied Lord Melbourne. 'But the King did not like the man.'

Then there was her own christening when her Uncle George IV (at that time Prince Regent) had refused to have her called Georgiana or Charlotte, and had insisted on Alexandrina Victoria.

'How do you think Victoria sounds as a queen's name?' she asked.

'I prophesy that it will one day seem more queenly than any.'

'I am glad Alexandrina is never used now. Victoria is much better for a queen.'

'Victoria,' said Lord Melbourne, 'is perfect for a queen.'

'Tell me what other names you like?'

Lord Melbourne considered. Alice he thought was charming. Louise also.

'Yes, I love them too. I wonder if I like Louise because of Aunt Louise. She is very charming.'

'She needs to be. I should think Leopold is a little hard to live with.'

Victoria held her breath. This was a kind of sacrilege, but it was like one god attacking another. It was true that Uncle Leopold *was* very solemn ... perhaps somewhat pompous? But only when compared with Lord Melbourne, who was a little racy and had had such experiences. How she wished she dared talk to him of them. She would have loved to hear from his lips stories of Lady Caroline Lamb, his wife, and those two women with whom he was involved. What a worldly man he was! No wonder Uncle Leopold seemed a little dull – oh, but Leopold could never be dull. Tame, perhaps in comparison – but only with Lord Melbourne.

'By the way,' went on Lord Melbourne, 'the King of the Belgians in that somewhat indiscreet letter to Your Majesty was obviously referring to the declaration Lord Palmerston made at the beginning of last month to the Prussian Government. I mentioned it to you at the time. You remember?'

She couldn't quite remember, she said.

'It may have appeared that we were ready to support Holland in this, but of course it is purely a matter of the advantages to this country.'

'Of course, but I should hate Uncle Leopold to think we are not on his side.'

'Has he written again?'

'No, there has been a long silence.'

'Ah, a little sullen, eh?'

'I don't know. He has always written such tender letters, except when he accused me of being irritable. Then he was hurt more than angry.'

'Ha! It is all he can afford to be with the Queen of England. Perhaps a letter from you would be useful. I am sure you do not wish to be on bad terms with such an old friend, even though you have ceased to be so intimate. Write and tell him that Cupid and I are anxious to see Belgium flourishing. I'll have a letter drafted out and you can put it into your own words if that appeals to you'

'Oh yes, it does. I *hate* to be on bad terms with Uncle Leopold.'

'It's just a little cloud. It will blow over. It's all due to this declaration to the Prussians. I notice you pronounce the "Pruss" part as in "brush" and I as in "Prue".'

'Yes, I have often noticed that. Which is correct?'

'Well, it's a matter of opinion, I dare say, and

158

pronunciation comes about through usage.'

'I feel it is important for the Queen to be correct,' she said.

'Queens have been known to set fashions,' said Melbourne, 'so it seems very probable that the fashionable way to say "Prussian" will very soon be in the "brush" manner.'

It was very easy to forget that unpleasant little contretemps with Uncle Leopold when in Lord Melbourne's sparkling company.

She wrote to the King of the Belgians as Lord Melbourne had directed:

'My dearest Uncle,

It is indeed a long time since I have written to you, and I fear you will think me very lazy; but I must in turn say, dearest Uncle, that your silence was longer than mine...

It would indeed, dearest Uncle, be very wrong of you if you thought my feelings of warm and devoted attachment to you and of great affection for you, could be changed. Nothing *can ever change them! Independent of my feelings of affection for you, my beloved Uncle, you must be aware that the ancient and hereditary policy of this country with respect to Belgium must make me most anxious that my Government not only should not be parties to any measure that is prejudicial to Belgium, but that my Ministers should, as far as may not conflict with the interests or the engagements of this country, do everything in their power to promote the prosperity and welfare of this your Kingdom.'*

That, Lord Melbourne had said, was the crux of

the matter, 'the interests or engagements of this country'. 'Your uncle will understand what is meant by that. We are his friends as long as it is not against the interest of England for us to be so.'

'I should like to think that we were always Uncle Leopold's friends,' she had said gravely.

Lord Melbourne had smiled at her tenderly. 'Your Majesty will realise that he will be our friend as long as that friendship does not affect the interests of his country. This is the difference between love of country and love of family. And it is one of the penalties of sovereigns and sovereigns' ministers that the country comes first.'

How right he was! As always, she thought. She went on:

'My Ministers, I can assure you, share all my feelings on this subject and are most anxious to see everything settled in a satisfactory manner between Belgium and Holland...

You may be assured, beloved Uncle, that both Lord Melbourne and Lord Palmerston are most anxious at all times for the prosperity and welfare of Belgium... Allow me once more therefore, dearest Uncle, to beseech you to use your powerful influence over your subjects and to strive to moderate their excited feelings on these matters. Your situation is a very difficult one and nobody feels more for you than I do. I trust, dearest Uncle, that you will at all times believe me your devoted and most affectionate niece.
Victoria R.'

There! She had written it.

'Sprinkle it lavishly with "dearest Uncles",' Lord Melbourne had said. 'It will remind him that while you still feel affectionate towards him as an *Uncle*, there must be no meddling in the politics of this country.'

She was surprised that she could nod in agreement. A short while ago she would have been horrified that she could have allowed anyone to call Uncle Leopold's interest 'meddling'.

But Lord Melbourne had taught her so much and Lord Melbourne was, of course, right.

The letter to Uncle Leopold appeared to have the desired effect. He wrote back to his dearest and most beloved Victoria to say that he was moved by her expressions of affection. He had not actually thought she had forgotten him, but it did occur to him that he had been put aside as one does a piece of furniture that is no longer wanted. He pointed out, though, how chagrined he had been by Lord Palmerston's declaration and naturally so, for the Prussians had become very imperious afterwards.

'...I am happy to say, I was never as yet in the position to ask for any act of kindness from you, so that whatever little service I may have rendered you, remained on a basis of perfect disinterestedness. That the first diplomatic step in our affairs should seem by your Government to be directed against me, created therefore all over the Continent a considerable sensation. I shall never ask any favours of you or anything that could in the least be considered as incompatible with the interests of England; but you

161

will comprehend that there is a great difference in claiming favours and being treated as an enemy...'

Uncle Leopold understood. She could not intervene in State matters for his sake.

He finished his letter declaring that she was never in greater favour with him and that he loved her dearly.

Dear Uncle Leopold! It was sad to think that she could ever regard him as a piece of furniture which was no longer of use! She remembered that when she was a child she had sometimes hoped that some dramatic opportunity would arise so that she could show him how much she loved him. Perhaps she might risk her life for him, perhaps even die for him. And now she could not allow him to interfere with her country's politics!

It was a new phase. But this was not the first time she had suspected that the closer she came to Lord Melbourne the farther she must draw away from Uncle Leopold.

Leopold declined the invitation to Victoria's Coronation. He thought that a king at the Coronation would be rather out of place.

There was no time to feel sad about his absence or to ask herself whether he was very offended.

'At a Coronation,' said Lord Melbourne, 'there is so much to do.'

Chapter 6

CORONATION

London was preparing for the Coronation.

This was going to be a coronation to make all others seem insignificant in comparison; the last two such occasions had been concerned with ageing and not very attractive old men and there was no Monarch so appealing at such a time as a fresh young girl.

From every part of the country people were arriving in London for the event and scaffolding was being erected along the route which the procession would take; houses fortunate enough to be situated there were being let at high rents and shopkeepers and traders looked forward to booming business. A fair had been set up in Hyde Park for the amusement of the visitors and to add to the general rejoicing. Patriotism, the gaiety of the occasion, and the summer weather made that a June to remember.

When Victoria rode out in her carriage she was often held up while the people expressed their enthusiasm. The roads were jammed with the carriages of visitors and, near the Park, all the coming and goings of the fairground people; there was noise, bustle and excitement everywhere and the general subject of conversation among rich and poor alike, was the Coronation.

163

'I feel quite *shy* to contemplate that all this is for me,' Victoria told Lord Melbourne.

'Shyness,' replied Lord Melbourne, 'shows a sensitive temperament – a great asset in a queen.'

'All the same,' she temporised, 'I should like to feel more assured than I do.'

'When you are in the Abbey you will enjoy it,' he said lightly.

'I feel very vague about it. I am not at all sure what I am supposed to do.'

Lord Melbourne waved an elegant hand. 'The Archbishop will explain everything, but it is all very simple.'

Lord Melbourne always made everything so easy.

'In the meantime,' she told him, 'there is such a fuss about the trainbearers. The Duchess of Richmond is arranging what they shall wear. Did you approve of the ladies I chose?'

'Your choice is mine – and I must say that you showed admirable perspicacity in the choosing.'

'I thought I *must* have Lady Mary Talbot as the daughter of the oldest Earl in the Kingdom and a Roman Catholic. I should not want people to think I am biased on religious grounds.'

'How wise!'

'And Lady Anne Fitzwilliam I chose because Lord Fitzwilliam has been so kind to me.'

Lord Melbourne nodded. 'Yes, yes,' he said. 'They and the other six are admirable.'

'I believe you regard the Coronation as a kind of puppet show,' she accused him.

'Not *your* Coronation,' he replied which she told him was a typical Lord Melbourne answer.

She went on laughingly to tell him about the fuss the Duchess of Richmond was in over the costumes.

'Really, I think she is not very competent. And a little arrogant. She has a very high opinion of her own judgement which is not confirmed by others.'

'Like almost everyone I know,' replied Lord Melbourne, and added, regarding her fondly: 'With one or two notable exceptions, of course.'

She smiled at him affectionately. 'They are wearing their hair in plaits over the ears.'

'A charming fashion,' said Lord Melbourne, because that was how Victoria wore hers.

'And can you guess what she wanted to do?' she demanded indignantly. 'She wanted them to be pale. She said they looked too robust which was not in keeping with the solemnity of the occasion. So she thought the leeches might be applied to draw off some of their healthy colour.'

Lord Melbourne laughed and Victoria's indignation vanished as she joined in. But she added firmly: 'Of course I would not allow that!'

'She must have thought your attendants should look like ghosts?'

'What a gruesome idea! She thought it would make them look *interesting*.'

'Wraiths risen from their tombs would certainly create great interest.'

'Lord M, you are joking about a very serious subject.'

'Serious subjects are the very ones to make jokes about because funny ones are a joke in themselves.'

'You are very profound, but this is *my* Coronation and the Duchess of Richmond has stated that she refuses to have the young ladies' Mammas interfering. They are to have no say in the matter whatsoever. Now she has decreed that they shall wear little flower caps as well as their silver wreaths and these *do* look rather odd. I should like your opinion on them.'

'As your Majesty's Prime Minister it is my duty to give it,' said Lord Melbourne with one of his most appealing grimaces that made her burst into laughter again.

However, she declared *she* was serious and sent a servant to request the Duchess to send in one of the young ladies to her wearing the head-dress, as she was anxious for the Prime Minister's opinion.

Lord Melbourne studied the head-dress very gravely and said it was pretty. But when they were alone he pulled one of his most comical faces and added that he thought it somewhat *curious*.

Oh, it was such fun to be with Lord Melbourne and she was so gratified because although they laughed and joked about such trivial matters, in the midst of the gaiety he would bring out some important official document such as a letter she must write to the King of Portugal about the suppression of the slave trade or an account of how she must receive members of the Clergy and what she must say to them.

'I am learning to be a queen,' she told him, 'in the most amusing and lighthearted way ... thanks to you.' And in the midst of a discussion on the

166

slave trade they would talk of people's noses (she was sensitive about hers, which was too large for such a small person). 'People with small noses never made much mark in the world,' comforted Lord M.

Later they would have to talk about Canada, he added, a slightly worried frown appearing on his fine brow; but for the moment they would devote themselves to the Coronation.

The weather was gloriously hot and foreign visitors were everywhere. The Queen's half sister, Feodora Princess Hohenlohe, and her husband had come, so had Victoria's half brother Charles, Prince of Leiningen. The Duchess was happy to have the children of her first marriage with her. They were a great comfort, she told Flora Hastings, when she considered her ungrateful younger child.

Lord Melbourne said there should be an entertainment to welcome them all, and what better than a ball since the Queen enjoyed dancing so much?

'What a splendid idea!' cried the Queen. 'We will dance until four in the morning and this time I hope my Prime Minister will be present.'

'Only a crisis or ill health will keep him away.'

The ball was fixed for the 18th June which, said Lord Melbourne, was a good date as it was ten days before Coronation day. He had completely forgotten that it was the date of the battle of Waterloo until it was too late to cancel the ball. The French visitors were offended. They referred to it as 'Le bal de Waterloo', and there were caustic comments in Paris.

Lord Melbourne shrugged this aside. It would soon be forgotten, he said in his easy-going manner.

At four o'clock Victoria was awakened by the guns in the Park. It was no use trying to sleep again; she was too excited. She prayed that she would go through this day as a Queen should, but she did feel rather nervous.

What a noise there was in the streets! People were already assembling and it was only four o'clock. Some of them she knew had spent the whole of the night in the streets.

She lay thinking of all this day meant and assuring herself that she must never forget that her first duty throughout her life would be to her country.

She was not quite sure what she had to do. The Archbishop of Canterbury was a bit of a bumbler (said Lord M), but the thing to do was to sail through boldly and she couldn't fail. He had told her of many amusing incidents from other coronations when the most odd things had happened. They had laughed a good deal, until she had said: 'But they were not funny at the time. It is only fair after that one would be able to laugh at them.' To which Lord Melbourne replied that the 'time' she referred to was brief and the aftermath long so that the short discomfiture was really well worth while. She did wonder though whether the people who had suffered the indignity ever really laughed as heartily as others. Well, said Lord Melbourne, they served their country by amusing it and there was nothing people liked better than to laugh.

'I'm a little apprehensive,' she had admitted.

'Oh, you'll like it when you're there,' he assured her.

It was not a matter of liking or disliking it. It was a dedication and she meant her people to know that this was how she felt about it.

'I want to dedicate my life to my people,' she told Lord Melbourne.

'A very proper sentiment,' was his reply.

The time was passing and at seven Baroness Lehzen came in through the communicating door.

'How does Your Majesty feel?' she asked anxiously.

'Well and strong.'

'Now you must try to eat.'

'That doesn't usually need a lot of effort, dear Lehzen.'

She was able to prove this with ease.

'The robes will be rather heavy,' she commented later to Lehzen. 'I do hope the train-bearers will manage the train.'

'They have their own trains to bother them,' said Lehzen. 'It was foolish of the Duchess of Richmond to give them trains. I told her so but she was so stubborn.'

'Well,' said the Queen philosophically, quoting Lord Melbourne, 'if anyone trips up or does something absurd we shall no doubt laugh at it afterwards.'

'Trip up! Be absurd! At your Coronation!'

'Dear, precious Lehzen, it could happen,' said

Victoria. 'And I am rather hungry. I did have rather a *little* breakfast, didn't I?'

Lehzen hurried off to get a further bite to eat and Victoria ate with relish and was ready to get into the State coach when it arrived, there to sit with the Duchess of Sutherland and Lord Albemarle. How exhilarating it was to ride through those streets with people everywhere, waving flags and cheering. She wanted to weep and laugh at the same time. Her dear, *dear* people. Oh how proud she was to be Queen of such a nation!

'It rained at six this morning,' commented Albemarle.

'But here is the sun again,' added the Duchess. 'It's going to shine on Your Majesty's Coronation day.'

Although she had left at ten it was half past eleven before she reached the Abbey. The cheers were deafening and smiling at her dear people she alighted from the coach and went into the small robing room where her eight trainbearers were waiting.

They were all young and looked charming in their white satin and silver tissue dresses trimmed with little pink roses. Their wreaths of silver corn-ears were very becoming but the little flower caps rather spoilt the effect. When the Queen was ready in her crimson velvet ermine-edged with a diamond circlet on her head, Lord Conyngham, who was in the robing room, showed the girls how to hold the Queen's train, and standing four a side they followed the Queen out into the nave.

All eyes were on the young girl who looked like a child, so small and slight was she in comparison with her trainbearers; but there was a dignity and assurance about her which was regal in itself and only the more insensitive could look on unemotionally.

Victoria was deeply moved. The Abbey decorated with crimson and gold was spectacular. On one side were the peeresses in their diamonds and robes of state; on the other, the peers in the costumes the occasion demanded.

When the anthem began the Queen went into St Edward's Chapel with her trainbearers that she might take off her crimson velvet and ermine robes and put on a little linen lace-trimmed garment in which she would be anointed and over this was put the supertunica made of cloth of gold. Leaving her circlet of diamonds behind she went back bareheaded into the Abbey for the anointing ceremony and in her clear voice beautifully enunciating her words she took the Oath promising to maintain the Reformed Protestant religion.

She was delighted to see Lord Melbourne, standing close to her throughout the ceremony, regarding her with such tenderness that she felt immediately secure and happy.

She took the regalia in her hands: she was wrapped in the Dalmatic robe by the Lord Chamberlain and then came the great moment when the crown was placed on her head.

It was as though the entire Abbey had burst into rejoicing. The trumpets began to sound, and outside cannon were fired. The organ then began to play *'The Queen Shall Rejoice'*, and at that moment the peers and peeresses who had been holding their coronets in their hands placed them on their heads and it was as though every one of the ten thousand voices in the Abbey cried 'God Save the Queen'.

She glanced at Lord Melbourne, whose emotion seemed almost too great to be borne. The Duchess of Kent was openly weeping in the royal box, nodding her head so vigorously that Lady Flora Hastings, who was in attendance, had difficulty in holding the coronet on her head. Victoria gave a quick glance up at the box over the royal one and there was Lehzen leaning forward, looking so proud and so tender that Victoria's heart melted with love. Dear, dear Lehzen, she thought, she shall always be with me, *always*.

Now was the time for the Enthronisation and Homage when first the Bishops, then the Royal Dukes (her uncles) and afterwards the peers in order of precedence should touch the crown and kiss her hand. She was glad that she had insisted on the crown's being adjusted to fit her small head for if she had not she was sure it would have rolled off, which would have been considered a very bad omen.

There was one unfortunate incident when poor old Lord Rolle, who was very ancient, had to be helped up the steps to the throne on which she sat, but alas as he was about to reach for the Queen's crown he slipped away from his supporters, fell down the steps and lay on the floor caught up in his robes.

There was a titter and a whispering for it

seemed strange that the man who should have rolled down should be called Lord Rolle. His friends lifted him, and determined to pay his homage he started up the stairs again. His face was red, his breathing difficult, so Victoria, feeling sure he was going to fall again, rose and went to meet him, giving him her hand to kiss.

It was a charming gesture and the congregation in its present mood were ready to adore their little Queen. A cheer went up and, pink and smiling, Victoria returned to her seat to receive the further homage.

She was delighted when it was Lord Melbourne's turn to kiss her hand and touch her crown. How gracefully he performed this duty! And how clumsy were the old Bishops and Dukes; and how dignified and handsome he looked. When he had touched the crown and kissed her hand, he pressed it and raised his eyes to hers (full of tears) and there was such tenderness and pride in them that she no longer felt tired and she believed that she could happily go through a hundred such ceremonies just to win his approval. Then she thought of the Lord Rolle incident and how they would laugh about that tomorrow.

The Duke of Wellington was loudly cheered too when he paid homage. People still remembered him as the hero of Waterloo.

She *did* notice of course that certain of her trainbearers were giggling and whispering together during some of the most sacred moments of the service. Later she would let it be known that she was aware of it.

When the Homage was over the members of the House of Commons cheered the Queen and cried: 'God Save Queen Victoria;' and the Queen took off her crown for the receiving of the sacrament

It was a little bewildering because there were moments when no one seemed to know what she was to do next. Neither the Bishop of Durham nor Lord John Thynne, the Sub-Dean, who were supposed to be guiding her through the ceremony, seemed to have very much idea; and the Bishop of Bath and Wells cut a piece out of the service by inadvertently turning over two pages.

It was a relief to go back into St Edward's Chapel to prepare for the procession and fortunately Lord Melbourne was at her side to take care of her so that everything was all right.

'You were magnificent,' he whispered; and she was happy, even though the crown which she had put on after taking the sacrament was so heavy and the stupid old Archbishop of Canterbury had crammed the ring onto the wrong finger and it was hurting.

Victoria was rather startled to see that on the altar in St Edward's Chapel sandwiches had been laid out with bottles of wine. She looked about for Lord Melbourne to mention that it seemed like sacrilege when she saw him helping himself to a glass of wine. She noticed then that he looked very tired and she was all concern.

But he had seen her watching him and put down the wine to come at once to her side.

'Was the crown heavy?' he wanted to know.

She told him that it was and he suggested that

174

it be taken off for a moment.

'A little respite,' he whispered.

She told him about the ring and he said it was that bumbling old Archbishop. It wouldn't come off, she said; he had crammed it on so fiercely and already her finger was becoming swollen. That would not do, said Lord Melbourne, and added that very cold water must be brought immediately for he could not allow the Queen to suffer discomfort. There was more of the ceremony to be endured and she must appear smiling and fresh to her subjects in spite of all she had endured.

So ice-cold water was brought and the ring finally but painfully eased off and while this was happening the Archbishop himself burst into the Chapel in a fine flurry crying: 'Where is the orb? I should have given it to the Queen.'

'I already have it,' said Victoria coldly.

The poor man looked so confused and upset that she was immediately sorry for him, but when he went out she caught Lord Melbourne's eye and they exchanged looks of secret mirth.

'At least,' whispered Lord Melbourne, 'his cope is very fine. It was worn at the Coronation of James II.'

How knowledgeable he was! And how light-hearted everything seemed when he was near!

It was time to leave for the procession back to the Palace and the eight trainbearers took their places. Out into the Abbey they went and to the strains of organ music, the heavy crown weighing her down and the trainbearers having a little trouble with their own trains so that they were

175

not very efficient with hers. But as soon as she was outside she forgot such minor details, for there were the dear people waiting to cheer her and show their loyalty. It was so touching.

Through the streets she rode in the golden coach with its glass windows specially designed so that the spectators could have a good view of their sovereign. It was indeed a magnificent coach with its elaborate carvings of lions' heads and the great crown on the roof. Lord Melbourne, that mine of information, had told her that it had been built for her grandfather and used for the first time at his Coronation.

How pleasant to sit and not feel conscious of her lack of inches; she bowed her head and smiled and now that she was sitting she felt as fresh as when she had started, although the crown was so heavy and her finger still smarted from that foolish Archbishop's bumbling mistake.

The cheers, the bands, the trumpets, the smiling faces of her people – all proclaimed her triumph. She felt exultant and her determination was intensified to do her duty by this *dear* country and her *dear* people for as long as she lived and to do all in her power to make sure that they never, never regretted this day.

The coach had arrived at the Palace. The crowds keeping their respectful distance, cheered wildly. She smiled, showing her delight and yet never losing that regality which was so much a part of her.

What a relief though to be in her own room, to remove the heavy crown and to say to herself: It is over and I did it well.

Dash came running to her barking fiercely. He had been in the garden digging again.

'Oh you dirty Dash!' she cried. 'Now you will have to be bathed at once.'

Lehzen was in the room. They flew at each other.

'My precious little Queen. I am so proud.'

'Oh, dear Lehzen, I was all right, wasn't I?'

Being overcome with emotion, Lehzen could only nod.

'I saw you watching me, dear Lehzen.'

'I didn't have my eyes off you one moment.'

'And I was remembering lots of things ... how we used to play with the dolls ... our reading while my hair was being done... It was a strange time to remember things like that.'

Lehzen could only repeat: 'I was so proud ... so proud.'

'Now look at this wicked Dashy. He is filthy.'

'Someone will have to bath him,' said Lehzen.

'Someone! You know Dashy never allows anyone to bath him but me. Come, help me out of these things.'

'But not on your Coronation day!'

Victoria shrugged objections aside and half an hour after her return from the Abbey was seated at the bath with an unrepentant and resentful Dash sending his mistress into shrieks of laughter because he would not stay still and had made up his mind that if he were going to be immersed in his bath he would at least see that she had a good drenching.

The sound of her laughter and Dash's occasional barks filled the room. Lehzen, hearing it,

177

shook her head.

'Who would believe she had just been crowned Queen of England,' she said.

There was not much respite, for dinner was at eight. Not that it was a ceremonial occasion, for just the family were present with one or two guests, including Lord Melbourne. The sight of him made Victoria's spirits rise. He was at her side immediately.

'I must congratulate Your Majesty,' he said, and the tears were in his eyes. 'It was a brilliant day. Everything went off well.'

'Everything?' she laughed, showing her pink gums.

'Well,' said Lord Melbourne, putting his head on one side in what seemed to her a very comical way, 'John Thynne didn't know which way to turn; the Bishop of Bath and Wells *did* cut out a piece of the service; the Archbishop wasn't sure what had happened to the orb and put the ring on the wrong finger; the Bishop of Durham wasn't sure of anything; the trainbearers were too much involved with their own trains to manage the Queen's; and Lord Rolle gave a charade of his own name.'

Oh how *amusing* was Lord Melbourne!

'And you call that going well?'

'Yes, because the performance of these minor players only accentuated the perfection of the leading role.' Lord Melbourne could switch from rather cynical fun to sentiment with the agility of an acrobat. Tears trembled in his eyes. 'It was a magnificent Coronation, and I was so proud to

178

be part of it.'

At dinner Victoria was delighted to have Lord Melbourne beside her; on his other side was her half sister Feodora and it was such a pleasure to talk to her and Lord Melbourne of the old days. Lord Melbourne knew so much about them and could entertain them with endless stories of Victoria's relations which were often so amusing. The manner in which he could turn from the serious to the comic was so comforting (as she remarked later to Feodora) because he made everything so amusing and after one had laughed immoderately one would find oneself discussing some very serious matter, which prevented one feeling too frivolous.

The sword of state, he told them, had been very heavy and he had been glad to lay it down. 'I do not use the term metaphorically,' he added. 'I hope I shall continue in my position as long as Her Majesty desires.'

'I shall *always* desire it,' the Queen vehemently assured him.

Then he discussed some of the peers in that light and chatty way of his and how far some of them could trace back their ancestry. Such and such came over with the Conqueror and somebody else had descended direct from the Black Prince. Victoria was glad that Feodora was discovering what a clever man Lord Melbourne was and as she said afterwards, his erudition sat so lightly on him.

After dinner the Queen sat on a sofa and chatted with her half brother, Prince Charles of Leiningen, and of course Lord Melbourne joined them.

The Duke of Wellington was giving a ball at Apsley House that evening in honour of the Coronation and Lord Melbourne said that he supposed he was expected to put in an appearance.

'You must be very tired,' said the Queen solicitously.

'Not as tired as Your Majesty. When I consider the weight of those robes, not taking into account the crown and the regalia, I marvel. And you did it all so beautifully ... every part of it, with so much taste.'

'It was your advice which was so useful to me.'

'Oh, good taste is something no one person can give another advice about. It must be left to a person.'

As she said afterwards to Charles, to hear such compliments from a kind *impartial* friend was so gratifying.

He gently advised her that she should go to bed. 'For,' he added, with that charming solicitude, 'you are far more tired than you think you are.'

'Well, I did sleep rather badly last night.'

'The Coronation was on your mind,' he replied. 'Nothing keeps people awake more than the awareness of a great event and being somewhat agitated about it.'

So Lord Melbourne took his leave and there was nothing after that to stay up for.

Several of the party had gone on to one of the balconies to see the illuminations. Victoria did not join them but went alone to the balcony of her mother's apartments, where she could watch the firework display in Green Park.

As she stood there, she went over the events of the day, feeling very solemn and dedicated and so thankful that she had her precious Lehzen beside her and her dear good, kind, *impartial* friend, Lord Melbourne, to guide her.

She slept soundly that night and as soon as she was awake she thought of Lord Melbourne and wrote to him:

'The Queen is very anxious to hear if Lord Melbourne got home safe, and if he is not tired and quite well this morning.'

Chapter 7

PALACE GOSSIP

Nothing was quite the same after the Coronation. When she had ridden through the streets the people had adored their charming young Queen and she had reached the top of her pedestal, but it was going to be very difficult to stay there.

There had always been scandals about the lives of Royalty; the people had come to expect them; and though it might be difficult to imagine that anything shocking could be happening in the life of a young girl who was so clearly innocent, that did not stop malicious people from speculating on the situation at the Palace.

Victoria in her innocence was unaware of this.

She was enjoying her role, applying herself to it assiduously. She was sure that she possessed a natural aptitude for it and as long as she had her dear Prime Minister to guide her in public life and her precious Lehzen in private, what more could she ask?

When the Court was at Windsor, naturally Lord Melbourne and any other visiting Ministers had their own apartments there, but this was not the case in Buckingham Palace where it was easy for a minister to pay a brief visit whenever he was required to do so. As far as Lord Melbourne was concerned though, he was so often at the Palace that it seemed advisable for a set of apartments to be put at his disposal there; and he did in fact live more often at Buckingham Palace than Melbourne House. This was an ideal arrangement, said the Queen, for it meant that she could call on him so easily at any time. Lord Melbourne agreed with her.

Trouble was brewing in the Palace and at the heart of it was Sir John Conroy, whom Victoria had suspected of treachery before her accession. Her suspicions were now confirmed.

'It is not only the Duchess's financial affairs which are controlled by him; she herself seems to be,' commented Lord Melbourne.

He spoke very frankly to Victoria now because as he said they understood each other and it was only if he spoke his mind that he could let her know what was in it. The Duchess showed quite clearly that she disliked Lord Melbourne, so Lord Melbourne retaliated; and as he explained to the Queen, there was no point in his saying what he did not mean out of deference to convention.

'I should like to see Sir John out of the Palace,' said the Queen.

'We could not agree to his demands. You remember they were exorbitant. To do so would be submitting to black-mail.'

'Odious creature! I always knew I was right to hate him. Sometimes I think that it would be a good idea to get rid of him at any price. Suppose we made it worth my mother's while to go abroad? Back to Leiningen perhaps. Then That Man could go with her.'

Lord Melbourne considered this. 'Would she go? And if she did, you could not live alone without some chaperone. It might make trouble too. The people would not like to see an open rift between you and your mother. You manage everything so well by being affectionate towards her in public. It is best to continue like that.'

'It seems so insincere. I don't like it.'

'Ah, you are open and frank by nature,' said Lord Melbourne admiringly, 'but sometimes we all have to do things we don't much like ... particularly queens.'

'Mamma has been much more humble lately. I think she would like a reconciliation.'

'Let her begin negotiating for it by sending Conroy away.'

'She has written to Lehzen – such a *friendly* letter.'

'I don't doubt she is trying to win you back,' said Lord Melbourne. 'But it would be best for the Baroness to acknowledge the letter and leave it at that.'

So the battle continued and like good soldiers the ladies-in-waiting and other servants of the Palace fell in behind their leaders. On one side was the Queen, with Lord Melbourne, Lehzen and Baron Stockmar; and on the other side the Duchess with Conroy and Lady Flora Hastings who, because of her rather serious nature and a certain gift for acid comment, led the ladies.

The strained situation with the Duchess drove Victoria into an even closer relationship with Baroness Lehzen. She even declared that she thought of her as Mother and sometimes called her by that name; but of course, reasoned Victoria to herself, she is not my mother, so I shall call her Daisy which I think is a lovely *faithful* name.

The Baroness was delighted by these outward signs of the Queen's favour. She could endure the sly allusions to her origins from sharp-tongued Lady Flora; and the sneers about her German habits and her caraway seeds were shrugged aside. All that mattered was that Victoria loved her and had sworn that nothing could ever separate them.

Meanwhile plots fermented in the opposite camp.

Items in the press – not very prominent it was true – were suggesting that there was too much foreign influence at Court. The names Stockmar and Lehzen were mentioned, and of course King Leopold.

'This has been started by J.C., Mamma and her ladies,' said Victoria vehemently.

'It's nonsense,' replied Lord Melbourne lightly.

'Everyone knows that it is Your Majesty's ministers from whom you take advice.'

'One of my ministers at any rate,' smiled Victoria. 'It is true that dear Stockmar is kind and so devoted.'

'He is a good intermediary for dealing with Conroy.'

'Oh how I wish we could rid ourselves of J.C.!'

'He would go if we acceded to his blackmail. That is what he is waiting for.'

'I cannot understand why Mamma does not see through him.'

'If I may be very indiscreet...?'

'Dear Lord M, you never are.'

'Then if I may be exceptionally frank...'

'You have my permission.'

'Then I will say that I find the Duchess not very strong-minded and easily led by some. I do not think she is capable of any deep feeling.'

Of course it was wrong to discuss one's own mother in such a way, but Mamma *had* become a State matter and this *was* the Prime Minister.

'I fear you are right, Lord Melbourne.'

'Therefore, we must not allow her to dictate our actions.'

'Most certainly not. Lord Melbourne, what do you think of Lady Flora Hastings?'

'Frank again?' smiled Lord Melbourne.

'Yes, please.'

'I find her a disagreeable young ... or not so young ... woman. She must be past thirty. Her family are staunch Tories.'

'I could well imagine so,' replied Victoria distastefully. 'She seems to be *very* friendly with J.C.'

'That is understandable. I have always thought there was not an ounce of sense in the entire Hastings family.'

'I do not find Lady Flora handsome either.'

'She is positively plain.'

'I am at a loss to understand why Mamma thinks so highly of her.'

'A few simple deductions would make the answer clear,' said Lord Melbourne, and they laughed.

Then they talked of other things – light, frivolous things, and Lord M was so amusing that she could not get to her Journal quickly enough to record some of his witticisms before she forgot them.

The Duchess came to the Queen's apartments.

'I thought,' she said, 'that my daughter might perhaps wish to see me.'

'I always wish to see you *agreeable*, Mamma.'

The Duchess fingered one of the many bows on her dress. 'My dearest angel,' she said, 'isn't it time to put an end to this sad state of affairs?'

'What state of affairs is this, Mamma?'

'This animosity between us.'

'It is not between *us* exactly Mamma. It is due to the people who surround us.'

The Duchess leaned forward in her chair.

'That is exactly true. You see far too much of Lord Melbourne.'

'My Prime Minister!'

'Is he not a little more than that?'

'I don't think you understand these matters, Mamma.'

'Oh, I understand very well. You think very highly of that man, now don't you?'

'It is of the greatest importance that the Queen should have confidence in her Prime Minister.'

The Duchess's trouble was that she was unable to control her temper and, as Victoria had inherited a similar one, when these two clashed there were what the Duchess had called in Victoria's childhood, 'storms'.

'Well,' said the Duchess, 'that is one way of describing it.'

'Describing what and at what are you hinting, pray?'

'Your friendship with that man. He is no friend to me.'

'It is only necessary that he should be a friend to the Queen.'

The Duchess should have been warned that when her daughter continued to refer to herself as the Queen she was reminding her companion that she expected the respect the title demanded.

'Take care!' cried the Duchess. 'There are some who are saying that he is the King ... or would like to be ... and that *you* would like him to be.'

Victoria did not realise the significance of these words; she was only angry that her mother, who had come ostensibly to seek a reconciliation, should think she would obtain it by attacking Lord Melbourne.

'I am managing very well without your advice, Mamma!' said the Queen coldly.

'Yes.' The Duchess was in a storm of rage now. 'Then there is the way you obviously *enjoy* riding out and always doing it ... so that the people can

187

cheer you. And you eat far too much and show too much pleasure in your food. You *gobble.*'

'If I wish to ride out, Mamma, I shall ride out, and if I wish to gobble, *gobble.*'

'You laugh too loudly.'

'I shall laugh as I please.' Victoria rose. 'And now,' she said regally, 'the Queen sees no reason why this interview should continue.'

The Duchess felt impotent to protest. This was the Queen and there was no doubt of that.

She rose and went back to her apartments.

'I felt as though she would have ordered me to be sent to the Tower of London if I stayed longer.'

'She is quite capable of it,' retorted Sir John.

Lady Flora, who was present – she was often in the company of Sir John – hurried to find smelling salts.

'Of course, Your Grace,' she said, 'the Queen's unkind attitude towards her own mother comes from that ill-bred Baroness. Did you know that Her Majesty is now calling the woman *Mother?*'

'Oh, it is shameful ... shameful!' moaned the Duchess.

'We shall get even with them, never fear,' promised Sir John.

Victoria was in the blue closet listening entranced to Lord Melbourne's racy conversation. She had begun by scolding him, for during the recent thunderstorm she had seen him from a window standing under a tree.

'I was in a *fever* of anxiety. It could have been struck. You might have been killed. Anything could happen.'

'A sublime death,' replied Lord Melbourne.

'I was so *angry* with you.'

'Then I must immediately begin to worm my way back into Your Majesty's regard.'

'You will not do it by standing under trees in thunderstorms.'

Lord Melbourne believed his size would prevent his doing that. *One* tree was all that was needed to shelter him. It was his subtle way of correcting her; she often needed correction. Her grammar was frequently faulty, and Lord Melbourne was so erudite. He noticed such things. As for herself, she was never quite sure when one should say 'who' or 'whom' or 'me' or 'I', but it was often convenient to be able to substitute 'the Queen' for the latter.

Then he talked lightly and easily about Canada and how Lord Durham as High Commissioner was managing. There were outbreaks of rebellion in Canada which were causing some concern to the Government.

'Possession abroad means anxiety at home and those damned Tories are ready to exploit any situation for the sole purpose of bringing discomfort to Your Majesty's Government,' explained Lord Melbourne.

Victoria shivered at the use of the word 'damned'. She had heard that Lord Melbourne was noted for his colourful oaths, but in her presence he was usually restrained; she was delighted that he could feel so relaxed as to use a mild one now and then. But she noticed that when he did it it was always in connection with State matters.

'Lord Brougham is beside himself with glee, and if Durham fails to bring about the desired result, Brougham could ask for a vote of confidence.'

'I'm sure the whole country has as much confidence in her Government as the Queen has.'

'I wish I could be sure of that, 'said Lord Melbourne fervently.

'You dined at Holland House last night,' said the Queen.

'That was so.'

'I trust that it was a reasonably entertaining evening?'

'Your Majesty's trust is not misplaced.'

She giggled and went on, 'I wished that I were there sitting next to you and you could have amused me with some of your comments on the guests.'

'A somewhat churlish occupation,' replied Lord Melbourne. 'For after all one is invited to these occasions to help entertain, not to criticise.'

'But, Lord M, you are very critical.'

'If I have the permission to correct Your Majesty I would say that I am the most forbearing man in the world.'

'In some circumstances, perhaps. I am sure you would be very forbearing with Lady Holland.'

'I have never had occasion to exercise that trait in my character in connection with Lady Holland.'

'And I hope you never will be familiar enough with her to be called upon to do so. I think she has an extremely ugly mouth.'

Lord Melbourne smiled with cynical amusement. 'Your Majesty is very observant.'

'Yes, a *vulgar* mouth I should say. The Queen cannot understand why the Prime Minister finds the society at Holland House more entertaining than that at Windsor or Buckingham Palace.'

'The Prime Minister cannot understand why the Queen imagines that he does.'

'He goes there far too often.'

'Not as often as he is at Buckingham Palace and there are some who say that he is there far too often.'

'Naturally he has State business to discuss with the Queen.'

'Such as the appearance of Lady Holland's mouth, where he should stand during thunderstorms, his school days at Eton and the Queen's in Kensington Palace.'

She began to laugh. He could always make her laugh even when she was beginning to feel a little angry about his visits to Holland House.

Lord Melbourne became momentarily serious as he often did when the conversation became a little too frivolous. The civil war in Spain, he said, was causing Her Majesty's Government some concern. As for Portugal, that country was tottering on the edge of grave financial disaster.

'They are far away from us,' said the Queen.

'No country can be completely unaffected by what is happening in another and the European situation is of vital importance to this country. "No man is an island",' he quoted. 'Far less countries. We cannot afford to be unconcerned about any European situation.'

'I know that Uncle Leopold is most concerned.'

191

'Your Uncle Leopold likes to have a stir at every pudding.'

She laughed immoderately until she realised that she was laughing at Uncle Leopold, which seemed wrong.

She spread her hands and frowned at them, thinking that they would have been quite pretty if they did not get so red and swollen.

Lord Melbourne looked at them too.

'You don't like my rings,' she accused him.

'You wear far too many.'

'Well, you see my hands get red and I think the rings hide them.'

'They make them worse.'

'I don't wear them in the morning.'

'If you didn't wear them at all the fashion for so many rings would stop. And if you wore gloves when you are out riding your hands would not get red.'

'I can't get my gloves on.'

'So you see it is a battle between rings and gloves ... and you choose rings and cold hands against gloves and soft white ones.'

'That doesn't sound like a very wise choice.'

'I leave your Majesty to decide.'

More laughter in the midst of which the door was opened and the Duchess came in.

Lord Melbourne rose and bowed; the Duchess nodded her feathers curtly; she looked at Victoria steadily and said: 'I thought to find you alone.'

Victoria, coldly regal, replied: 'No, Mamma. I am not alone. I have urgent State matters to discuss with my Prime Minister.'

Even at such a moment she wanted to laugh for

the manner in which Lord Melbourne's brow shot up told her what he was thinking: urgent matters like rings and red hands and Lady Holland's vulgar mouth.

'I did not realise that you were so *busy*,' said the Duchess pointedly.

'Well, you now see that we are.'

The Duchess's rather insolent gaze swept the table and Victoria said: 'If you wish to see the Queen it is better to make an appointment beforehand.'

Lord Melbourne took a document from his pocket and laid it on the table (for all the world, the Duchess told Sir John and Lady Flora afterwards, as though I was not there) and Victoria went over and studied it, ignoring her mother.

Uncertain, angry and tearful, the Duchess turned and went out of the room.

'There you see, said Victoria, 'she was spying on me. She will go back at once and report to That Man.'

'She must not be allowed to walk in unannounced.'

'I will go to see her and tell her that no one is to enter my apartments without first obtaining my permission.'

'That,' said Melbourne, 'is the only way to settle the matter.'

The Baroness was rather angry.

'What is it, Daisy dear?' asked the Queen.

'It is that impertinent Flora Hastings.'

'Oh, that woman. In Lord Melbourne's opinion she is most disagreeable. They call her Scotty.

Whether it is a term of endearment I do not know. But I can't imagine *anyone's* finding *anything* endearing in Flora Hastings. What has she been doing now?'

'Oh, just making her unpleasant remarks.'

'About you?'

'Sly hints at us both and of course Lord Melbourne.'

'How dare she! And who are the Hastings? Lord M says they haven't an ounce of brains between them. They are Tories, too.'

'Scotty is very friendly with John Conroy.'

'Which makes her even more odious.'

'I've heard rumours that they are more than friendly.'

'I really think he is a very wicked man.'

'He looks at all the letters you write to the Duchess and all her replies to you are seen by him ... perhaps even written by him.'

I always hated him. Do you remember how he came to my bedroom when I was so ill and tried to trick me into promising to make him my secretary?'

'I remember a great deal about him and nothing good. I think it is unwise of you to put anything in writing to the Duchess. If you gave all our answers verbally he could not be so sure of what you had said.'

'She would tell him.'

'It wouldn't be so satisfactory to him because he knows the Duchess's tendency to inaccuracy.'

'How I wish he would go.'

'He won't until his demands are met.'

'Lord Melbourne says they are blackmail.'

'Lord Melbourne is right.'

'Lord Melbourne is always right,' said Victoria smiling. 'I will ask him what he thinks of your idea, Daisy. I have made her understand that she is not to enter without permission. I was obliged though to remind her that I am the Queen.'

'There are some people who need constantly reminding of that important fact,' commented Lehzen grimly.

Later Lord Melbourne told the Queen that he thought it an excellent idea to reply to the Duchess only by word of mouth.

Lehzen discovered by, as she said, keeping her ear to the ground that the Duchess was in debt to the sum of £70,000, a loan had been arranged for her at one of the banks, and that if this had not been done her affairs would have been in dire straits.

'Of course,' said the Queen, 'it is That Man again. He is supposed to be managing her affairs.'

'Mismanaging,' said Lehzen.

And the Queen agreed.

The ladies of both parties whispered together.

'The Duchess's financial difficulties are due to the fact that since she has had her increased allowance she has been paying off her husband's debts,' said Lady Flora's faction.

'So she should,' retorted the Queen. 'It is her duty to do so.'

The Duchess's ladies felt that since the debtor was the Queen's father it was the Queen's duty to settle the debts. The gossip was brought to Lehzen who took it to the Queen.

'It's That Man again,' cried Victoria indignantly. 'He is putting this about. And it's monstrous because I *am* paying my father's debts.'

'It should be made known that you are doing this. I shall see that it is.'

'Oh, no, please Lehzen, don't say anything. It would seem as though I was saying how good I am. I shouldn't like that.'

'But the villainy of that man should be revealed.'

'It will in time, Daisy dear. For the moment let it rest.'

And so the Palace war continued.

There was great astonishment throughout the Palace because one of the footmen who had descended to those regions below stairs where the silver and gold plate were kept, to be brought out on state occasions, had discovered a boy.

He was young, about eight or nine, decidedly grubby, inarticulate and unlawfully in the Palace.

Everyone was talking about him. His name, he said, was Jones. He had come in ... he couldn't say how or even why, except that he wanted to see where the Queen lived. He did admit, though, that he had been in the Palace for a week.

It was incredible. The Queen discussed it with the Baroness – who wondered whether it was some trick of the Duchess's faction; Lady Flora suggested that it might be one of the Baroness's relations who had come to look for her, which her friends thought very amusing. Lord Melbourne said that it showed security was not what it should be at the Palace and there was an enquiry.

The boy seemed not to care what became of him; he had achieved his purpose and had seen wonders which he could never have imagined. He had trodden the State rooms with their thick piled carpets; he had touched the heavy brocade curtains and pulled their gold tassels; he had sat on a sofa on which the Queen had sat; he had seen the throne room (and sat on the throne); he had walked down the grand staircase. If he had lived in the Palace for a week he must have fed himself so he would have made many journeys below stairs to the vast kitchens where he would have seen crystal cups ornamented with diamonds and rubies and Cellini vases; but no doubt the quantities of food would have been more exciting.

What could be done with such a boy? The press was full of the story and he was referred to as 'In I go Jones'.

Lehzen agreed with Lord Melbourne that this incident betrayed how easy it would be for people to get into the Palace. And suppose, she added, someone wishing to *harm* the Queen had got in!

'Nonsense, Daisy,' replied Victoria. 'A boy could slip in whereas a grown person couldn't.'

Lehzen said she would be very watchful in future. She was like a mother with a child, she said. The slightest sound, which might mean harm to her darling, would awaken her.

Victoria had always been on good terms with Lord John Russell and his family and his wife Adelaide had even become rather a special friend. Victoria was constantly inviting them to the Palace because she loved the children. And now Adelaide was expecting another.

It was delightful when the children came to the Palace. Victoria loved to listen to their chatter and enjoyed showing them the Great Drawing Room and the Throne Room. She would sit on the throne when they asked her to and they would gaze at her with awe and then one of them would want to play at being Queen.

'What fun to have children,' cried the Queen. 'I should love to have *ten*. But then I think I should never want them to grow up.'

Adelaide begged that if the new child should be a girl she might name her after the Queen.

'That would please me very much,' replied Victoria.

She said afterwards to Lord Melbourne that it was a joy to see them together. Lord John was so devoted to Adelaide and she was such a good mother. Lord John was her idea of a good husband too.

'He waited a long time before he took on the role,' said Lord Melbourne. 'So he gave himself plenty of time to learn how to play it.'

Victoria looked at him sadly. Poor Lord M who had had such an extraordinary married life. And what a *good* husband he would have been with the right kind of wife. She would have so much liked to talk to him of his past, but he never mentioned it so she could not. He would talk about his boyhood and his wonderful mother (although she was a little scandalous) and he would talk about his life as a widower but that very important section was always left out.

'I think Little Johnny was perhaps right,' said

the Queen. 'It is never good to rush into marriage.'

'And to choose a widow! That is probably wise. *Experto* crede. Trust one who has had experience.'

'Well, it certainly was right in their case. And if the child is a girl she is going to be called Victoria.'

'A great honour for her.'

'Oh, I am delighted. I can't wait for the infant to be born and of course I hope it's a girl.'

She looked at him quickly. Anyone else but Lord Melbourne would have been saddened by this talk of babies because surely he must be remembering his own son who had been an epileptic and had had the mind of a child all his life. What a blow to dear Lord M. Such a brilliant man must have longed for a son as clever as himself. But he gave no sign of the sadness this must have caused. He discussed Lord John's family lightly and pleasantly as though it had never occurred to him to envy them.

She was filled with tenderness towards him. How I wish he would confide in me! she thought wistfully. Such a *feeling* man must have suffered greatly and still does; but he hides it all under that careless exterior. Oh what a wonderful man Lord Melbourne was!

Lady John gave birth to a little girl in late October.

Victoria received the message while she was having her breakfast.

'Daisy!' she cried. 'Adelaide Russell has her

199

baby. It's a little girl, so she will be named after me. I shall go along to see her.'

But before Victoria could do this news was brought to the Palace that the Lady John was very weak and her life was in danger. Almost immediately after this message had been received, there came another.

Lady John was dead.

Victoria wept bitterly. 'Oh, Daisy,' she said, 'it is so sad. They were so happy, and this happens. If she had not had the child she would be alive today. Child-bearing is *cruel.*'

'It's natural,' said Lehzen.

'But to *die!* She was too young to die ... and all because of *that.*'

'It is, alas, an everyday occurrence.'

The Queen nodded sadly: 'An everyday occurrence,' she said. 'And now,' she added briskly, 'we must try and comfort Little Johnny.'

For days she could think of nothing but the death of Lady John. The ordeal of childbirth obsessed her. It was something she herself would have to face in due course – and that time perhaps not very far distant. They would bring her cousins over and she would be allowed to choose either Albert or Ernest, though she believed there were some people who would like to see her take her cousin, George Cambridge. Which I shall *not* do, she told herself vehemently. She had taken a great dislike to his mother, the Duchess, who had become over-friendly with her own mother recently. So the Cambridges had really taken sides in the Palace feud and the side they had taken was not the Queen's. No, it would have to be Ernest or Albert, she supposed. That was what Uncle Leopold wanted; but of course Uncle Leopold could not dictate policy to her. Yet she would have to marry.

Albert or Ernest. Ernest or Albert. Albert had pleased her more than his brother when they had visited Kensington before her accession. He was very good-looking and she felt that she could guide him more easily because he was a few months younger than she was. Yes, she had been delighted with Albert at that time and had marriage been suggested then she believed she would have been quite ready to agree. But she had grown up in the last years. She had become a Queen; she had emerged from her prison; she had benefited from the tuition of dear Lord M.

Soon, however, this question of marriage would arise, and she faced the fact that it no longer pleased her. She did not want anyone to interfere with the very pleasant relationship which existed between her and her Prime Minister. She was quite content as she was. And after this terrible affair of Lady John Russell, did she look on marriage and all it meant with a certain apprehension?

She wrote to Uncle Leopold, because they corresponded as frequently as ever, but there was a different tone in her letters now of which he must be aware. She was too open to pretend and their relationship had changed since she had been obliged to tell him that he must not meddle in English affairs.

But this was a personal matter. He had liked Lord John.

'*My dear Uncle,*
We have all been very much distressed by the
melancholy and untimely death of poor Lady John
Russell ... it is a dreadful blow to him *for he was* so
attached to her, and I don't believe two people ever
were happier together... He is dreadfully *beat down*
by it, but struggles manfully against his grief which
makes one pity him more... I had known her very
well and liked her, and I assure you I was dreadfully
shocked by it...'

Yes, she was dreadfully shocked; and she felt
something more than the loss of a dear friend
and pity for her husband and the children she
was leaving. She was vaguely depressed. The
pleasantest summer she had ever spent had
passed away; and she was facing realities which
did not look quite so pleasant to her.

I wish, she thought, that that summer could
have gone on and on and never ended.

But she did not speak of her misgivings, even to
Lord Melbourne.

Chapter 8

THE HASTINGS SCANDAL

Christmas followed closely on the death of Lady John. Several of the ladies-in-waiting went home to their families to spend the holiday and one of those who left was Lady Flora Hastings, who had gone up to Scotland to stay at one of her family's seats, Loudoun Castle.

Victoria had never recovered from the depression which had begun with the death of Lady John and she began to feel not so well and to worry about her health.

'I am putting on a good deal of weight,' she told Lord Melbourne.

'Oh,' he replied easily, 'plump people are much more comfortable to be with than thin ones. "I like not these lean men", said one of your ancestors, King Henry VIII to be precise.'

'It was all very well for him. He was tall. I am too short to be fat. Oh, how I wish I could grow!'

'Your small stature somehow lends you dignity which shows how naturally that very regal quality comes to you.'

'It could be even more noticeable if I were a few inches taller. And I hate to be fat.'

'You should eat less.'

'I know, but I do like food.'

'It is very often that we like the things which do

us most harm. Don't have your food so highly flavoured.'

'I like it so.'

'All Hanoverians are very fond of food. You take after your family.'

'That's what I'm afraid of. My grandfather went mad. Some said Uncle William really was.'

'I remember the gamblers making bets,' said Lord Melbourne. 'Would he be in a straitjacket before he could get to the throne?'

'And I believe it was hinted that even Uncle George...'

'Good God,' cried Lord Melbourne, 'what are you suggesting? It's madness... I mean folly. People go mad through worrying too much, so that is what you have to watch for. As for being fat ... walk more, take exercise. That will do it. Then you need not cut down on the food you like.'

'My feet get swollen when I walk.'

'Then walk even more and they'll get over it.'

'Some members of my family have walked a great deal and they are fat. I am getting rather lazy. I never want to dress in fine clothes now.'

'You must dress,' said Lord Melbourne. 'The people expect it. Besides dressing brushes up a woman.'

'I don't feel quite the same as I did.'

'You became Queen. It was a great experience. You were exultant, excited. It is only natural that the excitement wears off, and there follows a certain depression. Soon you will throw that off and settle down. Then you will discover what a fine thing it is to be queen of a great country.'

'I hope so. I hate to feel so lazy. Sometimes when I get up in the morning I don't want even to brush my teeth. I feel angry about teeth. They are such a nuisance.'

'Mrs Sheridan used to say that there were four commandments and that children should be brought up to obey them ... and if they did all would be well. They were: Fear God; Honour the King; Obey Your Parents; and Brush Your Teeth.'

Victoria began to laugh. Then she thought of Mrs Sheridan, who must have been the mother of Caroline Norton, that woman with whom he was involved in divorce proceedings.

She thought: How I wish he would tell me something of his past life – that very colourful, exciting and, some would say, wicked past of his, which has made him such a fascinating person!

Oh yes, there was something to make life agreeable even during this time of depression. Her meetings with Lord M.

The Baroness came into the Queen's bedroom through the communicating door. Her face was flushed and she looked as though she were rather excited about something.

'I must tell you at once. Flora Hastings is back.'

'Well, Daisy darling, that is not very good news.'

'She came back from Scotland, you know.'

'Yes, I heard she had gone to her mother's house for Christmas.'

'She came back in a post chaise which she shared with ... guess whom?'

'Daisy, what has come over you? Tell me what it is at once.'

'She came back *alone* with Sir John Conroy.'

'Well, of course there have been lots of rumours about them. They are often together and I am ashamed to say this – and wouldn't to anyone but you, Daisy – but people say that my mother is jealous of Lady Flora because Sir John pays too much attention to her.'

'It may well be that he has been paying *very* special attention to her.'

'What *do* you mean?'

'She is feeling most unwell. She has mysterious pains in her side. And there is no doubt that her figure has undergone a change recently. She had grown noticeably *larger*.'

'Oh no, Daisy, it cannot be!'

'I am certain it is. I hear that she is going to consult Sir James Clark.'

'Oh, how very shocking!'

'Well, what do you expect?'

'That man is capable of anything.'

'Now,' said Lehzen, not without glee, 'we shall await developments.'

The fact that Flora Hastings had travelled in a post chaise alone with Sir John gave rise to a great deal of gossip in both camps, and as she was visiting the doctor and her figure was somewhat enlarged, conclusions were being drawn in every quarter.

Lady Flora, too, seemed preoccupied and very pale; she was clearly worried.

Even her friends were asking themselves what the outcome would be. Lady Flora, the daughter of a very important family; Sir John married; and the Duchess either very jealous now or soon would be. What an exciting situation!

As for the Queen, who had begun to feel a little deflated, she was finding a new interest in life through the Lady Flora situation.

'If,' she said to Lehzen, 'it is proved that he is responsible for her condition, he will have no alternative but to leave the Palace and that is what we want more than anything.'

Lady Tavistock, Lady of the Bedchamber, who was in charge of the Queen's ladies-in-waiting, returned from visiting her family to find the scandal in full spate.

'It is disgraceful,' she was told by Lady Portman, second-in-command in the bedchamber, 'that the woman is allowed to go about in this state. Something ought to be done about it.'

'The Queen is aware of this, of course.'

'You should know what sharp eyes she has. She misses little. And it really is becoming quite obvious.'

'What a scandal! I'm glad it is one of the Duchess's ladies and not one of ours.'

'If it were one of ours we should have hushed it up by now and got her sent away ... quickly.'

'I wonder why Lady Flora didn't stay in Scotland?'

'Because she can't tear herself away from Sir John, I daresay.'

'I'll have to think what can be done,' said Lady Tavistock.

She could go to the Queen, but perhaps that was not advisable. The Queen could be very imperious. Lady Tavistock had been made uncomfortably aware of that when they had been out driving recently, and the Queen had suddenly declared that she must walk more because she was putting on weight and had been advised to take exercise. When the Queen walked etiquette demanded that her ladies walk also. The ground had been damp, and Lady Tavistock had returned to the Palace with wet feet and as her maid had the key to her wardrobe she had been unable to change. It had been most uncomfortable and a cold had resulted. She had complained to Thomas Creevey, that ubiquitous gossip, who had said with a chuckle, 'I daresay you thought her a resolute little chit.' And Lady Tavistock had agreed that she had. And Thomas Creevey had lost no time not only in noting the incident in his diaries, but discussing it with his friends.

Now there was the difficulty of taking what would seem the right action in the eyes of that 'resolute little chit' with regard to the Flora Hastings affair.

Meanwhile Lehzen and the Queen discussed Lady Flora continuously.

'Of course,' said Victoria, 'if I were on speaking terms with Mamma I could tell her about it because after all Lady Flora is in *her* household.'

'It would certainly be her place to deal with the matter,' agreed Lehzen. 'When I think of all the unkind remarks that woman has made about me...'

'It's her just reward, Daisy. I am sure very soon everyone will know.'

'We can only wait and see,' was the reply.

Thus when Lady Tavistock approached the Baroness to ask what action should be taken, for she believed some action was necessary, Lehzen could only reply that it was impossible for any of them to approach the Duchess since the Queen was not on speaking terms with her mother.

'But something will have to be done,' cried Lady Tavistock. 'We can't have a woman in the Palace flaunting such a condition.'

'Someone will have to be spoken to,' Lehzen agreed. 'And if it is not the Duchess, then who can it be? I can only suggest Lord Melbourne.'

'The Prime Minister! On such an *affair!*'

'Lord Melbourne is more than the Queen's first minister. He is on friendly terms with the Palace.'

'Then I will ask him to see me when he next calls,' said Lady Tavistock.

Melbourne looked at her with some distaste. Though she was connected with Lord John Russell and would be the Duchess of Bedford, Anna Maria, Marchioness Tavistock, did not attract him in the least. She was something of a mischief-maker, he believed, and he had heard the story of the wet feet. It was her own fault, Melbourne had thought, if she wasn't in better control of her maids; and a walk in the rain hurt nobody. Moreover it was disloyal of her to have discussed her mistress with someone like Creevey.

'I have to speak to you, Lord Melbourne,' she began, 'on a very delicate matter.'

He waited.

'It concerns Lady Flora Hastings.'

'Yes?'

'I have reason to believe that she is in a certain condition.'

'What reason is this, Lady Tavistock?'

'Well, it is becoming rather obvious and she has visited Sir James Clark.'

'You have spoken to Sir James Clark?'

'Yes, and he tells me that she would seem to be pregnant.'

'He is not sure?'

'He has not examined her fully.'

'And she has made no suggestion that she should leave Court?'

'She is one of the Duchess's ladies, but I am sure that had she intended to leave someone would have made me aware of it by now. If she is indeed in this condition I cannot have her here contaminating the young ladies of the Palace.'

'Quite so,' said Lord Melbourne gravely.

'I would like your advice as to what action should be taken.'

'Well, as you are not entirely sure that the lady is pregnant I cannot see that you can take any action. On the other hand if it is indeed so, time will soon make this plain. So all I can suggest is that you wait and see.'

Before leaving the Palace Lord Melbourne went to see Sir James Clark.

'I want you to tell me,' he said, 'what you think of your patient, Lady Flora Hastings?'

'I think that she may be pregnant.'

'Are you treating her for anything?'

'I am giving her a few pills and ointments.'

'What is the ointment for?'

'For a swelling of the body.'

'In a significant place, I presume.'

'Most significant.'

'But you are not sure what ails her?'

'I have not made a proper examination but all the signs are that she is pregnant. She appears to be nervous and a little afraid, but that could be accounted for by the fact that she is an unmarried woman.'

'Precisely,' said Lord Melbourne. 'Well, we can wait and see.'

When he left the doctor he called on the Queen and told her that he had spoken both with Lady Tavistock and Sir James Clark.

'There doesn't seem to be any doubt as to what ails the lady.'

'It is scandalous.'

'It's the last thing I would have expected to have happened to her. She is such a plain, disagreeable woman.'

'And wicked too.'

Lord Melbourne was inclined to be lenient towards her frailty, and Victoria went on: 'I can guess who is responsible. He is a monster.'

'I believe the Duchess to be already very jealous,' added Lord Melbourne.

'It is disgraceful.'

'He is very popular with the ladies ... your monster. Even your Aunt Sophia delights in him. So that is three ladies we know of who find him irresistible. Your Aunt Sophia was quite a character in her youth. There was a scandal about her. She fell in love with one of your grandfather's equerries and rumour has it that there was a child. Sophia was smuggled out of the Palace from under Queen Charlotte's nose and had the boy and came back as demure as ever.'

'It is hard to believe that of Aunt Sophia. She always gives me the impression of knowing so little of the world.'

'It is often hard to imagine that the lean and slippered pantaloon was the gay young rip of thirty years before. And it's not always easy for any of us.'

'Poor Aunt Sophia! It must have been very dull living with my Grandmother Charlotte. But she was discreet and slipped away to have the child ... if she did. This brazen Flora Hastings stays at Court and as for that monster ... I daresay he is laughing about it.'

'The only thing we can do is wait and see,' said Lord Melbourne. He was a great believer in allowing events to take their course.

The days passed and Lady Flora looked pale and clearly ill but she made no attempt to remove herself. The ladies in the Duchess's household were whispering about her now, for the rumours were spreading. She was noticeably larger and she certainly did look quite ill at times.

They discussed what they had heard of pregnancy symptoms and assured themselves that these were exactly those from which Lady Flora was suffering.

But why did she not slip discreetly away? She was not the first lady of the Court who had found herself in such a situation. Perhaps she thought that as Sir John Conroy was involved it was not

212

necessary to do this. He was such a power in the
Duchess's household that Flora had no need to
feel the qualms which would beset a woman with
a less powerful lover.

Lady Tavistock and Lady Portman were constantly talking of what should be done.

Lady Tavistock said: 'I don't like it. I am after
all in charge of these young girls. I can't have that
woman here, getting larger every day and
brazenly showing us all that she has no shame.'

'Something ought to be done,' agreed Lady
Portman. 'Do you think you should speak to the
Queen?'

'I might approach the Baroness again.'

'I think you should do that.'

'Lord Melbourne said wait and see.'

'Meanwhile she is walking around in this
disgusting state!'

'I'll see if the Baroness is in her rooms. Come
with me.'

The Baroness was and she was not averse to
discussing the shocking affair of the woman who
had so long taunted her.

'There can be no doubt,' she said. 'No doubt at
all.'

'Then why does she not go away?' demanded
Lady Tavistock.

'She feels that with the support of Conroy she
can snap her fingers at us all.'

'I feel that she should be made to know that we
are aware of her condition.'

'Yes,' the Baroness's eyes were gleaming, 'I
should like to be there when she is told that.'

'Perhaps Sir James could tell her that it is no

longer a secret.'

'He is undoubtedly the one to do it. And then let her try to brazen it out with him!'

'She is brazen,' said Lady Portman. 'We all agree to that.'

'He could put it very discreetly,' said the Baroness. 'For instance he could say: "You must have been married for some little time, and have told your friends nothing about it" ... or something like that.'

'That's an excellent idea.'

'Do you think he will do it?' asked Lady Portman.

'Of course he will because he will know that we have the Baroness's support when we ask him and that means that we have the Queen's.'

Lehzen nodded. 'I can give you authority to do this.'

'Then I shall do it immediately,' said Lady Tavistock, 'because although it is all very well to wait and see, I feel I am failing in my duty towards the Queen's young ladies in allowing this to go on.'

Sir James Clark had been very surprised when he had secured his position in the Queen's household. His medical skill did not warrant this, as he was uneasily aware; he always said that he believed in simple remedies; he could be sure that while they might do no good (and on the other hand they might be effective) they could at least do no harm. Feeling insecure he had a great desire to ingratiate himself with the Queen and he knew that the best way he could do this was to win the good graces of the Baroness Lehzen.

He was well aware of the gossip concerning Lady Flora, that Sir John Conroy was suspected of being her lover and that the Queen hated Conroy who had made such extravagant demands as the price of his departure that it had been impossible to grant them. Therefore by declaring Lady Flora pregnant he would be condemning Sir John Conroy, and it was very likely that if Lady Flora retired in disgrace Sir John would be forced to go also. Thus he would be rendering a service to the Queen!

He had not examined Lady Flora but he had prodded her stomach over her gown and there was certainly a protuberance; she was undoubtedly unwell. Everything pointed to pregnancy.

So now he had the Queen's instructions (for coming from Lady Tavistock that was what it meant) to tackle Lady Flora and get the truth from her.

He did not wait for her to come to see him but called on her.

She was alone in her apartments, looking very pale with dark shadows under her eyes; she was obviously worried and the swelling, he noticed with gratification, was obvious.

She showed some surprise that he should call on her so he said quickly: 'I am anxious about your health, Lady Flora, and have come to enquire how you are.'

'I still have the pain.'

'Lady Flora, I think you must be secretly married.'

Lady Flora stared at him for a moment and

then turned a fiery red.

'I don't grasp your meaning. Sir James.'

'I think you do.'

'Are you suggesting that I am ... with child?'

'It seems obvious.'

'But surely you ... a doctor...'

He looked steadily at her. 'I have not examined you closely, but it would appear from all I have seen that you are going to have a child.'

'That's impossible.' She put her hands on her swollen abdomen. 'The swelling is not always the same. At times it is larger than at others.'

Sir James looked dubious.

'You don't believe me. I can show you dresses I have worn recently. I could wear one yesterday which a few days earlier I could not have got into because I was too large.'

Sir James said he was no dressmaker. 'I think you should submit to a proper examination,' he added. 'You are either pregnant or have some very obscure illness.'

'Then it is some obscure illness.'

'You must submit to this examination.'

'I will not,' cried Lady Flora, clearly agitated at the prospect. 'I think you are behaving in a most unprofessional manner. It is not your duty to insult ladies who come to consult you.'

'You grow larger every day and the ladies of the Palace think so, too. They will only be satisfied with a medical examination.'

'The ladies?' demanded Lady Flora. 'You mean the Duchess of Kent? She has said nothing to me.'

'Lady Portman has spoken to me.'

Lady Flora said: 'Oh... the *Queen!*'

Sir James nodded. 'So you see that since Her Majesty is aware of your ... plight ... an examination is the only answer.'

'You mean it is Her Majesty's command that I submit to this disagreeable examination?'

'Clearly it is Her Majesty's wish.'

'I need time to consider this.'

'It is dangerous to delay.'

'In what way dangerous?'

'The rumours are growing. They have spread beyond the Palace.'

'Very well,' said Lady Flora. 'But I insist that another doctor is present. I have known Sir Charles Mansfield Clarke all my life. If he will take part I will submit.'

Sir James was a little deflated, for while she was declaring she would stand out against the examination he believed her to be guilty. Now he was not so sure.

He could only agree at once that Sir Charles should be called in and went back to Lady Tavistock and Lady Portman to tell them what had happened.

'With great reluctance she has agreed to the examination.'

They were all disappointed. They had been counting on a blank refusal which in their eyes would have confirmed her guilt. They went to the Baroness who in her turn went to the Queen.

'Lady Flora has most reluctantly agreed to an examination,' said the Baroness. 'Sir James had to force her to it.'

'How ... indelicate!'

'She is brazening it out. She thinks she is clever enough to outwit us all.'

'How can she, Lehzen? If she has a child we shall all know in good time.'

'These things can be arranged. She can declare her innocence, then when the affair has blown over, slip away and have the child and let some servant look after it. It's been done before.'

Yes, thought Victoria, Aunt Sophia.

'It is all a matter of time,' went on Lehzen. 'That is why Sir James was insistent about the examination.'

'I'm surprised that she agreed.'

'She wouldn't have done so, but when Sir James let it be known that it was more or less an order from Your Majesty that changed her tune.'

'It is all very shocking. I don't want to have to see her. Send an order to her that she is not to appear until her character has been cleared in the only manner it can be.'

After leaving Lady Tavistock and Lady Portman Sir James felt it was his duty to inform the Duchess of Kent what was happening to her lady-in-waiting.

The Duchess was horrified. She had been so immersed in her own affairs that she had been completely unaware of what was happening under her nose although the entire household was whispering about Lady Flora.

She sent for Flora at once.

'Is this true?'

'It is lies ... all lies,' cried Lady Flora. 'I am ill and because my body is swollen they are saying I am pregnant.'

'Who is saying this?' demanded the Duchess.

'The Queen's ladies started it. Tavistock and Portman.'

'Oh,' said the Duchess, 'so it came from that quarter.'

'I have explained to Sir James Clark that I am sometimes more swollen than others. Besides, I am a virgin. I trust Your Grace believes me.'

The Duchess was relieved. She did believe Flora. She had been jealous of her because Sir John had been rather too friendly with her. Sir John was so charming that many women found him irresistible and Flora had quite clearly been flattered, but they had all worked very well together. The Duchess believed she saw the motive behind this attack on Lady Flora's character.

'Do you swear that you could not possibly be pregnant, Flora?'

'I do. If your Grace will allow me to stay at Court I can prove it. People will see that at times I am larger than at others. I am sick, I know. But I will consult Sir Charles Clarke. I am sure his diagnosis will be different from that of Sir James.'

'Go to your bed and lie down,' said the Duchess. 'I will talk to you later, but let me tell you this: I believe you. This is some cruel plot which has started in the Queen's household. Don't worry, Flora. I will stand by you.'

The Duchess kissed her lady-in-waiting and the usually frigid Flora was almost in tears. '*They* will be sorry for this,' declared the Duchess; and Flora felt that with the Duchess's support she could face the ordeal before her.

Naturally the Duchess immediately sought out Sir John.

'They are accusing Flora of being pregnant,' cried the Duchess. 'It is all a hideous plot. The poor girl is almost demented ... although she bravely tries to hide it.'

'You know,' said Sir John, 'that they are accusing me of being the father of this non-existent child.'

'No, they cannot!'

'They have already done so. But then I am blamed for everything so I have become accustomed to that.'

'Is this child ... non-existent?'

'As far as I can say ... yes. Do you think Flora is the sort of woman to take a lover? Flora is as frigid as an iceberg.'

'You have tested this?'

'One does not have to submit her to that test. All the signposts are there to lead one to that conclusion.'

'Then she should refuse to submit to this distasteful examination, poor girl.'

Sir John was smiling one of his most cynical smiles. 'This is going to be one of the biggest scandals of the age. Our little Vic does not realise what a storm she is raising.'

'Should we try to tell her?'

Sir John laughed. 'Tell her? Certainly not! Let her get her little fingers burned. The people love her. She is so appealing, the dear little Queen – so kind to everyone, so innocent. Out she goes on her horse – and how well she looks on her horse – riding in her carriage, bowing, smiling. Oh yes, the people love their dear little Queen. But don't you see, this is her affair. She is at the root of it. She is hounding an innocent woman; she is accusing her of what society calls disgraceful conduct – more disgraceful of course when it is brought to light. If practised in secret it can be quite respectable. Oh, yes, they are playing right into our hands. I think this is going to be a victory for us.'

'I begin to see what you mean, but this can only come about if Flora is innocent.'

'I'm ready to stake my future honours and pension on her virginity.'

'You should know,' said the Duchess, a little tersely.

'I'm sure I do,' he said with a smile.

'Then what happens next?'

'Simple. There is an examination and Flora is proved to be a virgin.'

'That will be an end to the matter.'

'Oh dear me, no. That will *not* be the end of the matter. Flora will be cleared, yes, but others will be involved. Those who slandered her; those who have treated a sick woman to such indignity, humiliating her, tearing her reputation into shreds.'

'You mean ... the Queen?'

Conroy lifted his shoulders. 'Our Little Majesty could scarcely escape *some* censure, for those interfering old busybodies could not act without her consent.'

'And then?'

'The Court, the people will see that it is not all sunshine in the Palace. Perhaps they will question whether some of the hard things which have been said about others – such as the Queen's mother and that Comptroller of a royal household who was ready to be her good friend – have been entirely true. Moreover I do not think Lady Flora's family will let the matter be quietly shelved. And quite rightly. They will want no stories being put about that the matter has been hushed up to save Lady Flora's face.'

'You are making it look like a conspiracy.'

'That,' said Sir John, 'is exactly what it is.'

On the following Sunday when the examination was to take place tension grew in the Palace. The two doctors and Lady Portman with Lady Flora's maid were all present.

Victoria, like everyone else, was waiting for the result. She had realised that if they were wrong the situation was going to be rather unpleasant. She could not hope that they would be proved right, of course. And yet...

Oh dear, what a terrible position to be in! How had she become involved in such an indelicate affair? How much better if everyone had taken Lord Melbourne's advice to wait and see.

The Baroness came to her, her face blank with dismay.

'Is it over?' asked the Queen.

'Yes,' said Lehzen.

'The result?'

'The two doctors have signed a statement to say that she is a virgin and that the swelling is due to some growth of the liver.'

'Oh, the poor girl!'

'She is very ill but not pregnant.'

'At least,' said the Queen, uncertainly, 'this has settled the disagreeable matter once and for all. I am going to ask her to come and see me. I am going to tell her how very sorry I am that we misjudged her.'

'That is the best line to take,' said the Baroness.

The Queen wrote at once to Lady Flora inviting her to call on her. Lady Flora replied at once begging to be excused; the ordeal through which she had passed combined with her illness had brought her near to a state of collapse and she was unable to leave her bed.

Victoria answered kindly, suggesting Lady Flora visit her the next day.

The meeting took place. The Queen was in tears. It had been such a dreadful affair and she was afraid poor Lady Flora had suffered greatly. But she, the Queen, was so happy now that it was all over and she wanted Lady Flora to know that she had her deepest sympathy.

Lady Flora replied with guarded dignity, aware she said of the honour Her Majesty did her by her interest in her affairs. She added she felt very ill and would be glad to retire to her bed.

'Please do so at once,' said the Queen. 'I shall send someone tomorrow to ask how you are.'

When Lady Flora was gone she sighed with relief and told herself how glad she was that the matter was settled, but she would be very careful in future to make sure that she was in possession of the full facts before she accused anyone.

'I am grateful,' she repeated to the Baroness, 'that this most distasteful affair is now over.'

But of course it was not over.

'This,' said Sir John, 'is the beginning of the fun.'

He was going to exploit the situation to the full, so he went at once to see Lady Flora.

'So our Little Vic has made her apology,' he said.

'She was very gracious,' Flora told him.

'And very frightened, I daresay. And how are you, Flora?'

'A little better today.'

'Good! Well enough to write a letter?'

'To whom?'

'To your brother, of course. He may not have heard of this. In fact I am pretty certain that he has not. Knowing the young gentleman I am sure that if he had heard of the slanders aimed at his sister he would have been down with all speed to avenge the insult to his family honour.'

'He does not know, of course.'

'He is going to.'

'You are going to tell him?'

'No, you are.'

'I am heartily sick of the entire affair.'

'You know, Flora, in an affair like this even though one is proved innocent there will always be someone to believe the worst. In a few years' time they will be saying "What was that Flora Hastings affair? Immoral woman wasn't she? Found out and disgraced!"'

'But I have been cleared.'

'People believe the worst. You'll have to make such a noise about this that the facts are not forgotten. We want the right people to be blamed.

Take my advice, Flora. Write to your brother. Tell him how you have been slandered. Tell him to what you have had to submit. Your family honour is at stake, you know. People are going to believe the worst. Write off to Loudoun right away.'

'He is not at Loudoun. He's at Donington Park.'

'So much the better. Leicestershire is nearer than Scotland. Take my advice, Flora. Do this at once. Or do you prefer to stand meekly by and let them insult you?'

He knew that was not Flora's way. He brought her pens and ink and sat there watching her while she wrote the story of her wrongs. When it was written, he himself took it away and made sure it was despatched without delay to the young Marquis of Hastings.

When Lord Hastings received his letter he had just risen from a sick bed. Flora had written that she was ill, and because she was ill her honour had been in question. Certain ladies of the Queen's household had fabricated a scandal about her and since the Queen believed this scandal it had been necessary for her to submit to an embarrassing and humiliating examination.

The young Marquis, quick-tempered and hotheaded, decided that he would leave at once for London and very soon was in his sister's apartments listening to her story in all its most indelicate details.

'Of course,' he said, 'there is one person behind this, for this examination was tantamount to an order from the Queen and we know who advises the Queen on all matters. Lord Melbourne. I shall challenge that fellow to a duel.'

'Take care,' begged Lady Flora.

'I shall take care of our family honour. Lord Melbourne has questioned this. He has to answer for it. It is either his blood or mine.'

'For Heaven's sake be careful.'

'Don't worry about me. I'm a young man, which is more than Melbourne is. I'll warrant he is better at tattling scandal in the royal boudoir than handling firearms.'

Nothing Flora could say would deter her brother and she began to wish she had not listened to Sir John's advice and written to him. However, she was feeling too ill to care very much and Lord Hastings left her to go to his friend Lord Winchelsea to ask him to act as his second in the duel.

'Duel!' cried Winchelsea. 'You're mad, my dear fellow. Whom do you intend to call out?'

'Melbourne.'

'The Prime Minister?'

'Why not? If he assails the honour of my family he shall answer for it as any man should.'

'Now wait a minute, wait a minute,' cautioned Winchelsea. 'You are jumping to conclusions. Are you sure it's the Prime Minister you should be blaming?'

'I can't very well challenge the Queen.'

'Oh, so it is the Queen you wish to castigate.'

'If she were not royal and a woman my challenge would go to her. As it can't, it goes to her Prime Minister.'

'You're a hot-headed idiot, Hastings. Look here, go and see the Prime Minister first. Get an

226

account of the story from him. I doubt he had anything to do with the affair. This is women's tittle-tattle. Don't make a fool of yourself.'

Hastings was impressed with this advice and agreed that he would see the Prime Minister first before calling him out.

As soon as Lord Melbourne heard that Lord Hastings wished to see him he guessed for what reason. A disastrous affair, this Flora Hastings matter. What a pity they had not let well alone. The trouble was that the whole press had taken up and exaggerated the story and it was being suggested that the Queen was deeply involved.

'Now, Hastings,' said Lord Melbourne in his most bland and worldly manner, 'what is all this about?'

'I am sure you have a very good notion. I am disgusted by the way in which my sister has been treated.'

'Ah yes, yes. So are we all. A most unfortunate business.'

'Fabricated by malicious people! Flora's innocence has been proved.'

'At which I am delighted,' said the Prime Minister. 'Not that I had any doubts that it could be otherwise.'

'How unfortunate that you did not state this at the time, Lord Melbourne.'

'Oh, but I did by implication. My advice when Lady Tavistock came to see me was: "Do nothing." And since she and her friends were so certain she was right – which was clearly very rash and uncharitable of them – I begged them to wait

227

and see. "Wait and see." Those were my very words. For I knew that the only way in which I could make these ladies see logic was to point out to them that while Lady Flora remained at Court under their eyes she must before long produce the infant if that infant existed. I assure you, my dear Hastings, I did all I could to urge these ladies to act with discretion.'

Lord Hastings was temporarily subdued. He could see that he had been rash to think of challenging the Prime Minister to a duel. But he was not going to let the matter be thrust aside.

'I am determined,' he said, 'to get to the root of this affair and to discover who set these ugly and criminal rumours into motion; and as Her Majesty seems to be at the heart of the matter I shall ask for an audience.'

Melbourne was horrified.

'But you cannot ask the Queen for explanations!'

'I am determined to get to the root of this, no matter whom I have to ask.'

'I think,' said the Prime Minister, 'that the Duke of Wellington might be able to help you. I will tell him you are coming to see him and I will ask him to listen to what you have to say and advise you.'

Lord Hastings agreed and when he had gone, uneasy as Lord Melbourne felt on behalf of the Queen, he was relieved that he had been able to pass the rather tiresome young Hastings over to the Duke of Wellington.

The Duke of Wellington was always eager to give

advice. His fighting days were over, his popularity had waned (because he had stood against the Reform Bill); he was now a considerable politician but Parliament could never take the place of the battlefield. He was fast becoming a kind of figure to the country and it was a custom to call him in for consultation at any time of difficulty.

He was delighted therefore to advise the impetuous young Marquis.

'It was a shocking affair,' he conceded, 'and therefore best forgotten. There has been a great deal of comment about it already. It is much wiser therefore to let sleeping dogs lie.'

'This,' said the Marquis, 'is exactly what I don't intend to do. Sleeping scandal, you mean! Yes, sleeping! Just waiting until someone comes along and prods it to life. Then we shall have the old accusations again. No, I intend to bring it out into the open and kill it stone dead.'

He left Wellington and wrote at once to Melbourne. He could get no satisfaction from the Duke, he said; and he was determined to have satisfaction. Therefore he asked Lord Melbourne to arrange for him an interview with Her Majesty the Queen.

Impatiently he waited for a reply. None came. Furiously he sat down and wrote again telling Lord Melbourne that his patience was exhausted. As Lord Melbourne had told him that the Court ladies were responsible for the treatment of Lady Flora he was determined to ask the Queen for an explanation. He did not believe it was due to the deliberate actions of Her Majesty but put it down to baneful influences which were about the throne and which poisoned human feelings. He was addressing himself to the Prime Minister as the organ through which all things were now carried out at Court.

When Melbourne received this missive he realised that it would be dangerous to ignore the young man. Hastings was in a fighting mood and the matter needed the most delicate of handling.

He wrote back at once saying that he had been away and he would submit the request to the Queen, and at once went to Victoria.

'It is this distressing matter of Flora Hastings again, I fear.'

'Oh, surely not!'

'I think it will be necessary for you to see this young man.'

'I? But what have I to do with it?'

'He blames your ladies and seems to think that you are behind them in this.'

'What nonsense! Naturally I wanted to know the truth. If Lady Flora was an immoral woman I didn't want her at my Court. I have seen her and expressed my sympathy. I have sent to ask how she is progressing. Surely that is enough?'

'Oh,' said Lord Melbourne comfortably, 'if you will just see the young man he'll be soothed. You will know how to charm him.'

'I don't care to be forced into this interview.'

'There is no question of forcing. Who would attempt to force the Queen? I will just give you one of my pieces of advice. You have never been averse to listening to them at less stormy times. You may reject it of course but I am going to be my bold and uncompromising self and say that you are much too clever not to listen to an old man who has seen a great deal of the world.'

'*Dear* Lord M, why cannot everyone be as kind and understanding as you are?'

'I might ask why everyone cannot be as reasonable as Your Majesty.'

'So you are absolutely certain that I should see him?'

'I think so. Be noncommittal. Tell him you regret what happened and that you have nothing but respect for his dear sister and she will be treated with honour, etc., at Court. That will satisfy him.'

'So it is really a matter of placating this young man?'

'No, it's not as simple as that. It's a matter of placating the people. This affair – alas – has been widely reported in the press and of course wildly exaggerated. The people take sides in these matters and they are invariably on the side of the oppressed – the wretched Lady Flora – devil take her – in this instance.'

Victoria could not help smiling at Lord Melbourne's *quaint* expressions.

'I will see what I can do with the trying young man,' she said.

In her most regal and dignified manner she received Lord Hastings as she had said she would. She told him that she greatly regretted that such a matter should have occurred at her Court, and that it was most distasteful to her. She realised that Lady Flora was blameless, so she should be allowed to remain at Court while she wished to do so and would be treated there with the utmost respect. As far as she could see that ended the matter.

Lord Hastings found it difficult to argue with the Queen, so he came away dissatisfied; but even though the Queen had intimated that she wished the matter to be closed, he soon realised that this could not be so. The press brought out the story again and worried it like a dog with a favourite bone trying to get a little more meat off it. People were taking sides. The majority of them were with Lady Flora but an unpleasant rumour was started that she was actually pregnant, that this was not the first time, and that she had recently left the Court to give birth to an illegitimate child.

'I will not allow this,' cried Lord Hastings. 'I don't care for anyone ... not even the Queen. I am determined to make sure that no one is going to question the honour of our house.'

He wrote to Lord Tavistock demanding that he ask the truth of his wife; he also wrote to Lord Portman. Acrimonious letters passed between them. Lord Hastings believed he knew who was at the centre of the plot against his sister and it came from the foreign influences which existed at Court. This was an accusation against the Baroness Lehzen.

Lady Hastings, Flora's mother, took up the fight and wrote to the Queen, reminding Victoria that she was a mother defending her much maligned daughter and she wanted an explanation of the 'atrocious calumnies and unblushing falsehoods against her daughter's reputation'. She wanted to

232

know who had betrayed the Queen into following a course of action which had attempted to degrade the victim of their persecution. People looked for sympathy to a female sovereign, she added. This was not a matter to be hushed up.

The letter was sent to the Prime Minister with a request that he should deliver it to the Queen.

He took it to her himself.

'Is there no end to this tiresome business?' demanded Victoria petulantly.

'There is an end to everything but time and space,' said Lord Melbourne lightly.

'I hear that when the injured lady took a drive this morning she was loudly cheered in the streets.'

'Unfortunate,' said Lord Melbourne. 'And also an indication. But I think we should handle Mamma Hastings with tact.'

'Of course she *is* a mother and she writes as though she is *very* upset.'

'But the matter is done with and I should have thought she would have known better than to address Your Majesty in this way. It's a breach of etiquette. Will you trust me to reply?'

'Please do. But tell her that I am sorry it all happened and let her know I understand her feelings.'

Lord Melbourne gave her one of his tender looks and sat down to write the letter immediately so that she could approve it.

Her Majesty's allowances for the feelings of a mother diminished her surprise that Lady Hastings should address her thus. Her Majesty bade her Prime Minister convey to Lady Hastings her deep concern for the unfortunate occurrence and was anxious to do everything to soothe the feelings of Lady Flora's relations.

'That should settle the old lady,' said Lord Melbourne.

But it did not. In a short time Lady Hastings was writing once more – this time to Melbourne. She now demanded the dismissal of Sir James Clark.

This, said Lord Melbourne, was insolence; and he wrote to Lady Hastings telling her that her demand was 'unprecedented and objectionable' and that although she was a lady and the head of a respected family he would do no more than acknowledge that he had received such a letter.

'They will give us no satisfaction,' said Lord Hastings, 'and there is only one thing to do, unless we are to slink off with our tails between our legs. We will publish the correspondence.'

The press was delighted; so were the people. Here was a mighty scandal. The *Morning Post* had a scoop and it intended to make the most of it. The whole story was revived. The Tories were trying to make it a political issue. Some declared that Lord Melbourne should apologise to Lady Hastings for his discourtesy towards her. In the clubs, in the streets, in the taverns, the Flora Hastings affair was discussed and the three principal actors in the piece were said to be Lady Flora, the Queen and Lord Melbourne.

'It will die down,' said Lord Melbourne. 'These things always do.'

The Queen read the papers every day and was hurt and amazed to read criticisms of herself.

When she rode out in the streets the people were silent. They no longer cheered her; yet Flora Hastings's carriage was held up by people who applauded her and wanted to tell her that they were on her side.

It was astonishing. Victoria could not believe it. She was no longer their little duck, their dear little Queen; she was a wicked woman who had cruelly slandered an innocent one.

'Who would have thought such a little thing could change them towards me,' she cried.

'It is often the little things in life which are the most important,' said Lord Melbourne.

She was depressed.

'It'll pass,' said Lord Melbourne philosophically. 'It always does.'

'How right you were when you impressed on me how important this affair could become.'

'And you listened to me. Therefore let us regard it as a lesson.'

That lifted her spirits a little. Lord Melbourne said that any experience was worth while if one learned from it. She had certainly learned from this. And she still had dear Lord Melbourne as her companion.

And that, she reminded herself, was a great deal for which to be thankful.

Chapter 9

THE BEDCHAMBER AFFAIR

The Palace feud had intensified, and the happiness the Queen had experienced during the 'pleasantest summer' had completely disappeared. The Duchess was becoming more and more tiresome and seemed to do everything possible to make life difficult. She kept Lady Flora constantly in her company, was over-solicitous for her health as though to draw attention to her own compassion compared with her daughter's heartlessness. The Flora Hastings scandal was still discussed and of course by this time it was obvious that she would not be pregnant and was really ill.

Victoria was touchy, irritable, snapping at dear Daisy and sometimes being imperious even with Lord Melbourne. Of course his extreme tact and rather cynical jocularity overcame these moods and he would laugh at her in a funny respectful way, bow with exaggerated formality and call her *Majesty*, so that she would have to laugh and feel better for a while.

She raged against the Tories and their horrid paper, the *Morning Post*, which had blown up the silly Palace intrigue to a mighty scandal; she referred to Flora Hastings as that 'nasty creature'; she worried about putting on weight, her lack of inches and her health. She was getting really melancholy and that, she once told Lord Melbourne, was how it probably started with her grandfather.

Lord Melbourne said it was not in the least like her grandfather. He had had a rash and had been unable to stop talking. Lord Melbourne thought where she did show a lack of balance was in comparing herself with him. Yet look how angry she had been when she had been likened to Queen Charlotte and the Duke of Gloucester!

That made her laugh.

'Dear Lord M!' she cried. 'What should I do without you? Whenever I feel melancholy I remember that you will be coming in to see me and that makes me feel much better.'

Lord Melbourne looked a little thoughtful and wondered whether he ought to tell her about the uncertain position of the Government. Was it better to do so and prepare her or let the inevitable burst upon her? It would certainly do nothing to relieve her present gloomy feelings; on the other hand he did not wish it to come as a surprise.

Better perhaps to prepare her gradually.

'Colonies can try us sorely,' he said. 'There are troubles looming in Jamaica now.'

'I am sure my Government with you at its head will be able to handle them successfully.'

'Oh, I have the utmost confidence in Lord Palmerston. There are, however, so many questions to be settled. There is controversy over the apprentices there. The prisons are overcrowded. Some of the planters are far from humane and they clap their workers into prison for the slightest offence which results of course in this dreadful overcrowding. We brought in a Bill to improve all this but the Colonial Assembly were hostile to it. "Trouble! Trouble! Boil and Bubble." If it isn't Canada it's Jamaica. Who would have Colonies?'

'Having them we must look after them.'

'Quite so,' said Lord Melbourne. 'We are going to bring in a Bill to suspend the Jamaican Constitution temporarily but Sir Robert Peel and his merry men are not going to agree with us on this point.'

'How *tiresome* they are!'

He looked at her more closely. She had not grasped the implication. He had been trying to tell her for some time that the Whig Parliament was on the brink of disaster. One could not govern in the present circumstances. The strength of the Tories was increasing; that of the Whigs diminishing; and Sir Robert Peel was poised at the ready to leap into Lord Melbourne's shoes.

No, she was too sad for him to drive home the point now, but he had sown the seeds. She would go away and think about the Jamaican situation and the powerful Sir Robert Peel who could – and most probably would – in a very short time be here with her talking to her of the country's affairs in the place of Lord Melbourne.

He allowed the conversation to slip back to the Flora Hastings affair which, unpleasant as it was, would he knew be more tolerable to the Queen.

'When the press takes up a royal scandal we can be sure it will be with us for a long time.'

'That wretched *Morning Post!*'

'You should not take it to heart. The Tories are always looking for a chance to attack us and they are trying to make me the scapegoat of this affair.'

'I shall never allow that.'

This is one of the matters in which Your Imperious Majesty has no say, alas. This affair is making as much noise as the troubles of George IV and his wife.'

'She was tried ... for adultery. That must have been very shocking.'

'Yes, but the people like a heroine. They could hardly make one of her and your royal Uncle was scarcely cast for the role of hero at that time. It was very different when he was a young man. Then he was a real Prince Charming. When I was a boy I remember the talk of him. He was in and out of scrapes but the people adored him. He was good-looking and gallant and even when Mary Robinson threatened to publish his love letters they were still on his side against his virtuous and let us confess it rather dull father.'

'Poor Grandfather! And it seems so unfair that people should be loved and admired because of their good looks. Grandfather tried so hard to be good; and Uncle George didn't care – yet they were on his side.'

'The people love romance. When you marry, you will see how they adore you.'

She avoided his eyes. Marriage was a matter she did not wish to discuss with him. Uncle Leopold was constantly hinting at it and mentioning the virtues of her cousin Albert, and she had thought Albert most attractive when she had met him on his brief visit to England before her accession; but now she felt differently. A husband would interfere and she wanted no interference.

Lord Melbourne was aware of her feelings, but marriage like the results of a division on the Jamaican Bill was something which would have to be discussed sooner or later.

She was depressed at the moment so he would try to cheer her.

'I love hearing your accounts of my family,' she said. 'How wonderful to think that you lived through so much and saw it at first hand.'

'I am not so sure. It betrays the fact that I am a somewhat aged gentleman.'

'Some people are ageless. Dear Lord M, you are one of them.'

'Your Majesty is in a complimentary mood today.'

'You are cheering me considerably ... as you always do. Tell me about your family.'

'Ah,' he said, 'they are not illustrious like yours.'

She giggled. 'I fear some of mine have been far from illustrious. In fact they have been wicked and scandalous.'

'Not really more so than the less exalted,' he assured her. 'They have had power some of them, unlimited power, and how do any of us know how we would act with such a weapon in our hands? Now mine is a very much more sober history. Most of it is wrapped in obscurity.'

'Tell me what you know.'

'Well, it was like this: a fellow called Peniston Lamb was born in Southwell in the year 1670. He was poor but he managed to go to London and study law. He went into business and made a fortune.'

'That was clever of him considering he was

born poor.'

'Very clever. When he died he left his fortune to two nephews.'

'Did he have no sons?'

'No sons, only two nephews. One of these, Matthew, was my grandfather. He married a Miss Coke of Melbourne, a little spot not far from Derby. He knew how to multiply the money left to him and made a large fortune. He was knighted and when he died my father, who was Peniston after the founder of our fortunes, inherited his father's money and the title. My father became very friendly with Lord Bute, who was a great friend of your grandfather's mother, the Princess Augusta.'

Victoria nodded. 'I believe there was some scandal.'

'She and Lord Bute were *great friends*, particularly after the death of Augusta's husband, Frederick, Prince of Wales.'

'It reminds me of Mamma and Sir John Conroy.'

'It was rather similar. Lord Bute advised the Princess and your grandfather was then Prince of Wales, his father Frederick having died and George II (*his* grandfather) still being alive. Lord Bute was a man of great influence and remained so until George, having become King, threw him off. But what I wanted to tell you was that my father had some connection with Lord Bute, and Lord North (the Prime Minister who lost us the American Colonies, with the help of your grandfather of course) made my father a Baron and that was how he became Viscount Melbourne.

Then the Prince Regent (your Uncle George) made him a peer of England. There you have the Melbourne history and you see that it is not nearly as exciting as your own.'

'It is far less shocking.'

'Oh, that is because it is obscure.'

'There are too many quarrels in our family.'

'The Hanoverians were noted for their family quarrels. George II quarrelled violently with George I; Frederick, Prince of Wales, who died before his father and so missed the crown, quarrelled with George II; and George III lost his father so he couldn't quarrel with him, but his son George IV made up for it by quarrelling with *his* father and having the most gigantic public quarrel with his wife which ended in the famous trial.'

'And now there is Mamma and myself. We are carrying on the family tradition. Mamma is behaving very badly. Oh dear, it is all so depressing.'

And here they were back at the Queen's growing dissatisfaction with her life.

'If Mamma could be induced to leave the Palace then I think everything would be well.'

'The plain fact is that she cannot leave while you are unmarried, and there is only one way out of it. Since you find her so difficult to live with and cannot live without her, you see the alternative.'

'Marriage.'

'Exactly so,' said Lord Melbourne.

'I do not find the subject a very pleasant one.'

'Quite a number of subjects are so, I fear, but often when one gives them an airing and looks at them from various angles one grows accustomed

242

to them and familiarity breeds not always contempt as they say, but acceptance.'

'I am very young as yet.'

'You are the Queen.'

'And therefore should not be obliged to do what I do not wish.'

'Providing it is outside the interest of the State, of course.'

'And this...'

'Is a State matter. But let us look at it from another angle. You are unhappy in your ménage. You are an unmarried girl. You must have some sort of chaperone and who is reckoned to be better for that kind of post than a girl's own mother? You would like to escape from that particular chaperone. How could you do this? By marriage. You have noticed that owing to this unfortunate affair...'

'That *nasty* creature!'

'Exactly, but the people see her as a wronged heroine and they love wronged heroines. Your role has shifted a little. How could we restore it? There is nothing to appeal to the people like romantic love.'

'Could you so describe a State marriage?'

'State marriages are *always* so described.'

'But that is invariably quite false.'

'But we are discussing how such marriages are described, not what they are. A young queen, a husband whom she loves, a royal wedding! These are the things which would drive that "nasty creature's" martyrdom from their minds and it would rid you of your unwanted custodian.'

The Queen was thoughtful. 'I see that you

243

think it is my *duty*.'

'Well, it is bound to come sooner or later.'

'You know that Uncle Leopold is pressing for me to marry my cousin Albert. They are planning to send him over in the autumn.'

'And your mother? What does she feel about this?'

'I think she would welcome it too.'

'I daresay,' said Lord Melbourne significantly, 'she would welcome her own nephew. They might become very friendly. Do you think cousins are very good things?'

'Well, they might think the same in many ways.'

'The Coburgs are not very popular abroad.'

'Everyone speaks highly of Albert. When I saw him I thought him ... *admirable*.'

'And yet you do not seem very eager to see him again.'

'So much has happened since we last met him. Then I was very young.'

'And Coburgs...' Lord Melbourne made a wry face and shook his head. 'The Duchess is a Coburg.'

'Oh, the men are different.'

'Perhaps the English are not very fond of foreigners.'

'You mean the people would like me to marry an Englishman ... that would mean a *commoner*.'

'Which might not be satisfactory,' Lord Melbourne agreed.

'Is it necessary for me to marry just yet? There is plenty of time. I like to have my own way as you know.'

'I have gathered that,' said Lord Melbourne,

and they both laughed.

'You know my temper.'

'I know it well.'

'It would not be good if a husband roused it, would it?'

'It is not good when anyone rouses it.'

'But really do you not think that we could wait for a year or two?'

'Well, you have just said that you like your own way and I will say that if the Queen decides that she will wait three or four years then she will wait. But in the meantime perhaps it would be advisable for her to give consideration to the matter. It will take her mind from other things.'

She nodded smiling. He was thinking: Yes, from other things, from the possible defeat of Your Majesty's Government from which it would inevitably follow that these encounters which mean so much to us both may well soon be at an end.

Lord Melbourne was very uneasy. It seemed almost certain that in a few weeks he would cease to be the Prime Minister. He was thinking of the Queen. For the last two years they had seen each other every day. He knew she regarded him as a necessary part of her life, but, highly experienced in the ways of the world as he was, he understood their relationship far better than she did. Dear child, he thought, how innocent she is!

He knew that he had taken the place in her affections of Leopold. Was it due to the fact that she had never known her father that the father figure was glorified in her mind as the ideal to which she must give loyalty unlimited, and enduring affection. Had Edward Duke of Kent lived, it seemed possible that there might have been little differences between him and his imperious daughter, just as they had arisen between her and her mother; but he had died when she was a baby; therefore she had always felt the need for a father. She was a Hanoverian, and therefore overflowing with sentiment.

She loved him and he loved her. But this was a love affair with a difference. When she had shown her jealousy of Lady Holland and the Duchess of Sutherland he had been a little alarmed. When she had asked him pointedly whether he thought this or that woman beautiful he recognised the signals. He knew exactly to what they pointed. Had I been forty years younger – her own age – it would have been different, he thought. What arrant nonsense! Had he been forty years younger the situation would never have occurred. It was only as Her Majesty's Prime Minister that he had been admitted to her confidence and how could he have been in that position at the age of twenty? Pitt the younger was twenty-four. He was no Pitt and he was sure Victoria would have disliked that earnest young man. Pitt, who at seven had known he wanted to 'speak in the House of Commons like Papa', would never have taken time off from politics to study human nature which was exactly what William Lamb had done.

Oh yes indeed, their relationship was an extraordinary one which few people but himself would understand. He loved the Queen; he was moved by her. The tears which she so often noticed in his eyes were genuine enough. She was so young, so innocent, so unformed, and it had been his task to form her. Thus he had felt about Caroline ... and what disaster that had brought her to. When he had found himself *vis à-vis* with the Queen he had seemed to grasp at a second chance, to mould a young female creature, to guide her, to introduce her to queen-ship with a similar mocking tolerance and tenderness to that with which he had tried – and failed – to make Caroline into a happy woman. If to love a woman meant that she was the centre of his life then undoubtedly he loved Victoria. Without her life would be blank, dull, meaningless. It was significant that now he did not so much care that his Government was going to be defeated but that he was going to lose his intimacy with the Queen.

And she, in her open innocent way, loved him too. She would be content to spend the days with him; she asked no other companion. When she had first met that cousin of hers, she had been enchanted by him, he had heard, for Albert was a pretty boy. Now she did not wish to discuss marriage or even think of marriage. Marriage was distasteful to her. Why? Because it would interfere with her friendship with Lord Melbourne.

'It could not go on, William,' said Melbourne sadly to himself. 'It had to come to an end.'

Not yet though. Perhaps in three or four years' time, when she married.

No doubt it would be better to tell her by letter. Yes, he felt that would be safer. He would break the news gently.

On that dismal April day, for any day must be dismal when news of this nature must be broken, he took up his pen and wrote:

'Lord Melbourne presents his humble duty to 'Your Majesty and begs to inform Your Majesty that the result of the Cabinet has been a decision to stand by the Bill as we have introduced it and not to accede to Sir Robert Peel's proposal. The Bill is for suspending the functions of the Legislative Assembly of Jamaica and governing this island for five years by a Governor and Council. If Sir Robert Peel should persist in his proposal, and a majority of the House of Commons should concur with him, it would be such a mark of want of confidence as it will be impossible for Your Majesty's Government to submit to.'

When the Queen read the letter her temper flared up. It was those tiresome Tories again, led by that perfectly horrid man, Sir Robert Peel. Lord Melbourne and Lord Palmerston knew best what was good for Jamaica and if the Colonial Assembly had trouble in managing the affairs of the country, of course they needed a Governor and Council. It was just a plot to overthrow Lord Melbourne.

She discussed it with Baroness Lehzen.

'How very stupid they are!' she stormed. 'Of course they must do as Lord Palmerston says. Lord Melbourne thinks it is the only way.'

'Let us hope that Lord Melbourne gets his majority in the House because that is what he must have.'

'But of course he will.'

'I would say he seemed a little uncertain,' said Lehzen, for she, too, was fully aware what the cessation of Lord Melbourne's visits would mean

248

to her darling.

'I would never accept Sir Robert Peel and his Tories. I *detest* that man in any case.'

How gloomy it seemed in the Palace. Who would have believed everything could have changed so quickly? She wished that Flora Hastings would go away. It was really rather unkind of her to remain to be a reproach to them all.

Lady Flora looked like a ghost. She was so pale and the flesh seemed to be falling away from her bones; the ugly protuberance was obvious though, just the same as it had been when they had suspected her of being pregnant.

Victoria ignored her as much as possible, but occasionally she sent a message to her asking how she was. The Duchess continued to cosset her; there were still letters in the press. As Lehzen said to the Queen: Someone was determined to keep the affair alive and she suspected Conroy.

Lady Tavistock and Lady Portman told the Queen that Flora Hastings gave them the shivers. She was like a ghost walking about the Palace.

'She should really go home to her family to be nursed,' snapped the. Queen. 'That would be the best thing possible.'

'The Duchess has said that she will see that Flora is well looked after.'

She wants to keep her here, thought Victoria, as a reproach to me.

She found Lady Tavistock, pale and trembling, and asked what ailed her.

'It is that woman, Your Majesty.'

'Oh, that nasty creature, you mean?'

'I had a dream about her ... that she was dead and came back to haunt me.'

'You should put her out of your mind,' said the Queen sharply. 'After all, you only did your duty. There should never have been this fuss. There was an enquiry; our suspicions proved false and that should have been the end of the matter.'

'I have always been blamed,' said Lady Tavistock.

Lady Tavistock was inclined to see herself as a martyr, as the Queen had once remarked to Lord Melbourne.

'Nonsense!' said Victoria irritably.

Lady Tavistock dared not pursue the matter with Her Majesty but went away to tell the Baroness how she and Lady Portman had asked Flora to shake hands with them and say she forgave them. But Lady Flora would not. She just looked through them with that ghostly air and walked quietly away. 'I can't forget it,' said Lady Tavistock.

Lehzen did not mention this to the Queen. Poor darling, she had enough trouble coming to her as it was.

It came in the form of a letter from Lord Melbourne who could not bring himself to call and tell her.

'Lord Melbourne presents his humble duty to Your Majesty and has to acquaint Your Majesty that the division upon the Jamaica Bill which took place about two this morning, was two hundred and ninety-nine against the measure and three hundred and four in favour of it...'

That, thought Victoria, is a majority. Only five it is true, but a majority. So all is well. They have won. Her relief was so great that she had to read what followed twice before she could grasp its implication.

The words danced before her eyes:

'Lord Melbourne cannot conceal from Your Majesty ... leave Your Majesty's confidential servants no alternative but to resign their offices into Your Majesty's hands. They cannot give up the Bill either with honesty or satisfaction to their own consciences and in the face of such opposition they cannot persevere in it with any hope of success. Lord Melbourne is certain that Your Majesty will not deem him too presuming if he expresses the fear that this decision will be both painful and embarrassing to Your Majesty...'

Painful and embarrassing! He was going to resign. There would be another Prime Minister. He would cease to call on her. She would rarely see him – only perhaps at social functions. Oh, no, she would not accept his resignation. No one ... *no* one could take Lord Melbourne's place.

Lehzen came in to find her staring before her.

'My precious angel, what is it?' cried the Baroness.

Victoria threw herself wildly into the Baroness's arms. 'They are going to resign. I cannot bear it, Daisy. He will not come here again. It is all over.'

The Baroness led her to a chair and made her sit down.

'Perhaps it will not be so. Perhaps they can

251

come through this. After all they have not been defeated.'

'He says...' began Victoria and gave the letter to Lehzen. Lehzen read it as she read most of the Queen's correspondence.

'Oh my love,' said Lehzen, 'this is terrible!'

They wept together. 'I cannot imagine it without him,' said Victoria.

'You will find the new men easy to get along with. You will find someone as willing to advise you.'

The Queen stamped her foot angrily. 'I will find no one,' she cried. 'Do you think anyone could take *his* place?'

Her anger was more bearable than her grief.

Lehzen said: 'He was the Prime Minister...'

'*Was!* He still *is* the Prime Minister. He shall *remain* Prime Minister. I shall *refuse* to accept his resignation.'

Lehzen looked hopeful and the Queen went on. 'Am I the Queen or not? If I say I won't have these horrid Tories, I won't. Lord Melbourne is my Prime Minister now and nothing is going to change it.'

Lehzen shook her head sadly. 'It is no use,' she said. 'You know the Constitution.'

'But they haven't been beaten, Lehzen. They won by five votes.'

'You read here what Lord Melbourne says. He is summoning a Cabinet meeting this morning and he tells you what the Cabinet's decision will be.'

'I must beg them not to. Let them give up their Bill.'

'Even the Queen cannot interfere with State affairs like that. You know that, my darling. You are overwrought.'

'Oh, Lehzen ... darling Daisy ... I am going to lose him.'

Lehzen tried to soothe her. She must lie down. She must rest. She must remember she was the Queen. Malicious people would be watching. There was gossip enough. 'Oh, please, please my darling, control your feelings. Remember you are the Queen.'

'Daisy ... what should I do without you!'

'You have me until I die, my dearest.'

'But if I lose *him*, Daisy, I don't want to *live*.'

'What sort of talk is this? Is this how a Queen talks?'

'But he ... is going to leave me, and I cannot *endure* that Daisy.'

'Of course he is not going to leave you. He is still here. He will be the Leader of the Opposition, I suppose. He will not be far off. You will se him now and then. You speak as though he were going to die.'

That cheered her a little. 'Yes, I shall see him now and then. We shall be at dinners together. I shall invite him to my box at the opera.'

'There you see,' said Lehzen.

'But it won't be the same, will it? He won't be able to come here and we shan't have our chats ... alone. He will have to move out of the Palace. All our fun will be over. Oh, Daisy, you have no idea ... no one has ... how amusing he is. He makes everything so lighthearted and he is so good and kind and there is no one like him.'

'He will come and see you.'

'No, that horrid Peel man won't allow it. He will come instead and I won't have him.'

'Once again,' said Lehzen, 'I beg of you to remember that you are the Queen.'

'He would say the same, Daisy. He always reminds me that queens have to do all sorts of things that are distasteful to them.'

'Yes, if he were here now he would say what I am saying.'

'Oh, yes, dear Daisy, it's true.'

'And you would want him to be proud of you. People will be calling to see you soon. You must remember that you are the Queen. Have you forgotten how wonderful you were when Conyngham and the Archbishop came to tell you you were the Queen. Everyone said how calm ... how dignified ... how queenly.'

'But that was something I wanted to hear ... something I had been waiting for. Now I am going to lose my *dear* Prime Minister.'

'Let me bathe your eyes. I have a wonderful lotion. No one must see, must they? There would be gossip ... scandal...'

Victoria stared at the Baroness. Scandal! It was the first time she had thought that her relationship with Lord Melbourne might be considered scandalous.

She said brokenly, 'He is the best and kindest of men. I was fortunate beyond everything that he should be my Prime Minister.'

'And still is as far as we know.'

'For how long, Daisy, for how long?'

'Let's cross our bridges when we come to

them,' said Lehzen just as she used to when they were in the nursery together before Victoria was a Queen.

'Lord Melbourne has called,' said Lehzen.

The Queen clasped her hands together. She was trembling.

'He is waiting,' added Lehzen gently.

Victoria covered her face with her hands.

'Try and control yourself, dearest. You want to see him. Remember you are the Queen, and this is not goodbye to him.'

She nodded and went to him.

She held out both hands to him. He kissed them. When she raised her face to his she saw the tears in his eyes.

'It ... has happened?' she asked fearfully.

Lord Melbourne nodded. 'Lord John will be coming to see you. He will tell you that at our Cabinet meeting it was agreed that the Government should resign.'

'I shall lose you,' she said.

'I shall be close.'

'You will not forsake me, then?'

'You cannot believe that I would ever do such a thing.'

'I am a little comforted, but most unhappy.'

'Your Majesty does me too much honour.'

'But you know my feelings.'

'Yes, I know them. And I believe you know mine.'

'You could be here just the same?'

'Your Majesty's new Prime Minister would not allow the Queen to be in constant conference with the Opposition.'

'Those Tories!'

He smiled. Like Lehzen he preferred to see the flash of temper rather than the sorrow.

'You must try to get on with Sir Robert Peel.'

'I never shall. I hate the man: He is quite *loathsome* to me.'

'He's all right. Stiff and formal. But you'll get to know him.'

'I shall refuse to.'

'You will remember your duty, I know.'

'Why do you have to have this *miserable* Bill?'

'Well, you see, something had to be done for Jamaica. We believe we are right. They believe they are. That's politics.'

'But us ... our ... friendship. That was not politics?'

'I have been honoured as I never thought to be. I shall remember the esteem you have had for me as long as I live.'

'Esteem!' she cried. 'You are usually so good with words. That is not the right one, you know. Oh, dear Lord M, I will *not* let you go. I *will* not.'

He took her hand and patted it gently as he might a child's. 'I have explained to you what constitutional government is,' he said. 'A party that cannot rule must resign. This has been coming for a long time. Now we are going to show the world how a queen behaves. I know you will do that... admirably, and when I see you working with your new Government as you have with mine I shall say: There is indeed a queen. And I shall be so proud. I shall be arrogant and I shall deceive myself into thinking that I am in part responsible for my great little Queen.'

'Oh, my dear, *dearest* Lord M!'

'Oh come,' he said, 'it's not the end. We shall meet ... often.'

'Yes, we shall. I shall *insist.*'

'And of course we shall have to obey the Queen for her temper can be a little choleric and one has to be a brave man to risk arousing that.'

'*You* were always very brave in that respect.'

'I knew how kind and good a heart she has despite the flashing eye and frowning brows, and I always trusted to luck that I should not be dismissed from my Sovereign's presence.'

'That Peel gentleman will not find my heart so kind, I do assure you.'

'I would not wish you to be as kind to him as you have been to me. That would be asking too much of me. But remember he's not such a bad fellow and he is only doing his duty. I can assure Your Majesty that he is highly thought of in some quarters.'

'Not in the Palace, and he never will be. Oh, you are teasing me, you are trying to make me forget how unhappy I am.'

'I must leave you now,' he said, 'but if I have your permission to come back again this evening, I will by then have worked out a plan of action for you. Have I that permission?'

'I shall be waiting for you this evening.'

He bowed and smiled at her.

'All will be well,' he said.

She shook her head not trusting herself to speak.

'I knew it would happen,' said Lord Melbourne, 'some day.'

Then he was gone and she was alone ... desolate.

At three o'clock that afternoon there was another visitor. It was little John Russell for whom she had always had a special affection, partly because he was a supporter of Lord Melbourne, partly because she liked him for himself and partly because like her he was well below average in height.

She held out her hand to him with the tears streaming down her cheeks.

'Your Majesty!' cried Lord John.

'Oh, dear Lord John, this is *terrible*.'

'I cannot tell Your Majesty how it grieves me to inform you that your Cabinet must resign. I want to thank Your Majesty for all your kindness to me in my recent bereavement.'

'How are the darling children?' she asked.

'They are well but missing their mother,' said Lord John, which made her weep afresh.

'What a sad, sad world!' she sighed. Poor Lord John had lost his wife and she was about to lose her dear Prime Minister.

Lord John did not remain long. He had done his duty in giving her this unwelcome news and he was unhappy to be the bringer of such tidings. Lord Melbourne would be calling on her again that day, he added to cheer her up; and even he was surprised to see what an effect this had on her.

Another chance to see him! To try to persuade him to forget this wretched Bill. Were not the people of Buckingham Palace more important to him than those of Jamaica?

In the afternoon Lord Melbourne was back at the Palace. He had recovered most of his normal nonchalance, as though he had had a tussle with himself and come to the conclusion that he must not let his feelings get the better of him.

He kissed her hand; and she clung to his for a few moments fiercely as though she would not let him go.

'I have come to see Your Majesty,' he said, 'because I have been aware for some time that this was inevitable and I had already considered the advice I should give you when the day arrived.'

'Then,' she demanded, 'why did you allow this Jamaican business to happen?'

He raised those bushy but beautifully marked eyebrows and gave her that half-amused half-exasperated look which had so often enchanted her. 'Your Majesty forgets that our Ministry was never strong. Our majority was small and the Lords have never favoured us. Lord Brougham has constantly waited his opportunity to finish us off. It has been almost impossible to get any legislation through the House. Everywhere we have turned we have been baulked. This is a situation which cannot, for the good of the country, be allowed to continue. But for Your Majesty's kindness to me and my ministers I doubt we should have lasted as long as we did. So you see, we have been fortunate. Now I must tell you what I think you should do.'

'I do not want to see Sir Robert Peel,' said the Queen firmly.

'Your Majesty is not being fair to this man.'

'He is the man who has opposed you. It is because of him that you have to go.'

'He opposes me naturally because he is in Opposition so that is a perfectly logical thing for him to do. And my departure is by no means due to him. You must not blame him because he is a Tory.'

'I would prefer to see all people Whigs as we are.'

He looked at her sadly. Had all his teaching been in vain? Here was the child of the nursery. Then he was filled with tenderness. She is too young for such a burden, he thought.

'If you do not wish to send for Peel you can send for the Duke of Wellington. Tell the Duke, if Your Majesty feels this is so, that you were entirely satisfied with your late Government and that you part from them with reluctance.'

'Oh, *dear* Lord M, have you any doubt of that?'

'No, indeed I have not. Tell the Duke that as the head of the party which has been responsible for removing your late Government from office you turn to him to advise you as to the manner of replacing it and continuing with the country's business. Now if the Duke should decide not to do this Your Majesty will have no alternative but to call in Sir Robert Peel.'

'I can't bear to hear his name.'

'And first,' went on Lord Melbourne, 'you must overcome this aversion which in fact has no foundation in logic. For Your Majesty has scarcely seen the man.'

'Oh, I have seen him, but he did not have the

grace to present himself to me.'

'Then he was a fool ... but in that respect only. I do assure Your Majesty that he is far from foolish in the House of Commons. He is formal; he is self-conscious and it is for this reason that he did not present himself to Your Majesty. But he is an extremely able statesman and if the Duke refuses you must – for there is nothing else you can do – ask him to form a Government. But you should insist that the Duke of Wellington is part of that Government.'

'Are you sure there is nothing else I can do?'

He smiled at her tenderly, 'Ah, I can see that now you are accepting this unpleasant state of affairs.'

'I shall never accept it in my heart.'

'But you will remember you are the Queen. This is how it is with Sovereigns. There are times when we all have to act in a manner which causes us great sorrow; but this is particularly so with Sovereigns.'

'You will dine at the Palace tonight?'

'Your Majesty must excuse me, for I do not think that would be advisable.'

'You are still my Prime Minister until I have a new one.'

'Our actions are noted, commented on, exaggerated you know. I do assure you that it would be very unwise for me to dine at the Palace tonight. I have already accepted an invitation to dine at Lady Holland's. I think I should be there.'

She nodded. 'I shall see you again ... soon?'

'As Your Majesty commands,' he said.

Then he left her; and she went to her room to

weep quietly.

Lehzen came to her and there was some comfort in talking to her.

'It will not seem so bad tomorrow,' said Lehzen.

'It will never be the same,' she answered. 'All, *all* my happiness has gone! That happy peaceful life is destroyed. Lord Melbourne is no longer my minister.'

She stayed in her room. 'Which will be noted,' Lehzen reminded her.

'I don't care,' cried the Queen; and indeed she was in no state to appear.

Lehzen imagined the sly comments that were no doubt being exchanged in the Duchess's household; Conroy would be jeering, the Duchess gloating. But certainly the Queen could not appear with swollen eyes and silent grief, unable to eat.

In her own room Lehzen tried to tempt her with food but she could not touch it, but as the evening wore on she grew a little calmer.

'Lord Melbourne expects me to be calm,' she told Lehzen. 'He says I must behave as if this is merely a change of Government which it is obvious I would rather not have taken place, but I must show that I am ready to work with these people.'

'And Lord Melbourne is right. You used to say he always was.'

She sat brooding until midnight; then she went to bed and to Lehzen's relief slept soundly.

As soon as she awoke next morning she wrote to Lord Melbourne.

'The Queen thinks Lord Melbourne may possibly

wish to know how she is this morning; the Queen is somewhat calmer; she was in a wretched state till nine last night when she tried to occupy herself and to think less gloomily of this dreadful change and she succeeded in calming herself till she went to bed at twelve and she slept well; but on waking this morning all – all that had happened in one short eventful day came forcibly to mind and brought back her grief; the Queen, however, feels better now; but she couldn't touch a morsel of food last night nor can she this morning. The Queen trusts Lord Melbourne slept well and is well this morning; and that he will come precisely at eleven o'clock...'

She was sitting brooding in her room waiting for eleven to come when the Duke of Wellington was announced.

'It is not a bad dream,' she mourned. 'It really has begun.'

The great Duke was seventy and seemed quite ancient to the young Queen. The idea of his taking the place of her beloved Lord Melbourne was grotesque – yet just a little better than horrid Peel's doing so.

'Your Majesty!' said the Duke bowing.

'Pray be seated,' replied the Queen. 'Now I suppose you know why I have sent for you?'

'I have no idea,' replied the Duke.

A fine future leader of Government, she thought, who doesn't know what is going on!

'Lord Melbourne's Ministry, in which I had the *greatest* confidence, has resigned.'

'I am grieved to hear it.'

'As *your* party has been instrumental in removing them,' said the Queen with a flash of temper, 'I am *obliged* to look to you to form a new Government.'

'Your Majesty, I have no power whatsoever in the House of Commons. I can only advise you to send for the leader of the Opposition there – Sir Robert Peel.'

The Queen's lips tightened and the Duke went on: 'Your Majesty will find him a man of honour.'

The Queen ignored this and said that she hoped the Duke would have a place in the Cabinet.

'Your Majesty, I am seventy years of age. My prime is long past. I am so deaf that it is difficult for me to take part in any discussion.'

'I have more confidence in you than in any other member of your Party. You understand the...' her voice faltered ... 'the *great* friendship I feel for Lord Melbourne.'

'I do understand that,' replied the Duke, 'and I have the utmost respect for Lord Melbourne. I believe that he can continue to be of use to Your Majesty.'

'And now I suppose I have no alternative but to send for this Sir Robert Peel.'

The Duke assured her this was so.

When she saw Lord Melbourne at eleven she was less stubborn, he was glad to see. Her good sense was prevailing. She had been made extremely unhappy by what had happened but she saw that she would have to accept it.

'I am proud of you,' said Lord Melbourne with tears in his eyes.

Sir Robert was feeling very uneasy as he drove to the Palace in answer to the Queen's summons. He was fifty-one years of age, a power in the House of Commons and a natural reformer; but he was well aware of the great success Lord Melbourne had had with the Queen – it had been the talk of the Court and the country and was even creeping into the press – and he knew that he lacked those suave social graces which Melbourne possessed. Moreover he was conscious that the Queen did not like him.

She could convey her disapproval by a glance and a cold nod and these had come his way on the rare occasions when he had been in royal company.

He had talked the matter over with his wife Julia that morning. With her he shared his innermost thoughts; she understood him as no one else did, and therefore was well acquainted with the idealist who existed beneath the cold façade.

'I am inevitably being called to be asked to form a Government,' he had told her.

'Well, you will do exactly that,' Julia had replied with a smile.

'We shall be in a minority and the Queen will be against us.'

'The Queen, Robert, is just a child.'

'A child of some importance,' he had replied with a smile. 'And Melbourne is her god.'

'Which shows what a child she is. But queen or child when one Government falls she must accept another.'

'I fear it will be a rather trying interview.'

Julia had laughed. 'Oh, come now, you are not

265

going to be frightened of a chit of a girl.'

'If we were strong. If we were an elected Government with a big majority it would have been another matter.'

'Is this the great politician speaking – the man who revised the laws of offences against persons, and laws against forgers, who created the police force? Oh, come, Sir Robert Peel.'

'Everyone doesn't see me as you do, Julia.'

'Because you won't allow them to. You are going to see the Queen and you know that she will have to accept you. And if she is going to be annoyed with you because you have replaced Melbourne, well then she does not understand the Constitution which she is supposed to rule; and if she is wise she will very shortly learn that you are a greater statesman than Melbourne could ever be.'

'Melbourne knows how to charm her.'

'His job was to govern England not to charm the Queen.'

'He managed to do both it seems.'

'He certainly did not do both successfully for here he is forced to resign. What did Melbourne ever do but let things run along just as they were? You know very well he hates all change. That's no way to govern. And if the Queen likes him, the people don't. He's made himself very unpopular over this Flora Hastings affair.'

Sir Robert was thinking of this as he drove along. It was true that Melbourne was not the most successful of Prime Ministers and Peel was convinced that he himself would make a better one. Julia was right. What did it matter if Melbourne could make more of a show in a drawing-room? It was statesmanship the country needed – and the Queen would learn that.

He was too sensitive, and for that reason he presented this cold façade to the world. He was painfully aware of his social inadequacies, but it was true as Julia had said that he was a good politician. He had the welfare of the people at heart which was more than could be said for some, including the sybaritic Lord Melbourne. He had put on court dress which he hoped would please the Queen, and in any case the etiquette of the occasion demanded it, and as his carriage drew up he noticed that little groups of people stood about near the Palace watching for callers.

He heard his own name mentioned amid a buzz of excitement. 'That's Sir Robert Peel.' They knew why he had come.

They were not, of course, concerned about the Jamaican Bill. They were agog with excitement because the Queen's name was being linked with that of Lord Melbourne and if Lord Melbourne was no longer Prime Minister the Queen could not – without causing a great deal of comment – see him so frequently as she had hitherto.

He was shown into the yellow closet where the Queen was waiting for him. She had refused to see anyone in the blue closet. That was sacrosanct because it was there that so many of her meetings with Lord Melbourne had taken place.

'Sir Robert Peel.'

He bowed – *so* awkwardly, she noticed.

'At Your Majesty's service.'

He was tall, and his rather plentiful hair was untidy. Such a *fidgety* man, thought Victoria angrily.

267

'You know, of course, Sir Robert Peel, why I have sent for you?'

He bowed his head in acquiescence.

'I am grieved ... beyond words,' said Victoria coldly. 'I am filled with the greatest regret to be obliged to part with Lord Melbourne's ministry. Lord Melbourne served me well from the time of my accession.'

She looked critically at Sir Robert as though implying that he could not fail to displease her. She was the Queen, as she knew so well how to be and although when he had left his home he had agreed with his wife that she was only a child, he was overawed by her regality in the yellow closet.

He murmured that it would be the earnest endeavour of Her Majesty's new Government to serve her with all the power at its command.

The tilt of her slightly open lips suggested that she had no great confidence in his Party, and that she had in fact no great confidence in Sir Robert Peel, and she was wishing with all her heart that he had had the good sense not to oppose her dear Lord Melbourne.

'We believed in our late Government,' she said. 'We approved *all* that they did.'

It was very difficult to talk to such an imperious Sovereign who had made up her mind so definitely, but Sir Robert must get down to the purpose of his visit.

'I hope, Sir Robert,' she said sternly, 'that you are not going to *insist* on the dissolution of Parliament.'

'Your Majesty will know that in the circumstances this seems a reasonable course of action.'

'*We* should not wish that and I ask you to give me your assurance that you will not do so.'

Sir Robert was looking down at his feet and pointing his toe down on the carpet with his heels raised. He fidgeted. For all the world, thought Victoria maliciously, like some *dancing* master.

'Your Majesty will understand that it is impossible for me to give you such an assurance.'

'Impossible! *Why* impossible?'

'It will be a matter for the Cabinet to decide.'

'But if *we* do not wish it?'

Sir Robert continued to *prance*, as she called it. Lord Melbourne had told her that if they went to the country the Whigs would suffer a great defeat. At least, thought Victoria, they are not defeated yet; and she was *going* to resist this Sir Robert Peel with all her might.

'I am afraid, Ma'am, I can give you no undertaking on this point.'

She was longing for the interview to end and when Sir Robert suggested that he form a list of likely Cabinet ministers and submit it for her approval, she seized the opportunity to bid him to do this and return later with it.

He took his awkward leave and she gave an exaggerated sigh of relief.

She went at once to Lehzen. 'The dancing master has gone,' she said. 'What an unattractive creature! I still hope and pray that he will *never* be my Prime Minister.'

'But the interview went off well, I hope?' said Lehzen.

'It went off,' retorted Victoria with a burst of laughter.

'At least he has made you laugh.'

'With anger and horror to think that he should dare attempt to take Lord Melbourne's place.'

'It won't be very easy for Sir Robert holding office without a majority.'

Victoria was almost gleeful. 'That will show him! Oh, how dare he! I don't like his manner. How different ... how *dreadfully* different to the frank, open and most kind and warm manner of dear Lord Melbourne!'

After Peel had left Victoria did what she always did in moments of stress. She wrote to Lord Melbourne. Her facile pen flew over the paper; she was as effusive and impulsive in correspondence as her uncle King George IV. She told Melbourne how different Sir Robert Peel was from himself, how she disliked him, despised him and deeply resented his daring to take over from her dear Lord M.

Melbourne replied cautiously and tactfully. He begged her to try to overcome her dislike of Sir Robert, who was a very skilful politician. Her conduct, he wrote, was very proper and judicious but he must also admit that Sir Robert and Wellington appeared to have conducted themselves with propriety and sincerity. As for the dissolution of Parliament, he advised Her Majesty to reserve her opinion on that and not to give a promise to dissolve. At the same time she could scarcely say that she would not. He begged her not to judge Sir Robert by his manners. She must understand that he might in his consultations with her seem to harbour an animosity towards Lord Melbourne. This was not the case. When Sir Robert discussed Lord Melbourne – if he did – he spoke of him as the Leader of the Party to which he was in opposition. There was nothing personal. Sir Robert was cautious and very reserved. Few people really knew him but of one thing Lord Melbourne was sure – he was neither deceitful nor dishonest, and many people who appeared to be sincere were most definitely not so.

'Dear Lord Melbourne!' said the Queen on the verge of tears. 'He is so gracious to his enemies. But nothing even he can say would make me like Sir Robert Peel.'

She wrote at once to thank him and tell him that as soon as Sir Robert had returned with his suggestions for his new Cabinet she would write and tell him who had been selected.

Sir Robert Peel was ushered into the yellow closet.

Victoria regarded him imperiously and bowing he told her he had come in accordance with her command to prepare a list of his Cabinet. He now presented this to her.

She took it from him and scanned it. She noted with relief that the Duke of Wellington's name was mentioned as Secretary for Foreign Affairs. The Lord Chancellor was to be Lord Lyndhurst who had never been a friend of hers because he had supported the Duchess over the Regency Bill before her succession. Sir James Graham was the Home Secretary. A man I never liked, she had once told Lehzen, because he looks almost exactly like Sir John Conroy.

271

But of course, she thought, how could I possibly like any people who are trying to replace *my* Government.

She handed the list back to Sir Robert with a disdainful air and was delighted to see how embarrassed he was.

'Your Majesty approves the list?'

She nodded faintly.

Sir Robert looked relieved and ceased to point his toe at the carpet for a moment.

'Then I must broach the subject of Your Majesty's household.'

'My household?' she cried.

'The ladies, Ma'am.'

'You mean my personal household ... my bedchamber ladies?'

'Precisely, Ma'am. The ladies of your household were chosen by Lord Melbourne and they all belong to Whig families. Your Majesty will see that it is impossible to continue with such a household.'

'I see no such thing,' said the Queen, her temper rising.

Sir Robert stood his ground firmly.

'Your Majesty's Government would require you to show your confidence in them, and a change of household would be necessary.'

'Am I to understand, Sir Robert Peel, that you look to *ladies* for support in the House of Commons?'

Sir Robert looked as though she had struck him, and she immediately went into the attack.

'I will not give up *any* of my ladies,' she declared. 'Please understand this I have never imagined such a thing.'

'Does Your Majesty intend to retain *all*?' he asked in a shocked whisper.

'*All*,' retorted the Queen imperiously.

'Your... Your Majesty means the Mistress of the Robes and the Mistress of the Bedchamber?'

'All,' repeated the Queen.

'But they are the wives of the opponents of Your Majesty's new Government.'

'I cannot see that this is important and I never talk politics with my ladies. Some of them, in fact, are related to prominent Tories. This procedure has not been asked for before. It was never asked of Queen Adelaide.'

'Your Majesty is a Queen Regnant. This makes a difference.'

'*I* would never consent, and has it occurred to you, Sir Robert Peel, that in this hint that I should allow my ladies to interfere in politics there is an implication that *I* would intrigue against my own Government? That seems to me a gross insult and I cannot understand how anyone could suggest such a thing.'

Sir Robert Peel, amazed at the vehemence, seemed temporarily unable to stem the flood of royal indignation.

'This is a matter which I feel I should convey to my colleagues,' he said. 'Would Your Majesty grant me leave to retire that I may consult the Duke of Wellington?'

'With pleasure,' said the Queen emphatically.

When he had gone she immediately sat down to write to Lord Melbourne:

'*The Queen writes one line to prepare Lord Mel-*

273

bourne for what may *happen in a very few hours. Sir Robert Peel has behaved very ill and has insisted on my giving up my ladies to which I replied that I never would consent, and I never saw a man so frightened. He said he must go to the Duke of Wellington and consult him ... This is infamous...*

I was calm but very decided and I think you would have been pleased to see my composure and great firmness; the Queen of England will not submit to trickery. Keep yourself in readiness...'

'Lehzen,' she cried, 'what do you think that ... that *dancing* master is trying to do now?'

She hastily gave Lehzen an account of what had happened. Lehzen's face turned pale.

'You know what they are trying to do. They are trying to take me away from you.'

'Oh, no, Lehzen! That can't be. You are not one of the Ladies. You have no official post. How wise we were not to give you a label! You are just my dearest friend.'

'They have been constantly talking of foreign influence.'

The Queen's eyes were flashing with the light of battle.

'If this is true I am doubly determined.'

The Duke of Wellington arrived. The Queen received him graciously. After all, she had told Lord Melbourne, she *much* preferred him to Sir Robert Peel.

'I trust,' she said in a kindly voice, 'that you will accept the post which Sir Robert Peel is offering you.'

The Duke said he would do so.

'You do not feel it would be too much for you?'

'Your Majesty is good to be concerned but I feel perfectly capable. I hear that there has been some difference between Your Majesty and Sir Robert.'

'Oh, he started it.'

'Sir Robert has explained to me what took place. The opinions of your ladies is not important. It is the principle of the matter.'

'It seems to me that Sir Robert is so weak that even the ladies must be of his opinions.'

'Your Majesty will discover that this is not the case.'

'And Sir Robert must *discover* that I will not give up my ladies. I find the suggestion that I discuss politics with them quite offensive.'

'I am certain that you would not do this, but the public might think that you did. To have a Tory Government and a Whig household could cause a great deal of dissension.'

The Duke could do nothing; he retired from her presence and consulted with Sir Robert who was waiting in the Palace for the result of the interview.

Sir Robert then returned to the Queen and told her that he would have to consult his Party and asked for a few hours' grace in which to do this.

Meanwhile Lord Melbourne had received her letters and, knowing his imperious, obstinate and shrewd Sovereign, and also understanding what the effect of this obstinacy would have on Sir Robert, decided that action was needed.

He must call together his Cabinet immediately for a discussion, for naturally he could not act without them.

It seemed to him very possible that he and his Party might well be back in power, for unless Sir Robert could bring the Queen to his way of thinking he would be unable to form a Government.

They were scattered but by great effort he managed to assemble the greater proportion of them.

The position was invidious, said some. Of what advantage would it be to resume office when they had such a small majority? What would happen if they went to the country? Let Peel take over and see what he could do with a minority.

Melbourne read them the Queen's letters and the company was moved by them

'How,' it was demanded, 'could they abandon such a queen and a woman?'

As a result of that meeting, Lord Melbourne was writing to the Queen:

'The Cabinet ... after much discussion, advises Your Majesty to return the following answer to Sir Robert Peel:

"The Queen having considered the proposals made her yesterday by Sir Robert Peel to remove the Ladies of her Bedchamber cannot consent to adopt a course which she conceives to be contrary to usage and which is repugnant to her feelings."'

When Victoria received that letter she was triumphant. Lord Melbourne and his Government were behind her. She was sure she had routed Sir Robert Peel.

She was right. Sir Robert believed that unless there were some changes in the Queen's household he must decline her offer to form a Government.

'We have won,' cried the elated Queen and seizing the Baroness began dancing round the room.

The Baroness cried: 'Is this the way for a Queen to behave! Is this the same one who was being so very much the Queen in the yellow closet with Sir Robert Peel a few hours ago?'

'One and the same,' cried the Queen. 'You see our dancing master is a coward. I knew he was afraid of me from the start. Now I shall write to *dear* Lord Melbourne and command him to wait on me at once.'

Lehzen was astonished at the cleverness of her darling and said so.

'It is the way you brought me up, dearest Daisy,' said the Queen.

At two o'clock Lord Melbourne arrived.

'Victory!' cried Victoria.

Lord Melbourne smiled admiringly.

'You always said I was stubborn. You said I was choleric. You know you did. Well, those qualities have served me well.'

'I salute them,' said Lord Melbourne; and she burst out laughing. Oh how good it was to laugh with pleasure again.

'Now I will show you our dancing master's letter. He regrets that in the circumstances he has to reject my offer to form a Government. He knows full well with what reluctance that offer was made.'

'Yes,' said Lord Melbourne, 'you made that very clear.'

Lord Melbourne took Sir Robert's letter and read it. He paused and looked at the Queen with some consternation.

'He says here that you refuse to make *some* alterations in the Bedchamber.'

'Yes, of course he does.'

'But you said that he was insisting on your changing them *all*.'

Victoria looked testy. 'All or some, what is the difference?'

'It could be a great deal.'

'Oh, don't let us quibble about such a small thing.'

'I'm afraid I must consult the Cabinet on this. They might not agree to support this since Sir Robert says *some*. It is in fact a very different matter from *all*.'

'It is exactly the same,' said the Queen petulantly.

'Nevertheless,' said Lord Melbourne, 'I must consult my colleagues.'

'How tiresome,' cried the Queen, but she was uneasy.

'Peel has met you halfway,' said Melbourne. 'He is clever. Don't underestimate him. This could beat us.'

The Queen answered fiercely: 'I will never yield. And I will never apply to Peel again.'

Lord Melbourne looked dubious and said he would tell his colleagues how she felt.

With that skilful oratory, never fiery but witty, sentimental and nonchalant, of which he was master – Melbourne persuaded his Cabinet.

The Queen was adamant. If Her Majesty could see no difference in 'some' and 'all', he suggested they should look at the matter from the same angle. The Queen felt she had been insulted by the suggestions that she would intrigue with the ladies against her Government. It was intolerable. He appealed to them. Could they desert such a gallant young Queen?

They decided they could not and Melbourne was able to tell her that his Cabinet were with him. Peel's refusal could be accepted.

'Then everything is as before this ridiculous affair occurred!' cried the Queen.

But of course it was not. For the country knew what had taken place. Nothing would ever be the same again. In the eyes of the people the dear little duck of a Queen had proved to be a forceful young woman, who had been arrogant and offensive to one of the senior Statesmen, Sir Robert Peel; and had defied that doughty old warrior, the Duke of Wellington. And she was not yet twenty. And why? Was it for the sake of the country? Certainly not. It was so that her relationship with Lord Melbourne might not be changed.

And what was the relationship?

The speculation which had been trivial before the Bedchamber affair flared up. Everywhere people were talking of the Queen and Lord Melbourne.

During the controversy over the Ladies of the Bedchamber the Tsarevitch Alexander, Hereditary Grand Duke of Russia, had arrived in England and the very night following the day when Victoria had routed Peel there was to be a ball at Buckingham Palace in honour of the Grand Duke.

Victoria, who loved balls more than any other form of entertainment, had lamented the fact that that wretched Peel was going to spoil this one entirely for her. But now that she was in such a mood of elation she prepared herself to enjoy it as she had never before enjoyed a ball. It will be a victory ball, she told Lehzen.

The Grand Duke was tall and very handsome, his manners charming, and he managed to convey very obviously that he thought the diminutive Queen delightful.

What a joy to dance with him and while she basked in the admiring glances of this royal personage to reflect that all was well, nothing was changed.

Lord Melbourne was present, looking a little tired she noticed with anxiety; but when she was dancing she was able to forget everything else but the pleasure that exercise gave her. How very fortunate that everything had been settled today so that she could throw herself wholeheartedly into this pleasure!

It was a quarter to three when the ball ended, and she recorded this with pleasure, for she loved to stay up late. It was because when she had been that poor little prisoner of Kensington Palace Mamma had always had such a stern eye on her and she was rarely allowed to do anything she wanted to.

She went off into a happy sleep as soon as her head was on her pillow but the first thing next morning she wrote to Lord Melbourne:

'The Queen is very anxious to hear that Lord Melbourne has not suffered from the ball last night, as it was very hot at first... The Queen danced the first and last dance with the Grand Duke, made him sit near her and tried to be very civil to him, and I think we are great friends already and get on very well. I like him exceedingly.'

There! She was doing her duty as Queen and she would continue to do so – as long as they did not try to wrest *dear* Lord M from her and attempt to replace him with that *odious* Sir Robert Peel.

Chapter 10

'MRS MELBOURNE'

But the Bedchamber controversy was by no means forgotten and it was unfortunate for the Queen that it had followed so closely on the Flora Hastings scandal. Although the names of Lady Tavistock and Lady Portman had been used freely in the press, it was generally accepted that these ladies would not have acted without the approval of the Queen and Victoria was regarded as the chief culprit. And now following on this was her behaviour in the matter of the Ladies of her Household.

Charles Greville, the Clerk of the Council, wrote in his diary that he was shocked because 'a mere baby of a Queen' had flouted the advice of that great man the Duke of Wellington. The truth was, he believed, that the Queen could not endure parting with Melbourne and this was a plot which had been hatched to prevent this happening.

This summed up the general opinion. Even Sir Robert Peel, that most discreet of men, could not avoid showing his indignation about the manner in which he had been treated. The Queen would have to learn that although she might be their Sovereign these men whom she had treated with such haughty disdain were some of the greatest statesmen of the age.

The press naturally took up the affair with many a sly allusion; Lord Brougham thundered away in the Lords attacking Melbourne and his Cabinet and not hesitating – though with expressions of loyalty to the *Crown* – to castigate the Queen herself.

Victoria refused to be concerned. She had won and was going to enjoy life. She had another birthday. Now she was twenty. It was not such a happy birthday as the last one, but she could congratulate herself that she still had her dear Lord Melbourne.

She threw herself wholeheartedly into entertaining her royal guest, the Grand Duke. What a charming man and such an expert dancer! He taught her to dance the mazurka – 'Very Russian and exciting. One is whisked round as in the waltz,' she told Lehzen afterwards. 'Alexander does it magnificently.'

It was all very gay and if entertaining foreign visitors was always like this she could not do enough of it.

'It is so good for me,' she told Melbourne.

'It might have the opposite effect,' replied Lord Melbourne.

But for once she did not agree with him.

She thought a great deal of the Grand Duke and wrote in her Journal: 'I am really quite in love with the Grand Duke. He is such a dear, delightful man.'

The Duke of Wellington and Lord Melbourne remained anxious about the Flora Hastings affair for Flora still languished in the Duchess's apartments at the Palace, growing more and more like a wraith every day, a general reproach to everyone, and in particular to Lady Tavistock and Lady Portman. The latter had recently miscarried and everyone said it was due to her remorse about Flora Hastings, for it was very unpleasant to think that one's conduct could be hastening someone to the grave.

The Queen was uneasy too and to comfort her Lord Melbourne insisted that Flora was pregnant after all.

'We shall see,' he said, with a look of wisdom, and Victoria tried to believe he might be right.

Wellington decided that at all costs they must rid themselves of Conroy for without doubt he had been the instigator of the Hastings drama. But for him it would have been just a matter of suspicion, a little gossip followed by the doctors' exonerating verdict. The Hastings family, of course, had done the harm, but it should never have been allowed to reach a stage when it was possible for them to act as they had. So, they must most certainly rid themselves of Conroy. The Duke would work on him. He should have the pension he demanded; the peerage he asked could be promised him.

'Whether he ever gets it would be another matter,' pointed out the Duke, 'for it may well be that you, Melbourne, will not be Prime Minister when the Irish peerage promised him is available. And as it will be you who promised it, another Prime Minister might not feel himself obliged to give it. It seems likely that at the next election, which surely cannot be long delayed, the Whigs will stand down for the Tories and then it will be Peel's affair.'

Melbourne agreed with an ironic smile that one of the matters he would be most willing to place into Peel's competent hands was that of Sir John Conroy.

'So, rid ourselves of that mischief-maker we must,' said the Duke and, as he went into the fight as though it had been Waterloo, he succeeded.

It was with great joy that Lord Melbourne was able to call at the Palace and tell the Queen what had been arranged, and that Conroy would shortly be leaving.

What a pleasure it was to sit and chat with Lord Melbourne again in the blue closet!

The only flaw was Flora Hastings, who was growing steadily worse.

'I visited her and she was so ill,' said the Queen. 'She made me feel quite wretched. I never saw anyone so thin; she was like a skeleton but her body is so swollen that she looks as though she were pregnant. I hear she is very sick.'

'Sick!' said Lord Melbourne with an ironic smile.

'She must be very ill to look as she does, but she took my hand when I offered it and said she was grateful for all I had done.'

'She always had a mordant sort of wit.'

'I think she meant it. She looked at me as though to say: "I know I shall not see you again."'

'Your Majesty is too tender-hearted. That woman has caused you a great deal of trouble. Shall we talk of something else? I do know more pleasant subjects.'

'Such as?'

'That dress you are wearing is very beautiful.'

'Oh, do you like it? It is rather nice. What do you think of the Grand Duke?'

'Agreeable.'

'I confided in him about that dreadful Peel. Was that unwise?'

'Unwise but natural.'

'Oh dear!'

'But I doubt it will blow up to a major affair now that Conroy will no longer interest himself in Palace affairs.'

'It will be sheer bliss to know that *he* is not there.'

Then Lord Melbourne began to talk of long

285

ago Palace scandals and how Lord Bute had tried to rule young George III as Conroy hoped to rule her. He was amusing and while he talked pulled his hair about making it rather untidy, which, as she confided to her Journal, 'made him look so much handsomer'.

The rejoicing at Conroy's departure was dampened by the departure of the Grand Duke. The Queen wrote in her Journal:

'I felt so sad to take leave of this dear amiable young man whom I really think (talking jokingly) I was a little in love with.'

Victoria was planning another ball when a note was brought to her from the Duchess. Her mother wished Victoria to know that Lady Flora was very ill and the Duchess believed that people would not be very pleased if the Lady Flora were to die while the Queen was gaily dancing at a ball.

Victoria shuddered when she read the letter. She had thought a great deal of Lady Flora; she could not forget that emaciated figure stretched out on the couch looking like a skeleton, her yellow skin drawn tightly across her bones – and that fearful protuberance of the stomach. Sometimes – she dreamed of Lady Flora and she was filled with remorse.

So when Lord Melbourne came she showed him the Duchess's letter and asked him what she should do about the ball.

Lord Melbourne considered for a while and said that this might be one of the rare occasions

286

when the Duchess was right. So the ball was cancelled.

Lord Melbourne adroitly led the conversation away from Lady Flora and it worked round to Sir Robert Peel – a not very happy subject in itself but not so depressing as that of Lady Flora, of course, because in spite of criticism the Queen believed she had acted rightly in his case.

'Neither he nor Wellington appeared at my levée, I noticed,' she told him. 'I think that was rather rude of them.'

'I don't think they meant to be rude,' said Lord Melbourne.

'I think Sir Robert Peel is a very foolish man.'

'Well,' protested Melbourne, 'he is considered to be a very able statesman. He has been responsible for many reforms and the people think highly of him, even those who oppose his politics.'

'I think he is foolish to behave like this. It makes me dislike him.'

'It's certainly ill-judged of him,' agreed Lord Melbourne. 'But he is not so accustomed to dealing with kings and queens as I am.'

'Do you have to deal with them in a *special* way?'

'Most certainly. Some of them have very uneven tempers.'

So now they were laughing again and it was very pleasant.

Lord Melbourne then began telling her stories of Uncle William's testy behaviour on more than one important occasion, and she quite forgot to be uneasy about Lady Flora.

Then a very disturbing incident occurred.

The Queen had come to Ascot for the races and it was a very brilliant occasion. She was aware during the ceremonial drive that the people were not as vociferous as usual, in fact looked a little sullen. How tiresome of them! They made her feel so uneasy when they behaved like that. Lord Melbourne had told her that George IV had been afraid to show his face on some occasions because the people not only were silent, they booed and jeered. How unpleasant! she thought. 'The mood of the people is like the uncertain glory of an April day,' said Lord Melbourne. 'All sun one minute and rain the next.'

She was thinking of this as she rode along bowing and smiling to the unresponsive crowd. And then – as she took her place in the royal stand she heard the cry: 'Mrs Melbourne.'

She flushed hotly and began to tremble. *Mrs* Melbourne. What were they suggesting? But she knew full well.

The cry was taken up. It sounded like a deafening roar. 'Mrs Melbourne!'

There was nothing to be done but pretend she had not heard, but she could not enjoy the races; she could only think of getting away from those wicked people.

'Mrs Melbourne!' she told Lehzen. 'They called me that.'

Lehzen said: 'Everything you do is noted. It's talked of and often exaggerated. He has apartments at the Palace. He dines here almost every night. And of course this affair of the Bedchamber Ladies... They are saying that the reason you made it impossible for Peel to take office was because you wouldn't part with Lord Melbourne.'

'But *Mrs* Melbourne!'

'Yes, Mrs Melbourne,' said Lehzen a trifle severely. She wanted to be first in the Queen's estimation and did not enjoy taking second place even to the Prime Minister.

Lord Melbourne called as usual. He had been at the races and had heard the hisses and boos and the epithet hurled at her. She was never one to hide her feelings so she asked him at once what he thought of it.

He shrugged it aside with his usual elegant ease. 'People will say anything.'

'I believe I know who started it. It was the Duchess of Montrose and Lady Sarah Ingestre.'

'Tory bitches,' said Lord Melbourne and for a second she smiled; but she was immediately grave.

'Others quickly took it up. Oh dear, they should be severely punished.'

'Your ancestors would have had their heads off.'

'It's a pity customs have changed,' said the Queen angrily.

'Are you sure it was these women who started it?'

'Quite sure.'

'They were really attacking me you know.'

'And me too. But you heard it. You know you did.'

'Yes, I heard it,' admitted the Prime Minister.

'It must have made you angry.'

'On your account, yes. I am used to being attacked on all sides. A Prime Minister is blamed for most things.'

She could not settle down to a cosy chat. She kept hearing those words echoing in her mind: 'Mrs Melbourne'.

One early morning in July Victoria wakened to find the Baroness at her bedside.

'What is it?' cried Victoria, starting up in bed.

'I have bad news,' said Lehzen, 'Lady Flora Hastings died early this morning.'

'Poor soul!'

'This will mean everything is revived, you know.'

'At least,' said the Queen, 'it will be an end of the matter.'

'There will be a post mortem,' said the Baroness. 'She has left instructions that there shall be one performed by any doctor, providing he is not Sir James Clark.'

'That will surely settle the matter,' said the Queen as Lord Melbourne would have said.

But she knew it could not be settled immediately. There was sure to be trouble. The press, the Tories, the scandal-mongers and the Hastings family were not going to let it rest.

The autopsy was presided over by five distinguished doctors and the verdict was that Flora had died from a large tumour on the liver which pressing downwards had produced an enlargement of the abdomen.

The Hastings declared publicly that bowed

down with grief as they were, at least their honour was vindicated.

The *Morning Post* came out openly against the Queen; so did Lord Brougham in the Lords, who tried to induce Lord Tavistock to defend his wife's character at the expense of the Queen's. Pamphlets were written against her. ('There have always been the pamphleteers to write against Royalty,' said Lord Melbourne comfortingly.) The Queen saw one of these which made her shiver. It was called 'A voice from the Grave of Flora Hastings to her most gracious Majesty the Queen'.

Victoria wept with rage and despair. Life had become wretched. She wondered whether she would ever be happy again. She even remembered that Lord Melbourne had advised her to act as she had and told herself she should never have allowed the scandal to persist. She should have given Flora the benefit of the doubt.

An alarming thought had come to her. Was it possible that Lord Melbourne could be wrong?

When she ventured into the streets she was hissed. She strained her ears for the taunt, Mrs Melbourne. How different from what it had been like such a short while ago when the people had smiled and waved and loved her.

She wondered whether she should go to the funeral and asked Lord Melbourne when he called.

He thought it would be unwise for her to go personally but her carriage should be sent in the procession as an honour to the living Hastings and a mark of respect to the dead one.

'But,' said Lord Melbourne, 'we shall have to

proceed with great care. The press are working the people up to a fever of excitement and that is not good. Heaven knows what they might do if sufficiently worked up.'

'I know,' said the Queen, 'that my uncles were shot at once or twice and so was my grandfather and he never did anything that he thought was not good for the people.'

'The mob is unpredictable and like the poor, always with us. No one should know whether or not your carriage will be following. Unfortunately the lady died here in this very Palace which is most awkward. How much more convenient it would have been if she had gone home to the bosom of her family to expire.'

'That was Mamma. She was determined to keep her here to die.'

'And discountenance us!' said Lord Melbourne. 'Never mind. We will put it out that the coffin will be removed from the Palace at six a.m. and shall arrange for it to go at four. We will have the Guards and Life Guards on duty the night before ... all through the night and until the coffin is safely away. This will be to show respect to the dead of course ... and we will make sure of protection at the same time.'

'She is going to be taken up to Scotland, you know.'

'Yes, tiresome of her. But in view of all the fuss the sooner she gets there the better.'

There was a lack of ease throughout the Palace. *How* everything is changed, sighed the Queen.

In the early hours of the morning of July 12th

crowds of people were waiting outside the Palace. Even though it had been said that the body of Flora Hastings was to be removed at six, people had waited all night so there were many to see it leave at four a.m. Sir Robert Peel's police force were out in strength too. The first contingent would accompany the procession to Temple Bar where the City Police would take their place.

As the cortège progressed the crowds grew thicker and some of them were bent on mischief. The press had worked on their emotions with their diatribes against the Queen and her scandal-mongering ladies and the pamphlets like *The Victim of Scandal* and the *Palace Martyr* had had their effect. The crowd was all in sympathy with the dead and full of reproaches for the living.

The heroine of the occasion was without doubt Flora Hastings and the villainess the Queen.

As they neared the wharf where Lady Flora's coffin was to be placed on a ship to be taken up to Scotland someone threw a stone at the royal carriage; others followed but fortunately the stone throwing was not taken up with much enthusiasm and the people contented themselves with words.

'What's the good of her gilded trumpery after she has killed her?' called a voice.

And another: 'This is the victim. Where's the murderer?'

Another: 'This is a case of murder against Buckingham Palace.'

But at last Lady Flora's coffin was placed on board the ship which was to take it to Scotland and the danger was over.

'Just a few repairs to the royal carriage,' said Lord Melbourne lightly when he reported to the Queen.

'The indignity!' she cried. 'They stoned *my* carriage.'

'A mercy that you were not in it.'

She was angry. 'Oh how dared they! They misunderstood. I only wanted to be kind to her ... at the end.'

'At the end,' said Lord Melbourne. 'But that was *after* all the fussing.'

'I visited her. I asked her if there was anything I could do for her and she was grateful to me. She was indeed.'

'She was honoured of course, but it was an unfortunate business.'

'Thank God it is now done with.'

'Yes,' said Lord Melbourne, 'providing the Hastings will let it die down. They've got so used to hounding a scapegoat that it might be hard for them to do without one. They will doubtless decide on poor old Clark next.'

'Is there no end to this affair?'

'It's like a stone being thrown into a pond,' said Lord Melbourne. 'The ripples go on for a long time afterwards.'

She could not settle down. She was restless and ill at ease. Perhaps she was more upset by those words which had been flung at her than by anything else. Mrs Melbourne!

There was only one meaning to it. It disturbed her. But I am only twenty, she thought. I suppose I ought to marry.

Lord Melbourne was having his portrait painted. It was at her request that this was taking place and she had imperiously commanded that it should be done at the Palace so that she could watch the work in progress. Moreover she could talk to Lord Melbourne while he sat and that as he said would kill two birds with one stone, for naturally a busy Prime Minister would have little time to sit for his portrait.

'I want a picture of you,' she had told him, 'so that I can look at it when you are not there. Therefore I shall need a good likeness.'

She would sit watching the artist at work with the utmost amusement.

'Lord Melbourne,' she told him severely, 'you are *not* a good sitter. Is that not so?' she demanded of the artist.

The artist looked a little embarrassed and Lord Melbourne said, 'Oh, it is always wise to agree with the Queen.'

'That is not only wise but true. You are always being told to hold your position and keep your head where it was. You move continually. Mr Grant,' she said to the artist, 'Lord Melbourne is *not* a good sitter, is he?'

'His Lordship is solemn one moment and appears to be deep in thought and the next he is amused and laughing aloud. No, Your Majesty, it is certainly not easy to catch him.'

'There, Lord Melbourne. You see you are not easily caught.'

'Oh, I am very elusive,' said Lord Melbourne.

She was happy watching the work progress. And it was fun to take one of the dogs with her –

usually darling Dashy who was particularly fond of Lord Melbourne, but dear Islay sometimes went. And Lord Melbourne would talk to Dash and Dash would put his head on one side in such a way which drove her into fits of laughter and the poor artist into despair.

'It is an *exact* likeness,' she declared, which made Lord Melbourne grimace and Mr Grant so happy.

As she later wrote in her Journal: 'It will be such happiness for me to have that dear kind friend's face which I do like and admire so. His face is so handsome and his expression and there is his *air*. It is all just as he is with his white hat and cravat, waistcoat and coat ... all just as he wears them.'

It was hard to tear herself away from the room. But even those sessions had been spoilt by the memory of those words: Mrs Melbourne.

It was some time now since Baron Stockmar had at Uncle Leopold's suggestion left England to become the companion of the Queen's cousin Albert. She had not given Albert a thought during all the anxieties of the last months but those words heard at Ascot had brought him back to mind. She had recently reached her twentieth birthday; Cousin Albert would soon be celebrating his. It was a marriageable age.

Uncle Leopold had made up his mind that she was going to marry Albert. It was true that at one time she had not been displeased with the idea. Long ago – that was how it seemed but it was in fact three years – before her accession, Albert and his brother Ernest had visited her and she had been delighted with her cousins, particularly Albert. Uncle Leopold had reminded her when they met that she had written to him – he still had and treasured her letter – that Albert 'possessed every quality which could make her happy'. So she had thought then. But three years ago she had been a child. She hardly knew herself when she looked back – a princess instead of a queen, a captive instead of a power which could dismiss Sir Robert Peel, an ignorant girl who had never drunk from the fountain of Lord Melbourne's wisdom.

And now she could not get out of her mind the thought of those words 'Mrs Melbourne'; and she knew that it was time she married.

But whom should she marry? The answer from Uncle Leopold would be Cousin Albert of course, but Lord Melbourne had taught her that Uncle Leopold did not rule England. He had tried to interfere politically once before and Lord Melbourne had told him diplomatically, with such tact, that the affairs of England were for England's ministers and her Queen to decide.

And, she thought, if I do not wish to marry Albert, I shall certainly not do so merely because Uncle Leopold wishes me to. Nor anyone else for that matter. But the truth was that she was unsure. She did not think she wished to marry at all – perhaps never. She would be like Queen Elizabeth – whom she had never liked – and remain, single all her life.

If the people would not be so foolish and grow to like her again, and if she could keep Sir Robert Peel at bay, and if Lord Melbourne was her constant companion, that seemed a very happy prospect.

But, she thought vehemently, I will not be hurried into marriage in any circumstances.

Cousin Albert had made a grand tour of Europe in the company of Baron Stockmar and she knew that Uncle Leopold meant his next visit to be to England. Then her decision would be expected. She had three months of freedom. What a way to look at it. Freedom! Was she going to become a captive again? As far as she remembered Albert appeared to have been gentle, but of course one had to get to *know* people before one was sure.

Perhaps she should prepare Uncle Leopold. He must understand that she would not be coerced into anything – not even to please him.

She would write to him *now* and send the letter by courier. There were certain things she must know. How far was Albert aware of the family's intention? Was he coming over to inspect her as she would inspect him? Oh surely not! A somewhat obscure German Prince would jump at the offer of the hand of the Queen of England. It was for her to decide. She could be sure of that. But of all else she was not at all sure... because as Uncle Leopold must understand so much had happened since that naïve outburst of three years ago.

She sat down and wrote to Uncle Leopold:

'First of all I wish to know if Albert is aware of the wish of his father and you relative to me. Secondly if he knows that there is no *engagement between us... If I should like Albert I can make no final promise this*

year, for at the very earliest any such event could not take place till two or three years hence... Independent of my youth and my great repugnance to change my present position, there is no anxiety evinced in this country for such an event... I may like him as a friend, *and a* cousin *and a* brother *but not more; and should this be the case (which is not unlikely) I am very anxious that it should be understood that I am not guilty of any breach of promise, for I never gave any... Were this not completely understood I should be in a very painful position. As it is, I am rather nervous about the visit for the subject I allude to is not an agreeable one to me...'*

There! That stated her feelings exactly; and having despatched the letter to Uncle Leopold she felt much better.

Naturally she talked the matter over with Lord Melbourne.

'I have written to Uncle Leopold. He seems to be so certain that I am going to like Albert.'

'Cousins are not very good for each other.'

'Most royal people are cousins.'

'And most of your cousins are Germans.'

'And Germans are not good for one either?' demanded the Queen.

'They are inclined to be solemn.'

'Shouldn't we all be on some occasions?'

'They are solemn on all occasions. Besides, they don't wash as frequently as we do.'

'I should enjoy washing less frequently,' said Victoria with a laugh.

Oh it was fun to sit with him and watch the expressions flit across his face and the way in which he ruffled his hair without realising he was doing it. Now, he looked quite mischievous, now very much the Prime Minister; now like his portrait.

Oh *dear* Lord M! she thought. Why can't we go on like this forever? We don't need interruptions.

'Something is on your mind,' said Lord Melbourne suddenly.

'It is this visit of Albert's. It's definitely planned for the autumn. Albert's father, Uncle Ernest and Uncle Leopold are very anxious for it.'

'They would be,' said Lord Melbourne. 'But it is not they who would have to marry Albert, is it?'

She laughed at the thought. 'Marriage! Why do we have to talk of marriage?' she demanded. *'You* don't think it is necessary for me to marry yet.'

'Not for a year or two.'

'And if I do not like Albert?'

'Well then Albert will be sent back to Saxe-Coburg.'

'And all will go on as before.'

She was so happy at the thought that he could not tell her then that sooner or later it would be her duty to marry, nor remind her that the victory they had snatched from Sir Robert Peel was in fact a respite. Life could not go on as it was. Change had to come from some direction.

The Queen was becoming fretful. Her temper flared out at the slightest provocation. Her ladies were sometimes afraid to speak to her. Even dear Daisy was snapped at.

She dreamed of Lady Flora Hastings now and

then; and the memory of that emaciated figure stretched out on the couch with the reproachful eyes regarding her stayed with her.

The Hastings would not let the matter rest and were now taking up the case against Sir James Clark. When she drove out she had come to expect a few hisses from the crowd. Often she thought of that first summer of her reign – the pleasantest she had ever spent in her life – and asked herself why it had changed.

She even became irritable with Lord Melbourne. Sometimes in the evening when they were sitting together and the rest of the company were playing games or listening to music and the Duchess sat at her interminable whist, Lord Melbourne would not answer when she spoke to him and she would realise that he had fallen asleep.

It was a habit of his, for although he could be very lively if there was an interesting discussion in progress he would go straight off to sleep when the conversation became trivial. It had amused her to try all sorts of ruses to awaken him without calling attention to his somnolent state; and it could be very awkward when she wanted to go and he was not ready to stand up and bow. She would twit him about it afterwards and he would say the funniest things. It could be so embarrassing – in a comical sort of way.

Now it began to irritate her.

Of course, she thought, he is getting *old*. But immediately she would be conscience-stricken. Men like Lord Melbourne never really grew old. Their minds remained alert and it was a man's mind which was important.

One day she tackled him on this habit.

'Lord M,' she said, 'you should not go to sleep when you are in the company of so many people. It is most disconcerting.'

'Oh,' he replied, 'they are so full of their own affairs that they don't notice much what I'm doing.'

'Of course you do occasionally *snore*,' she pointed out.

'That would proclaim it too much,' replied Lord Melbourne and she had to laugh.

That was the point. *He* could always make her laugh as no one else could. Perhaps that was why she wanted everything to remain as it was and she was so perturbed by the idea of Uncle Leopold's protégé, Cousin Albert, coming to change it.

Chapter 11

THE QUEEN'S RELUCTANCE

When King Leopold received Victoria's letter in which she stated her reluctance to marry for a few years he was alarmed; he decided that he must see her without delay, and on a hot August afternoon the Queen received a letter from him in which he proposed to leave Ostend one evening and arrive at Brighton at about ten in the morning. He would stay only a few hours and return to Ostend the same day, but during that time perhaps he and his beloved niece could meet at the Pavilion and have a talk, which he felt was very necessary

Victoria was astonished. She knew, of course, that her letter setting out her feelings about Albert was responsible for this and she could not bear the thought of Uncle Leopold and Aunt Louise, who was a poor sailor, making such a long trip just so that she and Uncle Leopold could talk for a few hours. Moreover Uncle Leopold would no doubt wish her to commit herself and she had no desire to do this. It would be much easier to elude awkward decisions over a little space, of time.

How kind, she wrote back, of her Aunt and Uncle to wish to see her so much that they could contemplate coming over for a few hours. However, she herself did not feel equal to travelling to Brighton so soon after the prorogation of Parliament which was to take place on the 27th August. Her Uncle would know what an exhausting business that could be. Moreover she had had such a trying time lately. Her Uncle would know about the controversy with Sir Robert Peel because she had written to him and told him about it. Then there had been this distressing Hastings matter. It had really made her quite ill. She would *hate* not to feel absolutely well so that she could entertain her dear Uncle in a manner suited to his importance and for that reason – and that reason alone – could wish him to postpone his visit. If however he could stay a little while and come to Windsor, that would be delightful.

Leopold decided that the urgency of his business was such that he must comply with her suggestion. He would make preparations for a longer stay and would be coming to Windsor in a few weeks' time.

When Uncle Leopold was due to arrive she was in a fever of excitement, so eager was she to see him. She tried to calm herself by reading despatches and carrying on in the normal way. But it was no use and as soon as they arrived she rushed down to throw herself into those loving avuncular arms. She insisted on waiting on them and taking them to their rooms. This touched Uncle Leopold very much.

'I had begun to fear that you regarded me as an old piece of furniture which had once been quite useful but no longer was.'

'Oh, dearest Uncle, how can you say such a thing now? You said it once in one of your letters and I thought I had convinced you.'

'I needed to be convinced verbally,' said Uncle Leopold.

So there were more embraces and loving assurances.

But she was quickly realising how very solemn Uncle Leopold had become – or perhaps he always was so and she had not noticed it before. Aunt Louise had lost her gaiety and Victoria had developed a taste for it; she could not help comparing Uncle Leopold with Lord Melbourne and secretly finding Leopold a little dull in comparison. One could not burst into merry laughter with Uncle Leopold around. He was sentimental though, and reminded her of how close they had been in the old days at Claremont and they were able to shed tears over the death of dear old

304

Louie; and he talked again of her cousin, the Princess Charlotte. But again – secretly – she was a little sorry for Charlotte because although according to Uncle Leopold she had loved him devotedly, Uncle Leopold did not approve of so many things which Victoria discovered she approved of very much. Dancing for instance. Uncle Leopold thought that rather frivolous, but indeed why should one not indulge in a little frivolity after following the serious occupations forced upon rulers? She thought a little relaxation was essential when one considered just for one thing, all those papers one was forced to sign and all the ministers one had to see – and they were not all as easy to talk to as Lord Melbourne. Lord Melbourne, on the other hand, believed that a little gaiety was good for one. That was the difference between Lord Melbourne and Uncle Leopold, Lord Melbourne was such a man of the world that he was more understanding. He certainly understood her.

But how churlish to criticise Uncle Leopold – even to herself– who had meant so much to her in her childhood. He soon came to the real purpose of his visit.

'Baron Stockmar sends me such excellent reports of our young gentleman,' he told her.

'I am so glad. I am sure Albert is very good.'

'I remember how taken you were with him when you met him.'

'That was three years ago.'

'He has improved ... for the better.'

'I feel sure that with you to watch over him and dear Baron Stockmar too, he could not have failed to.'

'A match between you two has always been one of my dearest projects. When it takes place I shall say to myself "Lord now lettest thou thy servant depart in peace".'

'Dearest Uncle, do not talk of leaving the world ever.'

'My precious angel, it was a form of speech. I mean that it would be the realisation of one of my most cherished dreams.'

'Well, perhaps we shall like each other. But there is plenty of time. I am very young yet, Uncle, and Albert is even younger.'

'Albert does not understand why there is not a formal betrothal. He feels that this waiting is somehow a humiliation to him.'

'But the last thing I should wish to do is humiliate Albert.'

'That's what I have told him, but there *has* been this shilly-shallying. When you saw him last time you really did like him so much.'

'Let him come here and perhaps I shall like him as much again. Lord Melbourne says that I need not hurry into marriage. I can wait three or four years if I wish.'

'Do you think that would be advisable?'

'I do, Uncle. It is too important a matter to be hurried.'

'I do not think Albert would be prepared to wait indefinitely.'

'What does he mean by that?'

'He feels that to be kept hanging about and then refused would perhaps spoil his chances elsewhere.'

'He seems to be rather calculating.'

'You misjudge him.'

Leopold was thinking how obstinate she had grown since those days when she was such an enchanting little girl who had adored him and been so eager to please him in every way. And she had become somewhat regal in her manner too, as though she were reminding him that although he might be the King of the Belgians she was Queen of a somewhat more important country.

He abandoned the discussion for the time being and decided to come back to it later.

Uncle Leopold's visit coincided with that of another Coburg uncle – Leopold's and Mamma's own brother Ferdinand with his sons, Augustus and Leopold, and his daughter Victoire. They also brought with them another Coburg cousin, Alexander, whom Victoria thought was quite fascinating. She was soon on nickname terms with them all and they played games which Uncle Leopold would have thought quite childish but which to her were the greatest fun. Even Lord Melbourne could not play such games.

She told them about the visit of the Tsarevitch of Russia who had been so amusing, and had danced so beautifully.

'There is a German dance. Perhaps you know it. The men have to jump over a pocket handkerchief.'

They all declared they did know it.

'And each lady and gentleman has to duck under the pocket handkerchief. I rarely saw anything so amusing in my life.'

So they all danced it and there was a great deal of laughter. Victoria enjoyed dancing most with Alexander as her partner.

'What a charming young man Alexander is,' said the Queen in her chat with Lord Melbourne. Lord Melbourne said yes, he was. He was the son of the Princess Sophia of Saxe-Coburg and a French émigré and so therefore not entirely German. That, suggested Lord Melbourne, might be why he was more attractive.

'Uncle Leopold would not be pleased to hear you say that,' said the Queen. 'He has a very high opinion of the Germans.'

'That is natural,' said Lord Melbourne, 'because he is one of them and we all have high opinions of ourselves.'

She did enjoy discussing her cousins with Lord Melbourne but to tell the truth he seemed a little *old* in comparison with them.

What a sad day it was when the cousins said goodbye. The Queen declared that she was going to be quite heartbroken without them. She went down to Woolwich to see them off accompanied by Mamma and Lehzen, and of course Lord Melbourne was present. The Duchess was in tears; she had been very unhappy since the departure of Conroy. There was no one with whom to scheme for her daughter's discomfiture and now even the Flora Hastings affair had lost its impact. The Duchess would have liked to be taken back into her daughter's favour. However it seemed it was too late for that. But this farewell was a family affair and outwardly Victoria was affectionate to her mother. Many tears were shed and Victoria exchanged handkerchiefs with Victoire to remind her of 'our handkerchief dance'. It was all very, very sad, and the journey back to the Palace was silent and sorrowful. The only person who was unaffected was Lord Melbourne, who didn't like Germans and had found the cousins too childishly boisterous for his taste. However at this stage he kept his feelings to himself and smiled sympathetically at the Queen whenever she looked his way.

Uncle Leopold would be leaving a few days later and he had made very little headway for he had counted on getting a definite promise from Victoria that she would accept Albert. He had not anticipated this difficulty, but he was learning that this was a new Victoria.

He came back again and again to the subject of the marriage.

It was necessary. It was her duty. Had she looked at it from that angle?

Yes, she had looked at it from every angle.

And did she realise that if she did not marry and have children the throne would go to the Cumberlands?

She was years younger than Uncle Cumberland and she did not think she was going to die yet. No, Uncle Leopold could rest assured that Cumberland would spend his days as King of Hanover. It was not that she was against marriage, but that as she was only twenty she thought she had plenty of time and did not wish to hurry into such a state which was so very important not only to herself but to the country.

'It is not exactly seemly for a young female

monarch to live alone.'

'Alone, dearest Uncle! I am surrounded by people.'

'And your Prime Minister even lives at the Palace!'

'He has private rooms there of his own because it makes it so much easier when we have to discuss State matters.'

'That seems to me to be rather inviting criticism.'

Victoria flushed hotly. Cries of 'Mrs Melbourne' echoed in her mind.

'Lord Melbourne is my Prime Minister, Uncle. Naturally he has a suite in the Palace. I cannot see anything to criticise in that.'

'Yet am I right in assuming that there has been criticism?'

'There has been a great deal of senseless criticism. This distressing affair of Flora Hastings, for instance...'

'I was thinking more of the affair of the Bedchamber Ladies. You know it was said that you acted as you did because you were so fond of Lord Melbourne that you were ready to go to any lengths to keep on intimate terms with him.'

'What a wicked scandal!'

'It is, but we have to reckon with wicked scandals. A sovereign is in the arena to be shot at. A sovereign has to make sure that he – or she – gives no opportunities to people to cast slurs. You understand what I mean. Marriage is what you need, my precious angel. And soon.'

She was a little shaken but adamant. The fiery temper showed itself in her eyes though her voice was tender as always for dear Uncle Leopold.

'Dearest Uncle,' she said, 'I should never allow unworthy gossip to drive me into a situation which was abhorrent to me.'

'Abhorrent!' cried Uncle Leopold in horror.

'I was speaking generally, dear Uncle. Of course Albert is not abhorrent to me. I love all my cousins. Dear Alexander was delightful. So were Augustus and Leopold. I am wretched at the thought of parting with them. And I am sure Albert and Ernest are equally pleasant. I merely mean that I will not allow malicious people to dictate my actions.'

Nor even beloved uncles, she was implying.

Oh, she had indeed changed; and it was necessary to get Albert to England as soon as possible.

Uncle Leopold could stay no longer. He and Aunt Louise were due to start very early in the morning to catch the tide. Victoria, who had determined to say goodbye once more before they left although they had already said their farewells the previous night, arose at a quarter past four and went to their apartments. They were sitting in their travelling clothes ready for departure, eating their breakfast by the light of several candles. Sad as she was, Victoria's mouth watered at the sight of thin bread and butter and eggs and she could not resist joining them in their breakfast.

This was not the time, even Uncle Leopold realised, to indulge in further persuasion so he contented himself with a tender farewell; and from her bedroom window the Queen tearfully

311

watched them leave.

How very sad it was, to say goodbye to dear relations; but her sorrow was tinged with apprehension. Very soon Cousin Albert would be arriving and then she would have to make her decision.

She was touchy and irritable with Lord Melbourne.

'I believe you are pleased to see my cousins depart,' she accused him peevishly.

'They were rather noisy,' he answered.

'And of course they spoke in German which *you* do not understand. That must have been very tiresome for you.'

'Not at all,' said Lord Melbourne blandly, 'for I do not believe I missed a great deal.'

'I enjoyed their company very much.'

'Which was evident and made their visit worthwhile.'

'Poor Lord Melbourne! I believe their noise interrupted your little naps.'

'That is exactly the case,' agreed Lord Melbourne.

She burst out laughing. 'I am young after all. I don't think I see enough young people.'

'You certainly did during the visit.'

'A young person like myself must sometimes have young people to laugh with.'

'You lead rather an unnatural life for a young person,' admitted Lord Melbourne. 'It's the life of a man.'

'I do feel that is so sometimes. But the excitement did me good.'

'You may suffer for it afterwards. You must always take care of your health. You have complained of a certain listlessness. It would be dreadful if you were to take a dislike to your official duties.'

'You need have no fear, Lord Melbourne, that I shall ever fail in my duty,' she said coldly.

She was tense; she was apprehensive. The thought of marriage frightened her. Oh, why, she demanded of Lehzen, did everything have to change? She kept harking back to that happy, *happy* summer when everything was so pleasant and the people loved her.

'Nothing stands still,' Lehzen reminded her.

'I know that,' she snapped. 'I am not a child, although I am well aware that you sometimes think I am.'

Her ladies whispered together that she had changed. Once she had been so considerate to them; now nothing they could do seemed right for her.

Even Lord Melbourne displeased her. Understanding her better than anyone else and realising that it was fear of marriage that made her so irritable and bad tempered he sought to soothe her. He wanted her to realise that there was absolutely no need to consider marriage a necessity at this stage; he wanted to lull her into a peaceful frame of mind. All she had to do was inspect her cousins and if she did not like them she could send them packing.

She was aware of this and was afraid of marriage; yet she wanted to marry. She loved Lord

Melbourne, and she had never analysed her feelings for him. If he had been young and royal how easy that would have been! Lord Melbourne understood their relationship far better than she did and he was saddened because he knew that it had reached its peak and must now inevitably decline. Her present state of mind affected him deeply. He could not bear to see her unhappy. If she could marry now and make a success of her marriage and her life, his work had been well done. He knew – and had known all through – that his place could only be on the edge of that life, and he must now be ready to stand aside.

He tried to see less of her. This called forth abuse from her.

She was soon writing to him:

'The Queen was a good deal vexed at Lord Melbourne's not coming...'

This was to one of her dinner parties to which he had not received a formal invitation but it was regarded as the accepted thing that he should be present and he always had been in the past. She was miserable without Lord Melbourne to sit beside her and make his amusing comments and go to sleep and *snore* if he wished to. This last habit might displease her and sometimes embarrass her, but she wanted him there.

'The Queen thinks it is important that Lord Melbourne should be here at large dinners. She insists upon his coming to dinner tomorrow, and begs him to do so on Wednesday also, her last two nights in town,

as she will probably not see him for two days.'

When Lord Normanby changed places with Lord John Russell as Home Secretary, Melbourne, who had felt it wiser to avoid her company for a while, omitted to tell her and she learned of the change through Lord Normanby.

She was incensed ... and against Lord Melbourne.

'Lord Melbourne never told the Queen that this was definitely settled. This has happened before.'

Then remembering that he had looked a little tired at their last meeting and the old tenderness returning she added:

'The Queen has such unlimited confidence in Lord Melbourne that she knows all that he does is right but she cannot help being a little vexed at not being told things.'

When he came to her in the blue closet he could see from her expression that her mood was stormy and it was not his good friend who stood before him, but the Queen. So cold and regal was she – and nobody knew how to convey this manner better than herself – that he did not sit down in his usual easy manner but remained standing until she gave him permission to do so.

She withheld this and sitting herself, talked to him as he stood.

Realising suddenly how tired he looked she was filled with remorse and insisted at once that he sit down when she began upbraiding him for not taking enough care of *his* health. He was always talking about hers. She commanded that he be more careful.

She saw the tears in his eyes and then everything seemed just as it had been. She was foolish to worry about Albert's coming when she had this dear good friend to advise her.

The next day she sent him a little present.

'The Queen sends this little charm which she hopes may keep Lord Melbourne from all evil, and it will make her very happy if he will put it with his keys...'

She wanted him to understand that although she was going through a difficult stage, and although she appeared bad-tempered and nervous sometimes, her feelings for him could not change.

Sometimes she was quite herself and they talked in the blue closet.

'I feel very much *against* marrying,' she admitted.

'It's a very serious matter,' agreed Lord Melbourne, 'concerning as it does both the State and your personal happiness. To get the ideal man we should have to make one.'

That was typical Lord Melbourne and she was soon laughing while he conjured up a picture of the perfect man he would make to share the throne with Victoria.

'He must not be in the least stupid.'

'Of course not. Do you think I want a stupid husband?'

'Nor cunning.'

'Do you think he would get the better of me?'

'He would never do that.'

That made her laugh again and almost restored her old merriment.

'He would have to be equable in temperament.'

'And not have a quick temper?'

'One of those is enough in any family – royal or otherwise,' said Lord Melbourne.

He was *so* amusing.

'I have no great wish to see Albert.'

'You might change your mind when he comes.'

'I hate to have to decide.'

'Decisions which are so final can often be disagreeable,' said Lord Melbourne.

'Do you think I might decide never to marry?'

'I need notice of that question,' said the incorrigible Lord Melbourne.

She felt so much *better* talking to him.

'How I wish Albert were not coming,' she said.

But when Albert wrote to her and told her – without adequate reason – that he would be arriving three days late, her temper flared up.

'He does not seem very eager to get here,' she commented to Lord Melbourne. '*That* seems to me very odd. After all who is he but quite an obscure prince?'

'And a German,' said Lord Melbourne.

'And I am the Queen.'

'Of England,' added Lord Melbourne.

She was angered by Albert's apparent indifference which, said Lord Melbourne, was a little odd seeing that she was not in the least eager for him to come.

Chapter 12

THE BRIDEGROOM ELECT

Francis Charles Augustus Albert Emmanuel, otherwise known as Prince Albert, the second son of Ernest, Duke of Saxe-Coburg-Saalfeld, was not feeling very happy as the carriage carried him and his elder brother Ernest towards the dock where he was to take ship to England.

In fact only the company of his brother, to whom all his life he had been devoted, and that of his pet greyhound Eös comforted him.

Albert was reserved by nature and he hated all the preparation and fuss which had gone into making him a suitable husband for the Queen of England. He would have been glad if Ernest had been the chosen one except that he was too fond of his brother to want him to be submitted to what he had had to endure. He had been faintly surprised when he heard that he was the bridegroom elect. It had happened after that visit to England three years ago when he had first met his cousin Victoria, a very self-possessed young person of sixteen. Surely he had thought she would have preferred Ernest – besides Ernest was the elder. But no, it seemed her choice had fallen on him!

His Uncle Leopold, who ran the family affairs, was determined on this match. He had already succeeded in marrying other members of the family into the royal houses of Europe, but nothing, he had said, was as important to him as to see his niece and nephew united and ruling England together.

That was all very well, Albert reasoned to himself, but Victoria was the Queen and he could only be her consort, which he did not feel to be a very dignified position.

He had discussed it with Ernest who had retorted, 'Oh, yes, but you will have to see that Victoria obeys *you.*' When he remembered that rather regal girl of sixteen he wondered whether this could be achieved; and nothing else would suit him, of course.

Then he knew that Uncle Leopold had been trying to bring about a definite betrothal for more than a year and that Cousin Victoria had said that she did not wish to be definitely betrothed.

'It is somewhat humiliating,' said Albert to Ernest.

Ernest was less serious and more intent on enjoying life, whereas Albert wanted to do what was right and honourable and be respected.

'And if,' went on Albert, 'there is any delay I shall simply release myself from any understanding.'

'My dear Albert,' replied his brother, 'she will only have to take one look at your manly beauty and she'll succumb.'

But Albert was serious. Life to him was a solemn affair and he had first realised this at the age of four, when he had lost his mother.

There had been a mystery about his mother's

departure, for she had not died. She had simply gone away. Albert had adored her and he had been her favourite and for a long time he could not understand why she had left him.

He and Ernest had had whooping cough at the time and he remembered how he had waited for his mother to come and see them ... waited and waited.

'Where is my Mamma?' he had demanded, but all they would tell him was that she had gone away.

He remembered her as a supremely beautiful being. Warmhearted, and tender, who had loved her little boys, particularly Albert.

He learned the story later, of course. His beautiful mother in her very early twenties had been guilty of an intrigue with a gentleman of Jewish blood, a cultured man of some importance at her husband's Court. The Duke – who was years older than his young wife – had had so many mistresses that he lost count of them and the young Duchess Louise in desperation had turned to her lover. Not only had she committed adultery but she was *discovered* to have committed adultery. It was unthinkable that such conduct should be pardoned.

The story was similar to that of George I and his wife Sophia Dorothea who having taken the Count of Königsmarck for her lover was caught with him. Königsmarck was murdered and Sophia Dorothea sent away to a lonely castle where she spent the rest of her life as a prisoner. Times had changed, but while the Duke expected his wife to turn a blind eye to his countless amours he would not do the same to hers. So leaving the two little boys in the nursery she retired from her husband's house and was in due course divorced. Albert learned afterwards, that she had gone to Paris, where she had died when he was eleven years old.

He never forgot her. He became shy and thoughtful. As a consolation for the loss of that maternal love he became absorbed in his own illnesses and noted them all down in his diary. He did not know why this gave him so much satisfaction although he wondered now whether subconsciously he had believed that if he were ill enough his mother would come back. He had never liked women very much; he had always felt nervous in their presence; and when at the age of five he was at a children's party and a little girl had been brought to dance with him, he had burst into tears and refused to perform.

But as he grew up he showed a greater desire to absorb knowledge than Ernest did; Ernest was lazy and Albert was always determined to prove his point providing he thought it was a worthy one. He was intelligent without being brilliant; but what was most outstanding in his character was his moral rectitude. When he was only eleven years old, when asked what he wanted to be in life, he startled his worldly father by answering: 'A good and useful man.'

It was by no means an idle comment. Albert worked hard and painstakingly; yet he was prepared for a little fun of a sort. Lacking in humour and wit his jokes were of the practical kind but he and Ernest partook in all kinds of outdoor sports for their father was determined to make men of them; as long as the brothers were together they were content. Albert was a credit to his teachers. He was more sensitive than Ernest, who took after their father, and the effect of their mother's disappearance from their lives had had little effect on the elder boy. It was different with Albert. Loving his mother passionately, hearing vague reports of her mysterious past, he developed a great distaste for women and it was clear that he was going to be quite unlike his father in that respect.

Albert loved riding and hunting and enjoyed surprising his tutors with the painstaking excellence of his work; best of all he loved music. He had grown up considerably since his first meeting with Victoria, having been educated in Bonn and done a great tour of Europe in the company of Baron Stockmar, as well as being primed by his Uncle Leopold as to what was expected of him.

And now he was on the way to meet his fate.

The sea was very rough and he was never a good sailor. He lay sick and wretched wishing for death and asking himself why he had come.

He thought longingly of the little schloss near Coburg where he and Ernest – always together then – had spent their happiest times. Oh, to be there now – a boy with no ambitions but to be a good and useful man.

The heavy seas pounded against the sides of the paddle steamer until he thought his last hour had come. At least, he thought, it will rescue me from a difficult situation.

Ernest was prodding him.

'We're there, Albert.'

He noticed then that the violent rocking of the steamer had abated a little; he staggered up to see the white cliffs, which he thought forbidding rather than welcoming. But he did feel better as he stumbled onto land and the ride to Windsor began.

On the morning of the 10th October Victoria awoke little guessing that she would come to regard this as the most important day in her life.

She was feeling a little sick and she remembered that dinner last night had been somewhat rich. Had she over-eaten? Or eaten too quickly? The Baroness was always telling her that she did.

Lehzen came in as usual first thing in the morning.

'A stone was thrown at one of the windows early this morning,' she said.

'How tiresome!'

'There is not much damage done. Only a broken pane or two of glass.'

Victoria felt melancholy. How sad to think that some of her people disliked her so much that they were impelled to throw stones at her windows.

'I feel a little sick. I wonder if Lord Melbourne feels well. We both ate pork last night.'

'There is an "r" in the month so it should be all right,' said Lehzen. 'I'll send to see if the Prime Minister is well.'

The message came back that Lord Melbourne was suffering from a little internal disturbance which he felt was due to the pork. He intended to walk it off this morning.

Victoria sent a message back. She would walk off her pork with Lord Melbourne while he walked off his.

They strolled through the grounds together discussing the pork and from that Victoria changed the subject to Albert's imminent arrival.

'I still feel very uneasy.'

'It is so natural,' said Lord Melbourne.

'And if he does not think there is any hurry to see me I shall let him know that I feel no urgency to see him.'

'I should do that,' said Lord Melbourne.

'Then he can go back and we shall hear no more of the matter. I wonder if he will be as fascinating as my cousin Alexander?'

'Oh, that is hardly possible,' said Lord Melbourne, with a hint of mockery.

'Why, what do you mean?'

'You always speak of that young man as though he were Adonis.'

'Well, he is very handsome.'

'And you were completely fascinated by his handsome looks.'

'I like beautiful people. Beauty moves me deeply no matter in what form. I have always admired beauty.'

'That is true,' said Lord Melbourne. 'And you particularly admired Coburg cousin Alexander's.'

'As you must have done if you admire beauty.'

'Alas I must be insensible to it because Alexander's did not make much of an impression.'

'You were annoyed because you could not understand our conversation. You know you were. Well, never mind. This is very pleasant walking in the grounds here. Are you feeling better now?'

'I am walking it off,' said Lord Melbourne. 'And Your Majesty?'

'I am also walking it off.'

'And look, there is one of the pages running towards us. It appears that he has urgent news for one of us.'

'I daresay it is for you, Lord Melbourne. Some State business.'

'In that case it will be for us both.'

The page had a letter for the Queen. 'It's from Uncle Leopold,' she said. She read it.

'They are on their way,' she said, turning pale. 'Albert and Ernest will be here tonight at seven o'clock.'

The rest of the day passed slowly. She and Lord Melbourne had another chat during which she reiterated her determination not to be hurried into marriage and they agreed on the desirability of waiting for a few years.

At six o'clock, Lehzen helped her dress.

'They will be here soon, Lehzen.'

'You should look upon them just as another pair of cousins.'

'They will have to learn that I am the Queen and that I am the one who shall decide.'

'You will see that they learn that fast enough,' said Lehzen.

Seven o'clock. She went up to one of the towers and looked out. There was no sign of the, arrival yet.

Should she send for dear Lord M and beguile the time in pleasant chat? No, she did not even want to be with him.

She went to her own room and thought of other delightful Coburg cousins who had visited her.

I shall give a ball for them, she told herself but even the prospect of a ball gave her little pleasure.

Lehzen came in. It was nearly seven-thirty.

'They are approaching the castle now,' she said.

She had planned how she would receive him. She would stand at the top of the staircase and watch them ascend. She wondered whether she would know the difference between Ernest and Albert.

She rose slowly; she was in a regal mood. Albert must understand from the first that she was the Queen.

At the top of the stairs she waited. There were the two young men. Her heart began to beat so fiercely that the lace on her gown quivered.

He was mounting the stairs. She knew him at once. This was Albert. He was the most beautiful being she had ever beheld.

'Albert!' she said and held out her hands. And as soon as he touched her hand and lifted those beautiful blue eyes to hers she knew.

Ernest was there too but she did not see him. She saw only Albert, dear, beautiful Albert. There was no one else in the world.

She was quivering with excitement. Every little bit of resentment had disappeared. She was wildly, incredibly happy.

Nothing else mattered in the world but that Albert was here.

The Queen had fallen in love.

Chapter 13

VICTORIA IN LOVE

What an evening! There had never been one like it. How amusing, how delightful to get to know these *fascinating* cousins. Or should she say *cousin?* She had to admit that she, who usually noticed so much, was scarcely aware of Ernest. He was quite handsome, she believed; his eyes were very dark and he was pale. He was so different from Albert that one could scarcely believe they were brothers. But Albert ... Albert was divine. She could scarcely wait to get to her Journal to record what she saw.

He was beautiful as an angel and yet every inch a man. And his greyhound was delightful.

'How thoughtful of you, Cousin Albert, to bring him,' she cried. 'You must know how *I love* dogs. I am sure he and Dashy will be friends on sight. Islay is not nearly so good-tempered as Dashy. Do you think dear Eös will let me feed him? Oh, what a dear, *docile* creature.'

Albert did not speak much and they conversed in German which was easier for him and no trouble to her. Of course Albert spoke English. Uncle Leopold had insisted that he learn. Oh wise, wise Uncle Leopold!

Albert, it transpired, loved music.

'How very exciting. Do you sing, cousin Albert?'

Yes, he sang.

'Perhaps we can sing together ... duets.'

Ernest said that Albert had composed some songs.

She clasped her hands together. 'But that is so exciting. You must sing them to me, Cousin Albert. Perhaps we can sing them together.'

'There will be time to do that,' said Ernest.

Oh, what a happy, *happy* evening.

When she retired to her room that night she wrote in her Journal:

'It was with some emotion that I beheld Albert, who is beautiful.'

She wanted to be alone to think about this wonderful meeting. She wanted neither Lehzen's motherly fussing, nor Lord Melbourne's tender cynicism.

She knew something tremendous had happened and she wanted to be alone to consider it.

Another ecstatic day!

They had ridden together, Albert on one side of her and Ernest on the other. Lord Melbourne was just a little behind. There had never been such a ride. Her face was flushed with excitement, her little top hat rather jauntily askew with the veil flowing; her black velvet habit was becoming and she looked very pretty. She knew that she was always at her best on horseback and she was delighted that Albert should see her thus. He told her about the schloss in Coburg and she said that it was all *quite* fascinating. It was odd, she said, that he had no mother and she had no father; and they had been born in the same year. And all the time she was marvelling at his good looks. No man was ever quite so handsome, she was sure.

That evening they danced together. Albert was not so happy in the ballroom as he was out of doors. He was so manly, she supposed. That was the reason. But how she enjoyed dancing with him and when their hands touched a thrill ran through her. She hoped he felt the same.

Why had he not come before! She was appalled to think of all the time they had wasted; but what did it matter? Here he was at last and her mind was quite made up. There was none of the soul searching which she had expected. She only had to stand at the top of a staircase and look at him and she *knew*.

What joy! She wrote in her Journal:

'Albert has such beautiful blue eyes, an exquisite nose and such a pretty mouth with delicate moustachios and slight – but very slight – whiskers; a beautiful figure broad in the shoulder and a fine waist.'

She smiled as she wrote, visualising his perfections.

His voice was rather high pitched and not the sort of voice one would expect such a young man to have. Perhaps it was not the sort of voice a lot of people would admire – although they would all have to admit that his face was beautiful – but it was *his* voice and therefore to her the most pleasant in the world.

There had to be a session in the blue closet. Poor Lord Melbourne, he looked rather old and *tired*. Perhaps, she thought, that was because she was comparing his with Albert's dear young face.

'Dear Lord Melbourne.' She felt very tender towards him.

'I see that your cousins do not displease you,' said Lord Melbourne.

'Tell me do you think Albert beautiful?'

'I would say that he is very good-looking.'

'I think he is beautiful.'

'So I had observed.'

'Of course he's much cleverer than Ernest.'

'I would not say that,' replied Lord Melbourne.

'You can't mean that you think Ernest has the better brain?'

'Yes, the better brain I should say.'

The Queen was angry with Lord Melbourne. 'That is nonsense,' she cried imperiously. 'Albert has by far the better brain. He is of course under a certain amount of strain at the moment.'

'Very naturally,' said Lord Melbourne. 'I see that you no longer have the same aversion to the married state.'

'No, I have felt different about marriage since the arrival of my cousins.'

'Well, you have time to make up your mind completely. Perhaps in a week's time...'

She was not listening. She was so happy. She started to talk about Albert, his love of music, his handsome greyhound, his cleverness and above all his appearance.

'I have never seen such a *beautiful* young man,'

she said.

All that day Victoria lived in an ecstatic dream. She wrote to Uncle Leopold:

'Ernest is grown quite handsome; Albert's beauty *is* most striking, *and he is so amiable and unaffected – in short very* fascinating.'

She listened with delight to the brothers' playing. What a musician Albert was! She told him that the special treats of her childhood had been concerts and the opera, and that one of her birthday presents had been a concert at Kensington Palace and how she had learned Italian quickly because it was so useful for understanding the arias. Albert thought that very commendable.

Before the day was out she sent for Lord Melbourne.

'Lord Melbourne,' she said, 'I have made up my mind about marrying Albert.'

'Ah,' said Lord Melbourne. 'When will the marriage take place?'

'You do not doubt that I have decided in his favour?'

'I have no doubts on the matter whatsoever,' said Lord Melbourne with a smile. 'The question now is when will the marriage take place?'

'Not for a year perhaps.'

'That is too long,' replied Lord Melbourne.

She was pleased. 'Yes, it is far too long.'

'Once it is announced it should be fairly soon.'

'Yes,' she agreed.

'I believe it will be well received.'

'The people are being difficult at the moment. Remember they threw those stones only a few nights ago.'

'The people are easily swayed and there is nothing to sway them so quickly as a wedding. Give them a lavish ceremony, a young Queen-Bride and they'll love you for a while.'

'They are so *fickle.*'

'But they'll be faithful for a few weeks for a wedding, never fear. And after you will have the Prince to stand by you. You'll be in a much more comfortable position then. A woman can't stand alone for long.'

'Queen Elizabeth stood alone.'

'And I have no doubt that you would if the situation demanded you do so. But it doesn't. You approve of the Prince and you have made your decision.'

'Yes,' said Victoria softly, 'I have made my decision. Lord Melbourne do you think we are alike – Prince Albert and I?'

'Yes, there is a resemblance. I noticed it at once.'

'I am flattered. We shall be betrothed very soon.'

'Is he going to ask you to marry him?'

'There is a difficulty. Can he ask me ... the Queen? It is a very awkward situation for him.'

Lord Melbourne smiled. 'I daresay you will know how to handle such a situation.'

'Oh, I shall find a way.'

Lord Melbourne looked at her rather sadly, but her thoughts were too full of Albert for her to notice.

Nothing pleased Victoria more than to dance into the early hours of the morning and to dance with Albert was perfect bliss.

How strange that she had been feeling so depressed and had suddenly been lifted to the heights of ecstasy by the arrival of this wonderful cousin. Every time she saw him his beauty impressed her afresh; and that he was clever and loved music and was obviously already fond of her added to her enchantment.

She wanted the whole world to know of her feelings; although Lord Melbourne had said they should be a little discreet at first. And the marriage should be soon. Early next year, Lord Melbourne had said, would be a good time. She was sure dear Albert would agree though as yet the darling did not know of his good fortune.

She walked into the ballroom carrying her bouquet of flowers. Lehzen had said she looked enchantingly pretty with that fresh colour in her cheeks and her eyes dancing with happiness. Of course, she thought, although I *am* a little like Albert I am not beautiful as he is. But ... I am the Queen.

Albert was standing before her. How blue his eyes were and his lashes were magnificent. She had heard that he was the image of his mother, who had been rather a wayward woman. How wonderful of Albert to have inherited his mother's beauty without her waywardness.

In an excess of love she took some flowers from her bouquet and gave them to him; Albert took them, bowed, and his blue eyes looked straight into hers. He was in uniform so that he had no buttonhole in which to put the flowers. He took a penknife and cut a hole in his coat to receive them and during the whole evening he wore them.

Just over his heart, the Queen noticed.

Oh, dear, gracious, *gallant* Albert!

The next morning she was in a fever of impatience to be up. She had made up her mind.

After breakfast, which she took in her room, she asked where the Princes were and heard that they had gone out riding.

From her window she watched their return; and then she sent for Albert to attend her in the blue closet.

Albert came and her eyes lit up when she saw him.

'Dear cousin,' she said, holding out her hand to him, 'I trust you have enjoyed your ride this morning.'

Albert said that he had indeed and so had Ernest.

She said: 'I think you must be aware of why I asked you to come here.' Albert hesitated and she went on: 'It would make me *too* happy if you would consent to what I wish.'

Albert understood at once. The uncertainties were over.

He found her enchanting; her adoration had been so obvious; all the fretful delays were forgotten. She loved him, there was no doubt of that; and he was more than ready to love her.

He took her hands in his; she threw herself into his arms; she was laughing and weeping. Albert kissed her; she returned his kisses fervently.

'Oh, Albert,' she cried, 'life is so *wonderful*. Did you think it could ever be so wonderful?'

Albert had never dreamed that it could be.

They kissed again; she clung to him. 'I am so happy. Everyone will be happy. Oh, *dear* Albert.'

And suddenly she was aware of an unaccustomed humility which astonished her. She had believed until this moment that she was honouring him and now she thought of all that being a consort to a reigning Queen implied.

'Dearest Albert, do you understand what a *sacrifice* you are making in taking me for your wife?'

Albert laughed tenderly. All he knew was that he wanted Victoria to be his wife more than anything in the world.

'I am the Queen of England, dearest Albert.'

'To me you will be Victoria, my wife.'

What enchanting things dear Albert said!

Never in the whole of her life had she been so happy.

What glorious days followed! When she was not in his company she was impatient for a sight of him. She could come behind him and kiss the top of his head. Always demonstrative in her affections, she insisted on constant embraces. Not that Albert was loath. He was enchanted with her; and if she had fallen immediately and violently in love with him he was ready to follow at a more measured pace.

They talked about music and their respective childhoods, but they agreed that the past was unimportant compared with the future which they would share. What joy to dance with Albert, hands tightly clasped, smiling fondly. As she mentioned to Lehzen, she had never been so happy nor felt so humble. She had never thought it possible that she, the Queen, could be grateful to a man for marrying her.

'Of course, he will have a very high position,' she said.

'He'll also have his burdens,' added Lehzen.

Poor darling Daisy, perhaps she did feel that she was being pushed a little into the background. Albert seemed to take over so much of what she had done in the past. *He* made sure that she was not in a draught; *he* put a shawl or a cape about her shoulders; he would whisper that she should not do this or that as it might not be good for her.

What joy to be so cherished! But dear Daisy would always have a place in her heart.

It was different with Lord Melbourne. He remained her dear Prime Minister however much she was in love with Albert, and she must still have her daily meetings with him. It was true she took up a lot of time in discussing the perfections of Albert.

One day she mentioned Albert's reserve.

'Of course, *I* find it delightful. Do you know, I believe he is quite unaware of any of the other ladies.'

'Quite right and proper in the circumstances.'

'Oh, yes, of course, but I do not believe he has ever looked at a woman before.'

'That type often flirts later on,' said Lord

Melbourne rather waspishly.

'That,' cried the Queen angrily, 'is nonsense.'

'Oh, no,' insisted Lord Melbourne. 'I have known many such cases. A man is quiet and reserved in his youth and when he gets to middle age he changes completely.'

'Are you suggesting that Albert will do this?'

'Well,' said Lord Melbourne, 'there is a possibility that he will conform to that type.'

The Queen stamped her foot. 'That is a slanderous remark, Lord Melbourne.'

The Prime Minister looked startled.

'And,' said Victoria, the corners of her lips drawn down, her manner coldly regal, 'I expect you to say that you were talking foolish nonsense.'

Lord Melbourne replied that he was talking of a type.

'And you thought Albert might conform to this type?'

'I am sure that was a misapprehension,' said Lord Melbourne tactfully. And he added with one of his sly looks which Victoria was too put out – contemplating the possibility of Albert's infidelity – to notice: 'Albert is unique.'

'Of course Albert would not be like that. He is too dignified and too *loyal*. He will realise what it means to be married to the Queen.'

'Oh, yes, he will soon realise that,' said Lord Melbourne significantly.

'Albert is reserved, except with those he loves,' said Victoria tenderly, 'and he will *always* be like that.'

'The Queen will command it,' said Lord Melbourne with a courtly bow.

'He is not in the least like the Grand Duke of Russia.'

'Ah, there was a man whom Your Majesty admired very much.'

'He has had so many love affairs.'

'An affair before marriage is nothing,' said Lord Melbourne. 'As long as he doesn't do it afterwards.'

'I would never marry a man who had loved another woman,' declared the Queen.

'You wouldn't think of that if you were in love with him.'

'I should.'

'Then all is well for there is no question of your reserved and gallant Prince having so indulged.'

'There is no question at all,' said Victoria, her happiness restored.

There was so much to talk over with Lord Melbourne. Sometimes she would think of something at odd times and would summon him to her.

Dear Lord Melbourne! What would she do without him?

Once she sent for him in the evening. He was to come to her at once, was her message to him. He came in a very strange costume – light white and grey calico trousers; and she knew that he had been in bed and had been awakened to come to her.

She was full of remorse. She feared that in her newly found happiness she had neglected this friend.

'But you were sleeping,' she said tenderly.

He denied this, but she didn't believe him.

338

'I only wished to discuss some item about the wedding,' she told him.

'A most important subject,' he said with a smile.

'Dear Lord M,' she said. 'I fear I may have been a little short with you lately. It is all this excitement coming after that wretched time. But Lord Melbourne, always remember that I love you more than any of your other friends do.'

He did not look at her and she saw that his eyes were full of tears.

Her own gushed forth.

'My *dear*, dear friend,' she murmured.

And she thought: My overwhelming love for my *divine* Albert does not make me love this dear friend less.

Chapter 14

UNEASY PREPARATIONS

It was necessary for Albert and his brother to return to Coburg. Albert must make his arrangements for leaving the home of his birth, and preparations for the wedding must go forward at once if it was to take place in February. There was so much to be settled and the Queen urged Lord Melbourne to forge ahead with these matters.

In the first place there was Albert's position at Court to be considered, which was an affair of precedence of course; and then there was the question of his allowance. He would have to be naturalised too, for it was unthinkable that a foreigner should be the Queen's husband.

Lord Melbourne worked with all his might to meet the Queen's wishes but the Tories always opposed him and his tottering Whigs and as the Prime Minister had often explained to the Queen, it was often very difficult to get Bills passed because of this.

Uncle Ernest declared that he would not give precedence to a little Coburg Prince even if he was the Queen's husband. The Tories supported him and the other Royal Dukes who had followed him in protest, and the Queen was furious.

She raged against the Tories. 'I always hated them,' she declared. 'As for Sir Robert Peel I have always known that he was a low hypocrite. But I expected better of the Duke of Wellington. I shall certainly not ask *him* to my wedding.'

Lord Melbourne begged her to be calm.

'Calm!' she cried. 'When they behave so to my dearest Albert. That *angel* to be treated so by *monsters.*'

The Queen saw things in distinct shades of black and white, pointed out Lord Melbourne patiently. In Her Majesty's opinion people were either angels or devils, which was not true in this case. It was all a little more subtle than that.

'I should like to punish those Tory monsters,' she insisted.

'It is fortunate for them that we have a Constitutional Monarchy,' said Lord Melbourne wryly.

'Everything is too slow,' said the Queen. 'You

politicians don't work hard enough.'

Then Charles Greville, her Clerk of the Council, discovered that she could settle Albert's status by Royal Prerogative. This delighted her. Albert *should* take precedence over all Royal Dukes so that little matter was settled.

He was to be called the Prince Consort.

'The Prince Consort,' she cried. 'Surely the husband of a queen should be a king!'

'Not if he is a prince,' explained Lord Melbourne patiently.

'But his marriage will make him a king.'

'No, that is not so,' was the Prime Minister's reply. 'We should need a special Act of Parliament to turn a Prince Consort into a King Consort.'

'Then let us bring in this special Act.'

Lord Melbourne shook his head. 'It would be most unwise to give a Parliament the power to make a king; it would be a precedent. If it was as easy to make a king or queen, it would be as easy to *unmake* one.'

Victoria was thoughtful. Anything that was a threat to her Crown could not be ignored.

Albert should remain the Prince Consort.

It was necessary, Lord Melbourne told her, to make a formal announcement of her decision to accept Prince Albert as her husband and for this she returned to London and summoned her Privy Council to the Palace.

The Duke of Wellington, who had shortly before suffered from a stroke, was just well enough to be present. Her anger against him melted when she saw how ill he looked. The right side of his mouth was twisted a little and he could not use his arm. Poor old man, thought the Queen. How sad to be old and almost finished with life.

She had dressed herself in a plain gown and wore a bracelet to which had been attached a portrait of Albert.

She bowed to the councillors and begged them to be seated and then she read the speech which Lord Melbourne had written for her.

'It is my intention to ally myself in marriage with Prince Albert of Saxe-Coburg. Deeply impressed with the solemnity of the engagement which I am about to contract, I have not come to this decision without mature consideration, nor without a feeling of strong assurance that, with the blessing of Almighty God, it will at once secure my domestic felicity and serve the interests of my country.'

When she had finished reading she noticed that Lord Melbourne was looking at her with tears in his eyes.

Dear, *dear* Lord Melbourne. How often had she seen those eyes fill with tears for her!

That day she left the Palace for Windsor. Crowds collected to see her as she left. Now she could not complain of a lack of loyal cheers.

Lady Flora was forgotten. So was the Bedchamber Affair. Their young Queen was going to be a bride and her people were once more delighted with her.

But if the people were pleased at the prospect of a royal wedding the Tories had not forgotten the

Queen's insult to Sir Robert Peel and her uncon-
cealed animosity towards them which had been
so obvious during the time of the Bedchamber
Crisis. They seemed determined to make everything as uncomfortable for her as possible, and as
it was difficult to attack the Crown the best way
to annoy the Queen was to cast slurs on Albert.

There had been too many Germans in the royal
family, was their opinion, since the accession of
George I when the royal family had branched
from the Stuarts to the Guelphs. The country was
heartily sick of Germans. And now the Queen was
proposing to bring this young one over and marry
him and had even tried to make him a King
Consort. That had been satisfactorily stopped, but
it did not take the Prince's detractors long to find
a stick with which to beat him. In the Queen's
announcement of her betrothal to her Privy Councillors, the text of which had been published, there
had been no mention of the Prince's religion. This
could mean one thing. The Prince was not a Protestant. Was the Queen trying to bring a Catholic
to share her throne?

The King of Hanover, Victoria's Uncle Ernest,
who had always coveted the throne and had in
fact been suspected of sinister actions towards
the young Princess Victoria, was believed to be
behind the plots to disqualify the Prince and prevent the marriage. But for Victoria, Ernest would
have been King of England; it had always been a
sore point with him that he had been younger
than Victoria's father and so cheated of the
throne by a mere girl. He had never ceased to
hope that Victoria would die and he be called

over to take the Crown. That she had been so healthy had infuriated him; and now the thought of her marrying and having children who would come before him in the line of succession and so put the throne out of his reach for ever was more than he could bear.

And so his spies were ordered to put rumours in motion and the aggrieved Tories were not slow to make use of them.

The Queen was furious, far more angry than she would have been at an attack on herself. Her Uncle Ernest was an old wretch and the Tories were odious. How dared they attack her beloved! One day they should all be punished.

Lord Brougham, that old enemy in the Lords, made a pronouncement which was widely quoted.

'There is no prohibition to marriage with a Catholic. It is only attended with a penalty, and that penalty is merely the forfeiture of the crown.'

'Oh, how dare he!' cried the Queen. 'That man is a traitor!'

She was amazed that the Duke of Wellington did not hesitate to side with his Tory friends, and he actually led the attack on Albert in the Lords.

The Queen raged with Lord Melbourne. Why was nothing done? What were her ministers doing if they could allow the Queen to be so maligned? Were the Tories so foolish that they thought she did not know her own Constitution? Did they think she would ever marry anyone who was a Catholic?

'The noble Duke knows that the Prince is not a Catholic,' declared Lord Melbourne in the House of Commons. 'He knows he is a Protestant. The whole world knows he is a Protestant.'

Finally Baron Stockmar who had arrived back in England made a public statement that the Prince was a Protestant who could take communion in the English church, and that the only difference was that he was a Lutheran.

'So that matter is settled,' said the Queen.

These were difficult weeks. She missed Albert; she fretted for him; she made exciting plans about the wedding, and then she waited for letters from him and was miserable when they did not come.

The Tories and her other enemies were taking all the joy out of her betrothal. She was beginning to be irritable and bad tempered again.

'Never mind,' said Lord Melbourne. 'These matters have to be settled.'

There was worse to come. Albert was not a rich man; he had only an income of £2,500 a year and a small estate in Coburg.

'The fellow's a pauper,' said the Tories. 'He must not be allowed to get above himself.'

Lord Melbourne discussed the matter of the income which would be settled on the Queen's husband.

'He will be in a similar position to Prince George of Denmark who married Queen Anne,' said Lord Melbourne. 'She was the reigning Queen and he was a Prince of Denmark. The Parliament of the day settled £50,000 a year on him. The same amount was given to William III (only he was a king in his own right) and your Uncle Leopold was given a similar sum when he married Princess Charlotte. I think we should ask for the same for

345

Prince Albert. We will get Parliament to agree to that I'm sure.'

Even so Lord Melbourne secretly feared that the Tories would oppose this; and he was right, they did. £50,000 was too large a sum, they said. They would agree to £30,000.

When Lord Melbourne came to convey this information to the Queen he knew he would have to face a termagant.

He was right.

She raged and stormed. She would never speak to the Duke of Wellington again. She would take her revenge on Sir Robert Peel. They were saying that her clever, her *divine* Albert was not worth so much as foolish old Prince George of Denmark. How dared they insult her beloved Albert!

She turned on Melbourne. 'You should have arranged this better. You are the Prime Minister.'

'Ma'am, it is not in a Prime Minister's power to say this shall be done.'

'I know my own Constitution.'

'Then Your Majesty will know that these matters have to be decided by Parliament.'

'They shall be made to pay him £50,000 a year. He shall *not* be insulted.'

'The state of the country at the moment is not good. There have been riots in various places. The Chartists are making a fuss. There is a great deal of unemployment. The Tories know this and if there is much of a storm about this money – which would seem untold wealth to some of Your Majesty's hungry subjects – we could have a very ugly situation breaking out in the country.'

She was solemn. 'Riots! Hungry people!'

He looked a little sheepish. He had never wanted their happy relationship spoilt by these unpleasant matters. He had laughed at those ardent reformers, the Earl of Shaftesbury and the Duchess of Sutherland. 'Oh,' he had said, 'little children enjoy working in the mines.' And: 'Little boys have great fun climbing up chimneys.' 'People who are lazy go hungry.' It was such a pleasant theory and she had been only too ready to believe him.

Now he realised he had been wrong. He should have made her see the facts. Looking back he saw so many things that he might have done. It was as it had been with Caroline ... oh no, not such a disaster as that. Victoria was going to be a great Queen and his epitaph would be that he had helped to make her so.

She was grave at once.

'The people are unemployed. They are hungry. We must do something. I will talk to Albert about it when we are married.'

She looked at Lord Melbourne and she thought: It is not his fault. He has been led astray by others and all this political jangling. It will be different with Albert because Albert wants to be good and Lord Melbourne only wants to be clever, witty, amusing and *comfortable*.

She said soberly: 'I am angry that Albert should be insulted, but I see that he must accept this £30,000. When we are married I will explain to him and we will work together to help our people.'

The inevitable tears were in Lord Melbourne's eyes. She was slipping away from him as he had known she must in time and he thought of the years ahead when he would still serve her perhaps, but it would never be the same. Those years to come looked bleak and empty.

How difficult life was, thought the Queen. She had been so blissfully happy when she contemplated her union and was finding the details which had to be settled so depressingly tiresome. Lord Melbourne was different; vaguely she understood why. Nothing is changed between us, she told herself he is still my Prime Minister and very dear friend. But that was not quite true. Lehzen, too, was prickly. 'Now you will not have need of me,' she had said in that hurt, sad voice which was so distressing. 'Nonsense, Daisy,' she had replied briskly. 'I shall always have need of you.'

Oh why must they be so tiresome! She loved Albert beyond everything – but she was affectionate by nature and certainly was not going to forget her old friends just because she had found the great love of her life.

There were faint disturbances even from that quarter. Dearest Albert did not altogether understand what it meant to be a queen. She hated to have to remind him but sometimes she feared it was necessary.

Albert wrote that he longed for their marriage and he thought that when the ceremony was over they should retire to Windsor for a week or so where they could be absolutely alone. He was going to insist that they do this.

Insist. Dear Albert, he would have to learn that he could not insist.

How delightful of him, though, to *want* to be

alone with her all that time and to think of such things. She was glad that he had; but he could not insist of course ... to the Queen. Obviously he did not understand what being Sovereign of a great country entailed. How could he, the darling? He was only a Prince of little Coburg. She had to see her Prime Minister frequently. She had quantities of documents to go through and sign. How did she know what crisis was going to arise when her Government had such a tiny majority and were in some ways at the mercy of the wicked Tories led by that monster Sir Robert Peel in the Commons and that traitor the Duke of Wellington in the Lords. She wrote tender but chiding:

'You forget, my dearest love, that I am the Sovereign, and that business can stop and wait for nothing. Parliament is sitting, and something occurs almost every day, for which I may be required, and it is quite impossible for me to be absent from London, therefore two or three days is already a long time to be absent.'

A silence greeted this letter and she began to grow anxious. But in due course Albert replied. He was affectionate but never quite so demonstrative as she was and the honeymoon was not mentioned.

Another distressing contretemps had arisen. Albert had heard of the Bedchamber Affair and it was impossible to be with Victoria for very long without discovering her dislike of the Tories and her partisanship for the Whigs. Albert wrote that he believed a Monarch should be impartial. In a

Constitutional Monarchy the Government was the Government of the people and the Sovereign should stand aloof. He hoped that his household would not be composed entirely of Whigs as her own was.

Victoria was dumbfounded when she received the letter. She took it at once to Lord Melbourne:

'And what does Your Majesty think of this?' asked the Prime Minister.

'That, dear Albert has a great deal to learn. Tories in my household! He has never understood, poor darling, what those monsters are like.'

'Your Majesty will see,' pointed out the Prime Minister, 'that there should not be two separate households. This would lead to impossible rivalries. Look what happened with your mother's household and your own. The Prince should have a private secretary and as this is the most important position I suggest my own secretary, George Anson, who is a man of skill, tact and outstanding ability.'

'It is good of you, dear Lord Melbourne, to pass him over to Albert.'

'Oh, settling into a new country as the Queen's husband is a ticklish business. I can see it will have to be handled with care. Anson can serve us both, and that will prevent a great deal of misunderstanding.'

'I'll write to Albert and tell him not to worry his head about these matters and that we will settle them for him.'

When Albert received the Queen's letter he was both hurt and angry. It was clear that the Queen and her Prime Minister were going to make a puppet of him. He wrote to Leopold and told him that he was rather uneasy because he felt that he was going to be of no account whatever in his new life.

He must write to Victoria and tell her that he did not wish the Prime Minister's secretary to be his too. How could he have any independence if he were going to share the Prime Minister's secretary? He would refuse to accept this. He and Victoria must come to some understanding about his position before the marriage. Delightful, affectionate and charming as she was, she was demanding too big a sacrifice of a man by asking him to jettison his freedom of thought and his independence for the price of marriage.

He was secretly aghast at what he thought of as the licence of the Court. A certain amount of scandal was whispered. The affair of Flora Hastings was disgraceful. It was true that Flora was not pregnant but in a moral Court – as Albert saw it – the subject of pregnancy should never have been mentioned. He had seen some of the truly disgusting lampoons and items of gossip in the press. And for the Queen to have been involved, shocked his Lutheran soul to the core. Then there was the Bedchamber Affair. It was most undignified and it showed him clearly that Victoria's advisers were at fault to allow her to become involved in such a matter.

And this man Anson. He might be a good secretary but Albert had heard that he stayed up half the night *dancing*. He did not think he wished for a secretary who was noted for his dancing. The Queen, he knew, loved to dance. She would stay up half the night performing what seemed to Albert a somewhat pointless exercise. Albert liked to retire early to bed and rise at dawn. That was the best time for work for he grew very drowsy after ten o'clock. He could wean Victoria from her dancing – and other things – he had believed; but *if* she were going to behave all the time as though he were a humble subject and she was the Queen, how could he hope to do this?

He wrote to the Queen. He would like to appoint his own secretary and he thought that in their household a balance of Whigs and Tories would be a happy combination. He would like to appoint a man for the very important post of secretary who was of the highest *moral* standards.

The Queen received his letter at the same time as one from Leopold, in which were veiled criticisms of her treatment of Albert and advice on how to conduct their relationship. He and Princess Charlotte, he wrote, if ever there was a difference between them, never let the sun go down on their anger. It was a good rule and one of the most important for a happy marriage. He thought she should remember this in her relationship with Albert. He was surprised that he heard so little from her on the subject. She knew how dear both she and Albert were to him and he hinted as he knew them both so well and had been as a father to them, it was to him he expected them to turn for advice.

How distressing! She did not feel angry with Albert. That would have been impossible. The darling only had to learn. But Uncle Leopold *was* being rather tiresome.

She wrote to Albert:

'Regarding your wishes about your gentlemen, my dear Albert, I must explain to you quite frankly that it will not do. You may rely upon me absolutely to see that the people who will be about you will be pleasant people of high standing and good character...

I have today received an ungracious letter from Uncle Leopold. He appears to be disgruntled because I no longer ask for his advice, but, dear Uncle is inclined to believe that he must be in command everywhere...'

When he received this letter Albert's melancholy increased.

There were further difficulties. Victoria was eager that dear Albert should receive the Order of the Garter without delay; she had written to him on the subject of Anson. Her letters to Albert were written half in English and half in German. To write in German was to show her devotion to him for although she spoke that language fluently it was naturally not so easy to express herself in it as it was in English. Thus she tried to explain the Anson controversy. She fully understood his feelings but it was absolutely imperative that he had an Englishman at the head of his affairs; and therefore although she would not *force* Anson upon him, she asked him whether it was not better to take a man whom the Queen could personally recommend than a stranger of whom she knew nothing.

Albert, realising that he must concede, accepted

Anson (perhaps temporarily, he promised himself) but he did write and complain of the manner in which the Garter had been sent to him.

Surely his position as the Queen's future husband warranted a little more respect? He had to tell his dear and splendid Victoria that she should have sent a worthy envoy and that his father was anxious – and Albert understood this anxiety perfectly – because he feared people – especially in Berlin – would think he was being slighted.

The Queen was all contrition. Of course dear Albert was right. She could only blame those people who were handling the affair. She had no idea that anything had been done to hurt Albert and his father and the last thing in the world she would allow was that her dear Albert should be slighted.

That was a little better, thought Albert. Perhaps a firm hand was needed. His dear little wife-to-be was in the hands of her Ministers. That was something he would have to change. She was of course far too friendly with Lord Melbourne; there had been unpleasant rumours of which the two people concerned were no doubt unaware. They were without foundation of course but very unpleasant. Melbourne should never have been given apartments in the Palace. Albert could see that there was much work waiting for him; he would have to teach his dear little Victoria to be the docile wife that all good women should be – were they queens or commoners. When he had achieved this he was sure that great good would come of their marriage, to her, to him and to England.

But that was not the end of trouble. It seemed that whichever way they turned there was a difference of opinion.

Albert thought it very necessary that a more moral tone should be brought into the Court and that he and Victoria must in future set an example. Victoria had sent him a list of the bridesmaids chosen by her and Lord Melbourne, and was astonished when Albert wrote that he did not think them all suitable. For instance one was the daughter of Lady Jersey and that woman's reputation was notorious. Not only the bridesmaids themselves but their parents must be without reproach.

When Victoria received this comment she sent for Lord Melbourne without delay.

'The latest from Albert,' said Lord Melbourne, scanning his comment. 'But this is astonishing.'

'Dear Albert, he is so good himself, that he expects everyone else to be the same.'

'A notable characteristic of the good,' said Lord Melbourne. 'Now the bad rarely proselytise in the same way. They are perfectly content to enjoy their wickedness while others tread the path of virtue; the good wish others to suffer their self denials.'

The Queen tapped her fingers on the table impatiently; Lord Melbourne was a little odd nowadays, and if it were not for the fact that she used to delight so much in his company, and being not quite so enraptured by it now felt a little sorry for him, she would often have been much more short with him than she was.

'Of course,' went on Lord Melbourne, coming back to the business in hand, 'your bridesmaids will be chosen according to their rank.'

'I shall have to explain to Albert.'

'One should only take note of the characters of the lower classes,' said Lord Melbourne. 'You cannot do it with people of rank.'

'So then,' said the Queen, 'there is one law for the rich and one for the poor.'

'Certainly there is one law for the monarchy and one for commoners. Consider if we began to judge the Sovereigns of the past on their morals.'

Victoria agreed there were very few who would pass the test of morality.

Lord Melbourne looked at her earnest young face and his sentimental emotions gushed forth. She intended to be good. As for Albert, he was a puritan. But one could never be sure of what went on in puritanical minds in private.

He speculated on the future. Victoria would keep Albert in order – and how would Albert succeed in imposing his will on this rather pleasure-loving girl?

'I shall write to Albert to explain,' said the Queen rather sadly. 'Oh dear, it is rather *sad* constantly having to write and say No.'

Another rap over the knuckles for poor Albert, thought Lord Melbourne.

Chapter 15

VICTORIA AND ALBERT

February had come – the wedding month.

Albert was travelling across Europe full, as he had told Uncle Leopold, of misgivings. He could not visualise the future very clearly at all and the last few months had convinced him that his position might bring with it certain humiliations which he would find intolerable. The prospect of a wintry Channel crossing lay before him – and after that, what?

He tried to think of Victoria as she had been when he last saw her, her little face alive with affection and the manner in which she had flown into his arms and had told him he was beautiful and wonderful far beyond anything she had dared hope for.

Could that dear loving almost humble little creature be the arrogant Queen who had written to him saying: You will do this. You cannot do that.

All his hopes were in Victoria if she truly loved him. And how could he doubt that she did? She had protested it many times and she was too honest to deceive him. Of that he was certain. Victoria was honest and she loved him. She had, he believed, been led in certain ways by unwise counsellors. When he was her husband he must

357

be the one to advise. That was his only hope of happiness.

The Queen was equally uneasy. When dear Albert had been with her she had been so sure. It was all those horrid controversies which had made her so anxious, so apprehensive, so uncertain.

She was thankful to have Lord Melbourne at hand and there were constant meetings in the blue closet. There was so much to discuss: the ceremony; the bridesmaids; the procession; a new residence for Mamma because Victoria did not intend to have her living in the Palace when she married. Albert had implied that he did not approve of her feeling for Mamma. Albert was so good that he could not feel it was right for mother and daughter to be on bad terms. One day she would make Albert understand what her childhood had been like and how impossible it had been to live in harmony with the Duchess.

Lehzen had already gone to Windsor to make sure everything was in readiness for the honeymoon.

She herself had developed a horrid cold which everyone had feared was going to be measles. That would have spoilt everything; but it turned out to be only a cold and she was already feeling better.

Tomorrow, Albert would arrive and she was afraid that when she saw him again she might not feel quite so much in love with him.

She could discuss all this with Lord Melbourne.

'I feel a little agitated and nervous,' she confessed.

'Very natural,' said Lord Melbourne. 'It couldn't very easily be otherwise.'

'Such a short time ago I had made up my mind not to marry at least for a long time.'

'Depend upon it you are doing the right thing in marrying,' he said. 'It is in human nature. It is natural. Of course, it makes great changes in one's life and at times may be a little inconvenient.'

'When I saw him I was so *sure*.'

'Right and proper,' said Lord Melbourne.

'And now...'

He would not let her say that she was not now sure for he knew she would regret that. 'And now,' said Lord Melbourne, 'tomorrow when he comes you will be even more sure.'

She looked at him earnestly and it was as though she were the new young Queen again discovering her beloved Prime Minister. She felt as she had in the beginning, that all was well because he was there.

'You will not ... forsake me?' she said.

He laughed and she felt he was near to weeping; because he knew and she knew that they had come to an end of something very precious to them both.

'I shall always be here ... if you want me,' he said.

'Dear Lord M I shall never forget.'

She had turned slightly from him, her lips parted, her eyes wide; she looked very young and a great tenderness overwhelmed him. Fervently he hoped that she would be happy.

For himself ... he would be her Prime Minister

for a while ... a short while, it seemed evident. He would call on her in the blue closet; they would talk, but it would be different; her husband would overshadow their relationship and if she loved this husband he would take all the affection she had to offer – he knew well her loving heart, her tendency to idealise the dominant figure in her life to the exclusion of all others. He himself had briefly held that place in her heart, knowing all the time – old cynic that he was – that it could not last.

I had my day, he thought, and that day is over.

But not quite.

'We are going to Windsor for the honeymoon,' she said. 'You will come to see me there.'

'It will be of such short duration ... only a few days ... three at most.'

'Yes, I had to explain that to Albert. But I wish you to come It will make me happy to have you there. It always does.'

'But at such a time?' he asked, raising those beautiful eyebrows which she loved.

'I wish it,' she said.

'The Queen commands me,' he answered lightly, but she noticed the little catch in his voice.

She said earnestly: 'None of your friends are as fond of you as I am.'

She placed her hand in his and he bent to kiss it.

Albert was on the way. He would arrive at any moment. She was watching from one of the windows for his carriage. Eös, his greyhound, had arrived a day or so before and waited with her.

360

'He will be here soon, dear Eös,' she whispered. And there was the carriage. She saw him alight. Oh, how beautiful he was! Nothing ... nothing mattered but that he was here and tomorrow she was to marry him, and he was the most handsome, the most saintly man in the world.

Why had she doubted her feelings? She had been mad.

She ran down to greet him. She would have no ceremony.

'Albert ... *dearest* Albert.'

She had flung herself into his arms.

'How wonderful that you are here.'

They kissed; they clung together; then they drew apart to look at each other.

How foolish. How stupid to have doubted.

They only had to be together again to be sure.

She awoke early on her wedding morning, leapt out of bed and went to the window. It was raining.

February was such an awkward month for a wedding.

She picked up her pen and wrote to him.

'Dearest,
How are you today and have you slept well? I have rested well ... and feel quite at ease today. What weather!
Send one word when you, my most dearly loved bridegroom, will be ready. Your ever faithful
Victoria R.'

How slowly the time passed until she must get up

361

and prepare for the ceremony. She was going to look beautiful in her wedding finery, but I can never be as beautiful as he is, she thought. How wonderful he was! She was bursting with happiness. No one on earth had ever been so happy she was sure.

She was helped into the white satin gown with its deep lace flounces and her wedding veil of Honiton lace. Over it all was her garter ribbon. And of all the jewellery, the most important was the sapphire brooch which Albert had given her.

The crowds watched her drive from the Palace to the Chapel Royal at St James's; and there dear Albert waited for her, looking so tall and handsome in his uniform that she could have wept with emotion. Then she saw Lord Melbourne carrying the Sword of State and as he was looking straight at her his eyes filled with tears.

Dear, dearest Lord M! she thought. I owe you so much.

And then she turned to Albert and saw nothing but him.

She was trembling yet exultant, and when she was asked: 'Victoria wilt thou have Albert to be thy wedded husband?' her clear, young voice rang out firmly: 'I will.' And Albert was putting the ring onto her finger.

They were back at the Palace; there was so much to talk about, so many plans to make, she gave the Prince a wedding ring which he must promise to wear always and he swore he would love and cherish her till death did them part.

'There must never be a secret we do not share,'

he said.

'There never shall be,' she replied fervently.

In the afternoon they set off for the brief honey-moon at Windsor.

Soon she was writing to Uncle Leopold:

'... *I am the happiest being that ever existed. I do not think it possible for anyone in the world to be happier or as happy as I am. He is an Angel ... to look in those dear eyes and that dear sunny face is enough to make me adore him...*'

Albert came to look over her shoulder as she wrote.

He smiled as he read. Why had he had any qualms? Her affection was so wholehearted. He would mould her to his ways.

'Oh Albert,' she cried, 'how wonderfully happy I am! What joy to be here ... with you ... and to forget for a brief time that I am the Queen.'

If those were ominous words, he did not notice.

Bibliography

Argyll, The Duke of. *V.R.I. Queen Victoria, Her Life and Empire.*

Aubrey, William Hickman Smith. *History of England.*

Benson, Arthur Christopher and Esher, Viscount (edited by). *The Letters of Queen Victoria.* A Selection from Her Majesty's Correspondence between the years 1837 and 1843.

Creston, Dormer. *The Youthful Queen Victoria.*

Dunckley, Henry. *Lord Melbourne.*

Esher, Viscount. *The Girlhood of Queen Victoria* (A selection from her Majesty's Diaries between the years 1832 and 1840).

Gore, John (edited by). *Creevey's Life and Times.*

Greville, Charles C.F. (edited by Henry Reeve). *The Greville Memoirs.* A Journal of the Reign of Queen Victoria.

Jerrold, Clare. *Early Court of Queen Victoria.*

Longford, Elizabeth. *Victoria R.I.*

Maxwell, The Right Hon Sir Herbert (edited by). *The Creevey Papers.*

Newman, Bertram. *Lord Melbourne.*

Oliphant, Mrs. *Queen Victoria, a Personal Sketch.*

Pike, E. Royston. *Britain's Prime Ministers.*

Sitwell, Edith. *Victoria of England.*

Smith, G. Barnett. *Life of Her Majesty*

Queen Victoria.
Smith, G. Barnett. *The Prime Ministers of Queen Victoria.*
Stephen, Sir Leslie and Lee, Sir Sidney (edited by). *Dictionary of National Biography.*
Strachey, Lytton. Queen Victoria.
Tooley, Sarah A. *The Personal Life of Queen Victoria.*
Torrens, W.M. Memoirs of William Lamb, Second Viscount of Melbourne.
Wilson, Philip Whitwell (edited by). *The Greville Diary.*

The publishers hope that this book has given you enjoyable reading. Large Print Books are especially designed to be as easy to see and hold as possible. If you wish a complete list of our books please ask at your local library or write directly to:

Magna Large Print Books
Magna House, Long Preston,
Skipton, North Yorkshire.
BD23 4ND